BLOOD FEUD

BLOOD FEUD
RAISING CAIN

MARTIN ROONEY

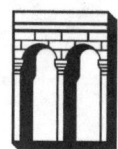

Arcade Publishing • New York

This book is a work of fiction. Names, characters, places, and incidents are the product of the author's imagination or are used fictitiously. Any resemblance to actual events, locales, or persons, living or dead, is coincidental.

Copyright © 2025 by Martin Rooney

All rights reserved. No part of this book may be reproduced in any manner without the express written consent of the publisher, except in the case of brief excerpts in critical reviews or articles. All inquiries should be addressed to Arcade Publishing, 307 West 36th Street, 11th Floor, New York, NY 10018.

Arcade Publishing books may be purchased in bulk at special discounts for sales promotion, corporate gifts, fund-raising, or educational purposes. Special editions can also be created to specifications. For details, contact the Special Sales Department, Arcade Publishing, 307 West 36th Street, 11th Floor, New York, NY 10018 or arcade@skyhorsepublishing.com.

Arcade Publishing® is a registered trademark of Skyhorse Publishing, Inc.®, a Delaware corporation.

Visit our website at www.arcadepub.com.

10 9 8 7 6 5 4 3 2 1

Library of Congress Cataloging-in-Publication Data is available on file.

Front cover by Martin Rooney and Mia Biehler
Jacket design by David Ter-Avanesyan

Print ISBN: 978-1-64821-138-6
Ebook ISBN: 978-1-64821-139-3

Printed in the United States of America

To Olympic Medalist Todd Hays
The toughest SOB I've ever met—if there's one man
Lee Cain would be afraid to fight, it's you.

PART 1
PREDATOR'S LAW

If your eyes face the side go run and hide.
If your eyes face the front go out and hunt.

The Bloodhound

The bloodhound is not a particularly impressive animal. It isn't fast, it isn't fierce, and it's not much to look at, either.

But there's one unique ability that sets the bloodhound apart. Something that makes it both powerful and useful.

Of all the possible tracks—the endless potential directions this hound can follow—all it needs is one sniff of a scent. Then just one path lights up brighter than a supernova. And once that track is lit, hell if you'll be able to stop that hound 'til he finds what he has set himself looking for . . .

CHAPTER 1

Thursday, January 12, 2023. 4:00 a.m.

New York City

W*hy murder a man with terminal cancer?*
On that crisp New York City dawn, before the "city that never sleeps" had a chance to wake up, a seasoned killer was already on the move.

Although his mantra was "every day was a good one for ending the life of another," this one began with an unusual feeling in his gut. Was it confusion? Nah—he knew the assignment. Was it compassion? Uh-uh—he was a professional. Because he couldn't put his finger on it, he settled on complacency: he felt a little off because this kill was an obvious waste of his skills.

After all, killing a guy who was already so close to the big dirt nap posed no challenge. Hit men of his caliber don't get called on to waste people already "hit" by an inescapable disease.

Let this fucker just die on his own, thought the assassin. But since half the blood money was already in his account, he quickly reminded that voice in his head that he didn't play God—he was just the guy that sent people off to meet him. With a little chuckle at that thought, he kept moving west down 31st Street toward the target. There was never any turning back. No refusing a contract once it was signed. And with the other half of the bounty waiting in limbo (a nice chunk of change, too), he sped up his steps on the cold concrete to get this job done and get out of this shithole city as quickly as possible.

He pulled over his black hood at the front doors of the Hope Lodge. Founded in 2007 by the American Cancer Society, the Lodge had sixty guest rooms available solely for people with cancer near all the best treatment facilities New York City has to offer. A supportive environment for people suffering with some of the worst prognoses—all for free. Once again, the assassin found himself in the unusual position of requiring a little motivation. He had been trained to slay soldiers on battlefields around the world—places hard men went knowingly to die. His mentors had succeeded in desensitizing him to erasing people from the earth. But this facility wasn't some terrorist cell focused on death—this was a sanctuary created to help people live.

After so many notches on his gunstock, he didn't have many feelings left—maybe just a couple of "feelers." But if there was a shred of humanity still left inside of him, it was pulling at him now.

To get in the killing mood, he reminded himself this would be a chance to get a little "creative." Instead of an impersonal bullet through the head from a thousand yards, the killer felt his pocket and smiled. "If you have to off a cripple, might as well get intimate and burn a few calories," he thought to himself. The prospect of using some combative skills—even if it was on a cancer patient—spiked his adrenaline the bit he was looking for.

"This place just became the No Hope Lodge for you, pal," the killer thought to himself with a smile as he walked past the sleeping doorman, who would have been a weak last line of defense. As he stepped into the elevator for the eighth floor, head facing down and away from the camera, he remembered something his platoon leader had always repeated in training: "Hope is not a strategy." As the elevator carried him above the city, he had to agree that the name of this place was sweet, yet stupid. The grim reaper ate hope for breakfast.

The contract killer's surprise from the moment he heard a resident with end-stage colon cancer was his next target had worn off. Now his only thoughts were on the task at hand. He moved right from the elevator, through the community kitchen area on the floor, and then down the hall to room 806. Picking 4:00 a.m. as the kill time was the right move. No one was stirring, not even a mouse.

At the target's room, the killer was actually excited the door was locked. This not only added a level of complexity to this already too-easy gig, but it also gave him a chance to work on some old skills. Since every resident is given an actual key instead of a keycard, the hit man used his gloved hands to pull out his tiny case of lock-picking tools. "The first sergeant always said these skills would come in handy," thought the hit man as he jiggled two metal rods in the keyhole. "That guy was always right."

After a little longer than expected, the hit man finally boosted the lock. He put away his trusted tools, entered the room, and silently closed the door behind him. There was a short hallway that opened into a little living area. Dawn had yet to break, so it took time for the hit man's eyes to adjust to the darkness. His boots were silent as he turned right for the bedroom door. He moved with a grace and smoothness that had come only with years of elite training.

He entered the bedroom and examined the target's soon-to-be final resting place—a simple dresser in the corner and a single bed lightly lit from the blinking of the IV machine on the rolling stand next to the bed. The killer figured this was the way most of the world went out these days—alone in a bed, hooked to a machine filled with expensive drugs designed only to delay the inevitable. As he reached into his other pocket and pulled out the syringe, he felt the power of knowing the expensive drug he wielded was going to speed up the process.

Like the ghost he had been trained to be, he wasted no movement. As he stepped to the bed, he was simultaneously removing the cap from the syringe. The use of a gun would have been impossible to cover up; a resident with the back of his head smeared across the back wall of a room at the Hope Lodge would be front-page news. But a cancer patient silently dying in the night wouldn't raise an eyebrow. A generous plunge of a needle, and it would all be over in minutes.

The hit man crouched into position and readied himself for a possible sleepy defense when the needle penetrated the sleeping victim. In one fluid motion, he yanked back the covers and drove the needle into what lay underneath. Instead of the groan or possible yell he expected to hear, the next sound that rang through the hit man's ears was the coconut clap of his own skull cracking against the cement wall. As he tried to make any sense of what had happened, a forearm had already slid across and under his chin. Right before he blacked out from the choke, he thought he heard a whisper: "Say hello to Jesus."

The hit man remembered just about everything his first sergeant had taught him. He was his hero. There was one thing he said that he always despised, but over and over he learned his teacher was right. "Always prepare; there is always someone smarter out there than you."

The first sergeant was right. The hit man forgot to listen.

CHAPTER 2

Thursday, January 12, 2023. 5:00 a.m.

Room 806, Hope Lodge

As the hit man came to, his initial assessment was a definite grade 3 concussion. He had had a few of those before and knew it would take a few weeks for his brain to heal. As his eyes opened and the fog continued to lift, his secondary assessment was definitely much graver.

When the killer realized he was lying on the bed on his side with his hands bound behind his back, his carefree daze was quickly replaced with concern. *Fuckin' A,* he thought to himself after he tried to move and recognized another cord was tied around both ankles and up to his neck, choking him if he attempted to straighten his knees. The pain in his shoulders and back from spending who knows how long knocked the fuck out in this position had his undivided attention. Being hog-tied with IV lines and lamp cords will tend to have that effect on a person. With his head pounding, the hit man began searching around the room for an escape plan. As he twisted, the ankle cord did its job and forced the killer to release an audible choking sound.

"Good morning, sunshine," said the smiling man as he turned from the TV to the bed. He picked up the remote and clicked off the TV.

"Been really looking forward to meeting you, shitbird. I was worried you might take the easy way out and never wake up."

The man stood and dragged over a kitchen chair, turned it backward, and sat down resting his elbows on the back. It was still dark in the room and after the blow to the head, the hit man couldn't identify much about him. But he could see the man continued to smile, and that definitely made him nervous.

"Now," said the man in the chair, "let's start with the easy stuff since the only thing I couldn't find on you was an ID. Who are you?"

"Fuck you," said the hog-tied hit man.

"Better check yourself, hoss," the man said in the chair with an even bigger smile. "If you haven't figured it out yet, looks like you been fucked already. Now, you cooperate and you just might get outta this one alive. But probably not. Maybe I will make it quick. If not, you are gonna suffer immensely."

The hit man was more well-versed on the other side of hostage interrogations. And even though he had prior captive simulation training, there was always the subconscious awareness that none of it was real. This scenario, however, was as real as it got. He ran through the stored files in his mind for a possible resolution. He was coming up empty.

"Not much of a talker, huh?" said the man in that jovial tone as he stood up and dragged over the small kitchen table. The hit man couldn't see what was on it, but heard the man moving some things around. The hit man tried to turn the tables the only way he could.

"Who are you?" the hit man asked.

"Nobody, shitbird. That's why I can't figure out what yer doing here. From what you're wearing and the shit I pulled off you, I know you are some kind of pro. Were you sent by the Sola brothers?"

"Who?" replied the hit man, obviously confused.

"Yeah, probably not. Was it the Whitlock family? I thought I cleared that whole mess up," the man in the chair said as he picked up the still-full syringe and showed it to the hit man. "Well, if you don't know who, how about we start with something you should know? What's in the needle?"

"Viagra," sneered the hit man as he forced his best smile.

"Yeah, well we'll see soon, won't we, smart-ass? I like yer style though. Better than going out like a little pussy. And if it is Viagra, at least you'll meet the devil with a boner," said the man as he quickly moved forward and brought the syringe down and near the man with the intention of injecting him. Since the hit man knew the contents, he reflexively tried to move out of the way, choking himself further as his entire body steeled itself for the deadly puncture.

Due to his response to the needle, the man said, "Yeah, that's what I thought. Doesn't seem to be Viagra at all, shitbird. Now I'm going to give you one last chance to save yourself. Tell me what the fuck is going on."

"Can't believe a fucking cancer patient got me," laughed the hit man.

"Believe it, shitbird. Got you pretty good, huh? Bet that grape of yours is stinging, too. And haven't tied any fools up in a while, so I had to look that shit up on Google while you were sleeping. Hope you appreciate that."

The hit man just shrugged and turned his eyes away.

"Well," said the man in the chair, now lifting the knife he found concealed on the previously unconscious hit man's ankle, "since you seem to know some things about me, why don't you tell me a little about you? Were you in the military?"

"Yeah," snarled the hit man.

"Nice!" exclaimed the man. "Now we are getting somewhere. See, shitbird, that wasn't so hard. I coulda told that from your boots and that slick military watch though. Looked that one up on Google, too. Pretty expensive for military pay. Since you obviously came here to kill me, am I right in assuming you're a hired gun?"

"Af-firm-a-tive," the hit man said slowly with a sneer.

"Take it easy. Take it easy," smiled the man. "You wouldn't want me to slip with this knife and bury it in your fucking skull, would you? So do the right thing, fuckchop. You know who hired you to kill me?"

"Contract killers are never privy to that information. We are only given the target, which obviously protects the person placing the hit," said the hit man from the bed as he was growing more uncomfortable by the second.

"I understand, and was worried that might be the case," said the man. "Not really worried for me, but for you. 'Cause if you can't really help me out, I guess you don't need to be breathing much longer. Or at least breathing with as many fingers and toes," said the man as he stood and placed his right knee hard into the hit man's rib cage, pressing him into the mattress. He then grabbed the hit man's right foot and sliced deep into the tissue below the smallest two toes, severing them.

The hit man grunted into the pain and tried to do his best to stay strong. He wasn't going to give this crippled son of a bitch the pleasure. But he definitely knew tendons were gone and this asshole meant business. He hadn't just reached the line between protecting information and survival with that knife cut—he blew right past it.

"Okay, okay," grunted the hit man as he started to perspire. "Even though I don't know who hired me, maybe we can figure it out. Did you see anyone different lately?"

"What do you mean, different?" Said the man in the chair.

"Did you change your contacts? Meet any new people in the last couple of weeks?"

"I been here seven weeks, and I haven't told anyone I am here," responded the man as he thought about the question. He muttered, "Can't be that kid or her family, right?"

But as he revisited his last few weeks of treatment, the light bulb went off.

"I know who it is!" the man said as he smiled.

"You think so?" croaked the sweating and now bleeding hit man.

"Yes," said the man. "Next question, where is your car parked?"

"In the lot on 30th, across from the jiujitsu place," replied the hit man.

"Thanks," answered the man as he picked up the syringe and flicked it with his index finger. "Now let's send you to hell with a hard-on, you piece of dogshit."

Before the hit man could offer a rebuttal, the man jammed his left knee into the hit man's rib cage and pinned him down with his right hand on the side of his head. Defenseless and with his neck exposed, the hit man could do nothing as the man jammed the needle completely into the side of his throat and depressed the plunger. He broke the needle off inside for good measure.

"Noooo!" gargled the hit man as he thrashed on the bed, choking himself further. As stars and spinning wheels were forming in his eyes and his muscles were tensing everywhere, he was able to utter, "Who the fuck are you?"

"Me?" The man smiled as he looked the hit man right in the dilating pupils of his eyes. "I'm Lee fuckin' Cain."

Those words and Lee's smiling face were the last thing the hit man ever heard or saw.

CHAPTER 3

Wednesday, May 14, 1985. 4:00 p.m.

Del Rio, Texas

There was something different about his older brother today—something downright scary. His brother had always been tough, but on that brown field, covered mainly in dirt and broken glass, the look in his eyes was at another level. Chris was saying things that scared twelve-year-old Lee—things that had obviously been bubbling below the surface for a while.

"Today it stops, little brother," Chris said with a grin as he pumped his fists up and down at his sides. He was in what Lee could only describe as some sort of angry trance. He was talking maybe to himself, maybe to no one. Pacing back and forth, continually looking toward the entrance of the field, readying himself for the upcoming fight. Psyching himself up for war.

Chris turned and grabbed Lee by the shoulders and looked deep into him. "Today it STOPS! Did you hear me? We will never be bitched again! We are the Cain brothers, and no one bitches us. If someone pops off, we pop them right in the mouth!"

Lee could feel how serious Chris was. He nodded in agreement.

"Now . . ." continued Chris in a hurry, "When these fucking greezers get here, there isn't going to be any talking. We are gonna start swinging right away. Those faggits will probably bring a whole group, and we have to be ready. Stay by me and keep swinging at their faces. Got it?"

Lee was scared. Sure, he had been in some scraps with his older brothers, and God knew his father had introduced him to the concept of pain, but he hadn't really tested himself yet. He worried as a child would worry—how many of the others were coming? Would there be kids watching? Would they get in trouble at school? Would he get laughed at?

Such stupid shit a young kid thinks. Where they were on the border town in Del Rio, Texas, he should have been more worried about knives and dying. But he was still too young and inexperienced for that. Luckily the kids coming to fight would be, too.

"Never again . . . never again," mumbled Chris to himself. Lee couldn't tell from his brother's face if he was smiling or crying. "No one will ever bitch the Cain boys again."

Chris looked over at Lee and sensed the fear in his little brother.

"Don't you be scared, Lee," said Chris a little softer. "This is gonna be fun. And it is gonna change things around here for us. You like being picked on at school?"

"No," replied Lee.

"You like being called 'white trash' and 'gringo'?"

"Hell no."

"You like getting spit on? Having our stuff stolen?"

"No," and Lee lowered his eyes, remembering the years of torment from being one of the few white kids from his area.

"Yeah, no one likes getting bitched. And from now on, no one bitches us. SAY IT!"

"No one bitches us," answered Lee.

"Louder!"

"NO ONE BITCHES US!" shouted Lee.

"That's right, little bro. Now like I said, when they walk up, just like Dad taught us. No talking. You just start punching. And stay near me. And don't stop 'til they are finished. You understand?" There was an urgency in Chris's voice. It was filled with concern and love only a little brother could understand. A protective love that would be a bond. An unwritten rule of, "when it's you versus me it's me, but when it's you versus them it's us." A mindset that would have them fight alongside and for each other forever.

As the group of Mexican kids crested the hill onto the field, Chris could barely contain himself.

"Okay, here they come. Worst mistake those fucking spics ever made. When they get closer, remember we go right at them. No talking, just punching."

The pack of kids walked slowly toward the two brothers, who were standing at the exact location Chris said they would be when he challenged them at school today: "After school, 4 o'clock, on the center of the field, you fucking homos."

The pack was larger than Chris had expected—five boys who were probably up for the fight and at least fifteen more boys and girls who couldn't resist seeing what was going to transpire. There weren't any fans rooting for the Cain boys, that was certain.

Thirteen is an interesting age for a boy. Hormones have often started flowing from biological maturity. Interest in the opposite sex can begin as a result. But another result is boys can start to grow in both muscle and bone. That had happened for Chris and he realized as the Mexican kids approached, he was finally as big as the rest of them. Their early mustaches weren't going to help them any longer.

Most people don't want to fight. They like to posture and puff up their chest and talk shit. Most like the powerful feeling that comes along with verbal intimidation. Most, unfortunately for the boys that came to the field thinking they were bullies that day, were not like the Cain boys.

Chris had already made up his mind. There would be no talking and there would be no more bitching. He didn't wait for the group to approach any farther. In the moment when a couple of the Mexican kids chuckled and a few taunts in Spanish from the cowardly back of the forming crowd started, the switch flipped inside of Chris—then and forever.

With a disarming smile on his face and his hands at his sides, Chris briskly walked up to the punk who had caused him considerable distress over the years. This was the cue it was time to talk. Before the kid got out the word "What?"—probably to begin the rehearsed tough-guy line of "what the fuck are you looking at?"—Chris's left hand shot right from his hip and landed cleanly on the kid's jaw. Chris's first throw was a clean knockout—pure and smooth. Easier to get addicted to than any drug.

As the boy collapsed unconscious and backward onto his backpack with his feet trapped under him, Chris wasted no time and immediately fired off on the boy to the right. Before the crowd of jackals could even register the shock of what was happening, Chris was already separating another boy from the group with a handful of black hair in his right hand guiding the head of the boy into uppercuts from his left.

Most people freeze up when bodies hit the floor. Few people really want to ever know what it is like to get punched in the fucking face. Hard. But a fight can also stimulate an attack response. And in this case two boys ran at Lee, probably correctly assuming he was the less dangerous of the two brothers.

Lee was watching Chris part in admiration and part in shock. The punch in the face he received for not paying attention to the other two boys woke his ass up quick. That first punch is a gift. It lets you know the fight is real—and you are alive. With the adrenaline now flowing and tunnel vision setting in, Lee reaped the benefits of human evolution. He didn't feel anything from the punch except provocation. And when you provoke a wild animal, you are probably gonna get bit.

Like he had scrapped with his brother before, Lee started wildly throwing haymakers into the face of the boy that hit him. They weren't good technical punches, but they were effective. As the mark stumbled backward, the other kid jumped on Lee's back and he went to the ground. The crowd was now in a frenzy yelling for the group to do damage to the brothers. As Lee struggled on all fours to get up, suddenly the boy on top of him went limp and rolled off to the side, compliments of Chris's work boot landing a direct soccer kick to the boy's face. As he rolled on the ground moaning and clutching his loosened teeth through a handful of dripping blood, Lee got to his feet to see Chris follow up with another kick to the nuts of the final kid standing. The kid folded like a lawn chair and with four boys now down and hurt, the crowd shut their fucking mouths knowing if they didn't, they would have theirs shut next.

Fights usually end as quickly as they start. The unwritten rule is when someone is hurt or gives up, the fight is over. Chris taught Lee on that day that the Cain boys operated under their own set of rules. A set for which most fools would never be prepared.

"Who's next, you fucking wetbacks?" screamed Chris in a fury. "Who else has some Spanglish bullshit to say, you bean-eating assholes? Ohhh . . . nobody that tough anymore? MUTHA FUCKIN' *PUTO PUSSIES!*" And with that roar, Chris turned and stomped the head of the original knockout victim, who was slowly rolling on the ground. Then he followed that with a gruesome toe kick to the face and the boy's elbows locked his arms out straight in front of him. There were gasps of horror that often come from seeing a defenseless person stomped into the ground. Chris then grabbed a handful of the barely conscious boy's hair and lifted his shoulders from the ground.

"You don't look so tough now, Hector!" Chris screamed in his face. And then he cleared his throat and spit right in the boy's face, throwing his already limp head back into the dirt.

In a fight, there are the alphas and there are the piranhas. Lee knew that Chris was the alpha that day, but a piranha has a job to do. Call it clean up, but it still sends a message. Lee booted the kid who jumped on his back in the guts and tore off his backpack, unzipped the zipper, and slung all the contents at the crowd. As some of the group was now dispersing and others were tending in horror to the downed combatants, Chris told Lee it was time to go.

"You okay?" asked Chris as they started walking back toward home. "Did any of them *putos* get ya?"

"I'm okay, Chris," replied Lee still breathing heavy and trying to process what had just happened. "But look at your hand!" He said in alarm.

The skin on the first two knuckles of Chris's left hand had been torn off from landing shots to the teeth and bones of his opponents. Lee was impressed that it didn't even seem to bother his older brother. After all, Cain boys were taught not to feel pain—and definitely never to cry.

"Just part of the game." Chris smiled, admiring his hand. "You see that fucking left and then that kick to the grape? I told you we were gonna squash those fuckers."

"We got them good," replied Lee with a grin. "But why did you pick today? What started it?"

"I don't know. Mr. Miller told me in gym that an airplane crashed today and killed twenty-two US amateur boxers. He said the saddest thing would be that they would never get to know how good they coulda been. I guess today was as good as any to find out about us. And I didn't want to go through life getting pushed around no more."

Lee let that sink in as they walked back home. As he absorbed the details of the fight, some part of him knew he would never be the same. "I think things are gonna be different now, Chris. But do you think we are gonna get in trouble? Will Dad be mad?"

"You kidding?" laughed Chris as he put his arm around his brother's shoulder, "I can't wait to tell him what we did. Just remember, nobody bitches the Cain boys," and he pushed Lee away.

But they didn't have to give their father the play-by-play that night at dinner. Because up on the hill behind the field with his old Army binoculars, their old man watched the whole thing with a proud smile on his face. And that grin only curved higher upward when Chris took out the boy on his youngest son's back with a boot right in the fucking face. Just like he taught them.

CHAPTER 4

Thursday, January 12, 2023. 8:00 a.m.

Gregory's Coffee, New York City

"It's good to be hungry. When you're hungry, you are always thinking. Always solving problems." Those were words Lee remembered his college coach saying as he started his second black coffee of the day. Since he was on another four-day fast from all food, this would be the only thing he put into his body—unless you counted rays of radiation and the poison from his daily chemo injections.

Even with the latest surprising development of having to kill a hit man, Lee could not let himself forget the overarching mission: kill cancer.

Colon cancer is a real pain in the ass, pun intended. It starts off innocent enough as a painless polyp you won't ever notice unless you are the type of guy into getting cameras stuffed up your butt. Lee Cain was not that type of guy. In fact, instead of being the proactive type about his health when he made it forty-five times around the sun, he let the one thing that kills most men like him work its black magic: neglect.

Now you could probably forgive a guy for getting his first colonoscopy a few years later than recommended, but Lee had no excuse for ignoring the blood he started to see in the toilet when he took a shit.

The red droppings started innocently enough and for months Lee kept telling himself what many tough guys might: Don't worry, it will get better.

Unfortunately, unlike many of the wounds Lee had watched heal on his body over the years, this was one that wasn't going to go away on its own. By the time he got tested and found out he had stage 4 cancer, there was only one bit of good news that the doctor was able to deliver: that it wouldn't progress further since there isn't a stage 5.

Lee had always been philosophical. He had also always been up for the greatest challenges. He interpreted his tumor as the universe's way of giving him the next great obstacle to overcome. During his last seven weeks of daily fasting, radiation, and chemo at the medical facilities around the Hope Lodge, Lee sometime wished he hadn't brought this challenge upon himself. It was severely testing his mettle.

Lee Cain, however, was never one to back down from a fight. He had learned that in order to take down an opponent, you ought to find out as much as you can about it— you study its weaknesses and its flaws. As Lee began to attack cancer from the perimeter, he began to understand more about his current foe. The possible causes and symptoms were easy—he had already checked those boxes anyway. The possible treatment solutions were much less concrete. No guarantees. But if all the doctors in the world didn't have the answer how to make this time bomb in his ass disappear, maybe he would be the one to figure it out. After all, those doctors definitely weren't as hungry to find the cure. And after losing thirty pounds so far with the goal of giving this cancer nothing to feed on in his body, Lee was fucking starving.

Lee was no fool, and he didn't believe in snake oil. Less than a few hours after he'd seen the pictures of the red mass in his colon, he had already discovered the best doctors in New York City, packed his bags, and secured his spot at the Hope Lodge. When you suddenly realize your days are numbered, you'll be surprised how much you can get done in one of them.

Yes, Lee was going to follow the recommended cancer-killing protocols of directed radiation and chemotherapy. Like a sniper, the radiation would be directed right to the exact tumor site, and like a carpet bomber, the chemo would be injected into his veins and injected into his stomach to kill the cells, not only in the tumor, but also hopefully in the lymph nodes to which they had spread. For many people, even in the face of impending death, this habit-changing regimen and exposure to daily discomfort would be almost too much to take. Some people just give up. Lee Cain was prepared to be so uncomfortable and make his body so inhospitable that the cancer would stop living before he would. Lee thought it was good he was never really known as "hospitable" in the first place.

During his own research (God bless Google), he identified that cancer had the sweet tooth of a fat kid. When he recognized that eating sugar could only make the problem worse, Cain began to investigate what other nutritional changes might increase his chances. That's when he discovered a theory around the additional combination of fasting, exercise, and the injection of medical-grade vitamins. The theory was by starving your body with controlled fasting while also performing the occasional high-intensity workout on the treadmill followed by the sauna, the cells of your body would go into a protective state. The cancer cells, however, did not have this ability. So, when the good cells essentially had their "shields" up, you blasted the cancer with radiation and poison and killed them off. The theory sounded good just as long as you didn't kill yourself in the process. And hitting the sauna after no food for a week felt as about to close as death as Lee could imagine. With all of that, there were no guarantees, but at least Lee had a plan. And that plan led him to the guy who may have ordered the hit man to kill him.

As Lee dove into his daily protocol and started shedding weight with the water fasting, he read a research study about the potential effects of a few promising supplements: black seed oil, turkey tail mushrooms, and intravenous vitamin C. If it had a chance to work, he was determined to give it a shot. The oil and the mushrooms were easy to get, but the vitamin C injections became his next hurdle. Doctors, it seems, don't always like when their patients bring new ideas to them. They like to help out even less when you ask them to write a prescription for something you are prescribing for yourself. The oncologist Lee was working with was not impressed enough by the data Lee showed him to write the 'script. Whether it was a question of pride or not liking to be made aware of things you don't know, that is no excuse to let the people under your care die. Lee wasn't about to let that doctor's inability to try something new stop him. So he started calling in favors.

Desperation leads to resourcefulness. Lee was desperate and reached out to his network. A buddy of his got him a phone number for a top IV doctor from a high-end coach with a major-league team. The coach relayed what Lee was to say in order to attempt to get an appointment. The coach said to use his name, but warned them an appointment with this doctor wasn't probable. That prediction turned out to be correct.

Lee was told he couldn't get in for six months. Lee politely told them he might not have six months to live. The secretary still made no exceptions—seems even impending death didn't move you up this place's list—especially someone as small-time as Lee. Undeterred by this, Lee decided he would go to the office in his free time (and he had a lot of it) and just see if he couldn't gain an audience with this doctor. All he needed was a damn 'script.

After two weeks of showing up every day, the squeaky wheel finally got the oil. A rare cancellation and an introduction later, and Lee was sitting in the doctor's office. Not one to mince words or waste the time of such an important man, Lee cut right to the chase. He asked about vitamin C injections and dug into this doctor about any cancer protocols of which he was aware. Perhaps he came on too strong. Hell, the guy just wanted to save himself and somehow it almost got him prematurely killed.

When Lee mentioned "cancer," the doctor seemed to grow cold. He said Lee needed his oncologist's approval and left it at that. He showed him the door like he couldn't be bothered. Well, there were two things Lee was now sure of: that doctor was the only new person he had met over the last six weeks and that son of a bitch was going to be bothered now.

As Lee sat and savored his black coffee as if it were filet mignon, he was sure he had his man. But why would this doctor want him dead? Yes, Lee was persistent and downright rude. But could that be the reason? The only way to be sure would be to pay the good doctor another visit. Last time he met with him, he couldn't use enough persuasion to get what he wanted from him. This time Lee was prepared to extract the information he wanted at any cost.

CHAPTER 5

Friday, February 22, 1980

6th Street, Del Rio, Texas

Whether or not he was half in the bag, Lee's dad was an all-in sports fan—currently the New York Yankees were his team. Jack Cain was not a lifelong fan because during his youth the Yanks had won more World Series titles than anyone. Actually, he didn't like them back then because they had that Oklahoma kid, Mantle.

Jack was a fair-weather fan who chose his teams not by the number of championships, but according to their leadership. He currently liked the Yanks because of the on-and-off manager from the last couple of seasons, Billy Martin. Word was he probably wasn't coming back to New York for the 1980 season, but he would follow the team where that guy went next—that fucking guy was a scrapper.

Yes, there were the stories of his World Series play, excelling when the chips were down, and those of him being a "drinker's man." And don't forget the press surrounding the notorious night at the Copacabana. But that wasn't what made Lee's dad a fan of the pinstripes. He was a fan because Martin didn't take any shit and rarely did he give a fuck. What won Jack completely over was an episode in 1966.

Back in those days, teams would share a charter flight out to the West Coast to save money. That night, Martin was the manager of the Minnesota Twins and they had just played his beloved Yankees. On those flights, it was also common for the players to have a little too much of the grape. Because the Yankee players got so out of control, one member of the Twins management told Billy to quiet his old team down. Billy refused. That man, Howard Fox, was steamed because no one told him "No," so he tried to pull a trick on Martin. When they got to the hotel, instead of following the unwritten rules of the time and giving the manager his key first, he made Martin wait until last. When Martin got angry, Fox threw the key in his face. Martin said he better watch it or that could lead to a fight. Fox said under his breath, "Well then, how about now?" And Martin knocked him the fuck out—earning Jack Cain's appreciation.

To put it over the top, even when he was playing pro ball, Billy had to stop playing and serve—twice! Now, Jack could forgive that Billy didn't do the kind of time he did. Jack was a disabled Vietnam Vet with not one or two, but three Purple Hearts. Those are the kind of medals you get when you run over a land mine in a jeep and break your neck. That claymore mine filled Jack's face with shrapnel. Some of those tiny shrapnel pieces the docs couldn't get were still lodged in his skull when he came home from the war. They abscessed at different times over the years and gave Jack the bright idea to pull his own teeth in front of his boys.

Even though Jack wasn't home much, when he was, he left powerful and lasting impressions. Because he rarely spoke to his boys, when he did, they had learned to listen and follow orders. So when he told Chris and seven-year-old Lee to report to the TV room at 1800, they were there on time and dressed in the best clothes they owned.

When they reported to the room at the appointed time, they found their old man sitting on the couch. Young Lee asked what they were doing.

"We're watching the Olympics, son," answered Jack.

"What's that?" questioned Lee.

"That's where our best go against their best," instructed Jack. "All the best athletes in the world get together to show which country's the best. And today the U S of A is taking on those commie Russians in hockey. And we are gonna take some time out and cheer them on."

Lee had never seen a hockey game before. Hell, he'd never seen ice in his life outside his father's whiskey glass. But as they watched that historic game unfold, Lee watch his father's usual demeanor change. As the US and Russian athletes battled on that frozen sheet of ice, Lee stopped watching the game and watched his dad. Instead of picking out his favorite athlete on the TV, Lee was most impressed with the athleticism of his dad. When the United States scored, he would jump out of his seat and yell and cheer. When the United States took the lead and then won the game, Jack wasn't just jumping any more, he was *leaping*. And he was hugging his boys and yelling, "We won! We won!" with the pride and joy you experience when your team wins the big game.

That night, the victory had already begun to wear off for Jack. The PTSD had begun to creep back in and the only cure-all he had found for it had been at the bottom of a bottle. But the victory was something Lee would ever forget. In fact, that game became one of the main internal drivers of the rest of his life. Lee would forever strive to be great at whatever it was he was doing. He would aspire to be the best—to be a winner. As he went to bed that night, he dreamed of ways he could do something so good that someday his father would leap for him.

Lee's father wasn't a man of many words. He didn't have to be. His presence alone filled a room, his quiet strength demanding respect. He'd spent his life working with his hands, and he had the build of a man who knew how to wield them—strong, unyielding. He was tough on his sons, especially Lee. But he didn't show his love the way other fathers did. There were no hugs, no kind words of encouragement. Instead, there were lessons. Lessons that hurt, but made you stronger.

One morning, when Lee was thirteen, he came downstairs to find two large buckets filled with rocks sitting by the front door. He stared at them, confused.

"What's that for?" he asked.

His father, sitting at the kitchen table with a cup of black coffee in hand, barely looked up. "That's for you."

Lee furrowed his brow. "Me? What am I supposed to do with 'em?"

"You're gonna get strong, son," his father said, setting the cup down and standing up. "You pick those up, and you walk. Walk as far as you can with 'em on your way to school. Then when you get there, you put 'em down. And on your way back, you carry 'em home. Every day, you go a little farther."

Lee had stared at the buckets, uncertain. They were heavy, and he could barely lift both of them off the ground at the same time. But his father's eyes were on him, and there was no room for weakness.

Lee picked up the buckets, his arms straining against the weight. His fingers barely wrapped around the handles, but he managed to hold on, determined not to let his father see him struggle. He walked out the door, his legs shaking as he made his way down the dirt road that led to school.

It wasn't far, but it felt like miles.

By the time he made it a few hundred yards, his hands were aching, the skin tearing at the seams from the strain. He wanted to drop the buckets, wanted to let go, but he couldn't. His father's words echoed in his mind. *You gotta get strong, son.*

So he kept walking. Every day, he carried those buckets as far as he could. And every day, he went a little farther. And every day, he brought the buckets back home. His hands bled, the pain searing through him, but he didn't stop. He kept pushing, kept going. Eventually, the skin on his hands toughened, calluses forming where the blisters had once been. His arms got stronger, his back straighter. The weight didn't feel as heavy anymore.

One day, after months of this, Lee made it all the way there and back. He dropped the buckets by the front steps, his hands shaking, but his chest swelling with pride.

His father walked out, took one look at the buckets, and without a word, added more rocks.

No celebration. No praise. Just earned a few more rocks in the bucket.

That was how you got stronger. That was how you survived.

As Lee callused his palms from carrying those buckets, he realized something. His strength wasn't just physical. It was mental. Every insult, every punch from the Mexican kids, only made him harder. They thought they could break him, but they didn't know what he'd been through. They didn't know how far he could push himself.

That hatred, that simmering anger, wasn't just directed at the kids who picked on him. It was at the world that let it happen. At a system that felt broken. At people who believed they were entitled to power, whether it was the Mexicans in Del Rio or the elites who thought they ran everything.

Lee's father never needed to tell him who to hate. Life taught him that lesson well enough.

And with every scar on his knuckles, with every callus on his hands, Lee learned one thing: you either fought back, or you got crushed.

And Lee wouldn't be anyone's bitch anymore.

CHAPTER 6

Thursday, January 12, 2023. 2:00 p.m.

Room 806, Hope Lodge

Lee knew the reason he'd had so many successful fight stories was that he was good at one thing besides beating down fools who deserved it: he was especially adept at covering his tracks. Sure, he had done a bunch of nights in local Mexican jail (which was nothing compared to the time he did in Cook County Jail), but for the most part, he felt he hadn't received a bee's dick of punishment in comparison to what the justice system might say he deserved.

With the box of heavy duty black garbage bags and two rolls of silver duct tape, Lee had returned to the Hope Lodge after his daily radiation and chemo injections geared up to make the hit man a long-term and unlisted resident.

Lee was drained from the acute infusion of poison into his body, but the sense of urgency from having a dead guy in your bed will surprisingly give you the burst of energy you need to keep moving. After confiscating everything of use from the hit man's body, Lee began to gift wrap the freshly killed killer in Glad bags. Even though rigor mortis had set in, with the hog ties still in place, it was a pretty easy procedure: put a bag over the top half, pull the drawstrings, and then wrap the body tight around the waist with duct tape. Then pull a bag from the bottom up over his legs and repeat in the same place with the tape. To make sure no one was going to get a whiff of the corpse, Lee layered bag after bag with more and more tape. After six bags on the top and bottom halves, he admired his work, sniffed up close and felt pretty sure he had bought himself a few days. Lee cupped one hand on the section of the package by its feet and another by the head and rolled the black mass off the bed. It slapped down on the floor like a tuna hitting the deck of a boat. Rolling the oddly positioned body over to the closet took energy, but Lee didn't mind. He was always up for new ways to exercise. "Damn," laughed Lee as he talked to the hit man. "If gyms knew how tough this was, you could probably save money stacking weight plates and just stack bodies instead."

As the closet door shut, his new roommate didn't have much to say back.

Lee got dressed, and admired his new watch, compliments of his victim. He then scooped up the hit man's knife and keys and placed them in his front two pants pockets. He left the killer's cell phone since he was unable to open it and debated on taking the gun. New York gun laws were especially tough, but fuck, he already had a dead guy in the closet. He packed the gun in his back waistband like he used to, but with all his recent weight loss, the gun slipped down over his cheeks. "Christ Almighty," laughed Lee. "That's all you need to fuck this up right now, Lee. Gun goes off and you shoot yourself in the ass." Lee slipped the gun into the inside pocket of his jacket, hung the Do Not Disturb sign over the outside door handle of room 806, and made his way to his daily meet-up. One good way to cover your tracks is to never appear like anything is out of the ordinary.

"If it isn't Mr. Tex-Ass," called the seated girl with green hair from across the lounge area of the eighth floor. "I was beginning to think you were pussing out."

Lee tried his best to control himself, but all he could do was smile. Over the last seven weeks that attitude of hers had really grown on him.

From their daily conversations, he knew she liked him, too. When you are both dying of cancer, misery really does love company—even if she was half his age.

"Nah, nah," smiled Lee as he walked over to her table with a chessboard at the center. "I was just deciding if it was better that I didn't show and give you another smackdown. How you feeling today, kid?"

"Like I got run over by a fuckin' bus," exhaled Julia. "How about you, Tex?"

As Lee sat down where they met up daily to shoot the shit, compare war stories, and play a little chess, he said with a wink, "Actually I got a little pep in my step. Maybe it's that green mop you got there."

"Yeah, thought it might turn on your old ass," smiled Julia as she seductively twirled a finger in the locks of the green wig.

Julia was a tough woman. You had to be when you had cancer most of your life and a couple of deadbeat parents. As Lee had learned, some people's bodies just seem to be the ones that cancer loves—a perfect host. Now skinny and hairless after the years of on-and-off treatments and experimental trials, Julia still had something in her DNA that just wouldn't shake cancer completely. She would battle and go into remission, only to receive the eventual news that the shit had cropped up again. Lee had a little spread into his lymph nodes, but Julia had had it all: lungs, kidneys, brain. And each time she beat it back, it would show up somewhere else. What she lost in muscle, she gained in fortitude—a necessary attribute when you were on your own. Her folks had split and given up. Having a child you love dying every day for a couple of decades can do that kind of thing. Each treatment was like a step forward and two steps back. Twenty-seven years old and she was out of steps, options, and time. There weren't any more trials that would accept her—or many people, for that matter. She was considered too sick for both. Her doctors had given her less than six months. That was almost five months ago. The last two of them she looked forward each day to talking with the cool guy who had told her he was from Texas.

"What? You wanna learn how to play some chess today?" Lee said as he sat down and pulled the board toward him.

"Fuck nah," said Julia. "I don't think I have the focus for that game. It was just sitting on the table. I really don't feel like doing much of anything."

"Gotta keep fighting, kid." said Lee in that slow southern drawl she had learned to love. "Three words I got for you today: go solve it."

"You didn't get that nugget from one of your football coaches, did you, big boy?" asked Julia with obvious sarcasm.

"Nope. Got that one from my old man," answered Lee. "One of the few things I got from the crazy sum bitch."

"At least you got something," sighed Julia with a frown.

"Yeah, well see if you like this lesson. One day when I was a kid, I had this bully who was always pushing me around. He was older and we had a scrap and I lost. Beat me up pretty good, but I wasn't hurt that bad, just a black eye and a fat lip, but my pride was hurt more than anything. And I sure as shit didn't want my dad to find out about it. So when I got home, my older brother'd already let my old man know what'd gone down. I tried to slip past him and get undressed in the room I shared with my brother. My dad called me out there, looked me up and down, and asked what I was doing. I said I was gonna take a shower. He said, 'Negative. The fuck you are. Yer gonna put your clothes back on and deal with this. You don't come into this house a loser. Go solve it!' And that's what I did."

"What did you do?" asked Julia really interested in the story.

"I put my clothes back on and went with my brother to the bully's house. I saw the kid in the front yard and walked right up to him and without a word I knocked him out. My brother curb stomped the shit out of him for good measure. Needless to say, when I was allowed to have dinner and a shower that night, I learned it's always better to end the day a winner."

Julia was speechless for once. Not because the story was unbelievable, but because she knew it had to be true.

"What I'm trying to say is," began Lee, "shit like cancer's going to beat you up. Life is gonna knock you around. You can sit around like a victim talking about it or you can go solve it. You can worry about and give energy to the cancer, or you can do your best to punch it in the fucking mouth."

With that Lee stood up and said, "Gotta go meet another doctor. Don't quit fighting, kid. I'm counting on you."

Julia could tell something was up. To stall Lee, she blurted out, "What did fighting ever solve?"

"Well," said Lee looking back with total seriousness. "Fighting solves just about fucking everything."

As Lee descended in the Hope Lodge elevator, he was putting together his plan of attack. His superpower had always been his ability to focus on the task at hand. Only this time, as he hypothesized how his next meeting might play out, a thought kept distracting him—his own daughter would only be a few years younger than Julia right now.

CHAPTER 7

Thursday, January 12, 2023. 4:45 p.m.

McCormack Clinic, 34th Street, New York City

You'd think a medical professional wouldn't be so shocked at the sight of blood. Doctors, it seems, are way better at handling the blood of others than they are their own. The blood, mixed with snot and tears, was obviously fucking up Dr. McCormack a bit.

Only minutes ago, Lee had been patiently sitting in the waiting room. He had watched members of the "rich and famous" get ushered in to see the doctor. Since he had become a fixture there for the last few weeks, even the bitch of a secretary had no cause for alarm. He even sat in the same chair so as not to signal anything new. *That poor asshole is gonna waste another day sitting for nothing,* she thought.

But although to her he looked bored with that far-off stare, he wasn't wasting time—he was doing some simple math. And little did she know, while she was contemplating the drink specials at happy hour, Lee was calculating answers that were life or death. Having sat through closing time at McCormack's office for a couple weeks, Lee already knew he would get a meeting with this prick. He also decided that how the good doctor responded when he first saw him would direct Lee exactly how this meeting was gonna go down.

It must have been the frozen look of surprise on McCormack's face when he ushered his last patient out of his office that keyed Lee into immediate action—he had his bitch. If the doctor's expression gave him the answer he was looking for, the way he stopped in his tracks instead of following the patient to the door confirmed his guilt. And him being too afraid to run also gave Lee the opportunity to walk the doctor back into his office before anyone knew what was going on.

Within thirty seconds, the secretary was told over the intercom that she could head out. The doctor would be locking up today. This might have been a little unusual, but since she already had on her winter coat and could taste the mojitos at La Esquina, she left unusually fast before the doctor changed his mind. Just separated by a wooden door and some drywall, the doctor's mind was racing—like one's mind does in extreme self-preservation mode.

Before the doctor could even get out the "What" of "What are you doing here?" Lee threw a straight right down the pipe. The doctor was like most people—he had never been punched squarely in the face. When someone takes a significantly hard shot to the chops, one of two things usually happen: a retaliation of violence, or a complete shutdown giving the other person complete dominance. The doctor showed he could still use that recently rattled brain in his head wisely—he chose option two.

IV specialists may have forgotten their first few classes of med school and how thin the membranes are in the nose. The way the blood was pouring out of his schnoz and down his white shirt and blue paisley tie, the knowledge was no longer theory, it was practical. He obviously wasn't up to date on not tilting his head back when you have a serious nosebleed. That's why it was hard to get the words out to send the secretary home since he was momentarily choking on his own blood. He still made sure he didn't play any games during that brief conversation. Lee gave the instructions while he flashed the gun.

"Okay, Doc," started Lee as the doctor was now sitting and trying to control the bleeding. "Now that I have your attention, I guess you can imagine I have a few questions since the last time we met."

Before the doctor could spit out an answer, Lee shut him up him by putting his right palm facing him and said, "And if I even think for a second what you're saying isn't true . . ." and Lee used one of his favorite strikes—he blasted the doctor across the left ear and jaw with an open-handed slap. A good slap will wake your ass up; one placed too good can knock your ass out. Lee made sure this one was right in between.

Lee filled both fists with the slumping doctor's bloody shirt and lifted him back into the office chair. While he brushed off the whimpering doctor's shoulders with a smile, he calmly said, "So you are going to tell me the truth, the whole truth and nothing but the truth so help you God, right?"

The doctor nodded in agreement.

"Okay," started Lee, "let's start with an easy one—I just want to know why you tried to have me killed."

"Wha—?" started the confused doctor, and not liking how the answer was beginning, Lee unloaded another vicious slap, this time with the left.

"Don't you fucking act surprised," spat Lee in his face as the doctor slumped again and started to cry. "Don't you dare. You know what you did cocksucker, now tell me why!"

Shaking his head, the doctor whimpered, "They're going to kill me . . ."

Lee again jerked the doctor forward by his soaked shirt snapping his head back and forth like a ragdoll. "Motherfucker, if you haven't figured it out yet, I'm gonna kill you. Now answer the fucking question!"

"You know why," said the whimpering doctor with a pout on his face. "You wanted me to give you the stuff."

"Stuff? What stuff?" shot back Lee. "I was here trying to get vitamin C!"

Though the doctor's face was quickly swelling, Lee was able to pick out an expression of shock and revelation.

"Oh my God . . . oh my God . . ." the doctor looked down and then looked up with a smirk, "You didn't know about it, did you?"

Lee didn't like to be out of the loop on things. He didn't like the pompous smirk, either, and rocked the doctor with a right to the left eye.

That succeeded in both removing the smirk and reminding the doctor the person with the most information was not the boss—it was the person most capable of violence.

That right got that dazed doctor talking again.

"All right, all right," he stuttered with his hands up, trying to defend himself from imaginary blows. "You don't know how far this goes. This is bigger than all of us. Bigger than the world." He sighed and whispered under his breath, "Now I'm gonna die for the King of Bahrain."

"What the fuck are you talking about?" asked Lee.

"Well, as you have probably noticed," began the doctor, trying to sit up and compose himself, "I built a practice that services a unique clientele—pro athletes coming in under fake names, movie stars, politicians, and, in this case, royalty."

"Go on," prodded Lee.

"I was notified by a doctor friend of mine that the King of Bahrain was bringing a family member to New York for a medical procedure. He asked if I could do an infusion here at my office for him—and when you get a chance to work with sheikhs, you always say 'yes.' They deal in cash, and my friend said I didn't have to do anything but put a bag in him."

"A bag of what?" questioned Lee, very interested where this story was going.

"That's just it," answered the doctor. "The King showed up after-hours with his entourage. Instead of me preparing the contents for him, one guy already had the bag with him. That guy didn't seem to be part of the group and the way he transported the bag in a metal suitcase and handled the bag giving it to me, I . . . let's put it this way, I knew it was serious. He was there to witness the bag being administered by me after he was the one to hand it over. It was a really weird scene."

"Then what?" asked Lee.

"Then when the procedure was over, the guy that produced the bag and head of security left first to discuss something outside with the King.

I was just in there with the king's brother or some shit when he must have thought I knew."

"Knew what?" asked Lee, growing more curious and impatient.

"What was in the bag. But at the time I didn't. What he said while we were finishing up was something I couldn't forget: 'when people say an ounce of gold can't buy you an ounce of time, they are wrong, aren't they, Doctor?'"

"So what was in the fucking bag?" questioned Lee.

"I don't know," responded the doctor. "When I finished up, the man that handed me the bag came back in the room with his suitcase and took the whole setup, needle and all."

"So why the fuck did you try to have *me* killed?" as Lee grabbed another handful of shirt and raised his right fist.

"I didn't!" panicked the doctor. "I swear it! It was weeks later someone asked me if I had seen the King of Bahrain. I told them 'yes' and then they told me they read in the paper that the King's brother had defied the odds and was now cancer-free. That was when I connected the dots."

"Are you saying there is a cure for cancer out there? Do you expect me to fucking believe that horseshit?"

"Well, what do you think? I panicked when you started asking me questions, waiting for me day after day. I thought it was some kind of test of something. These are powerful people! So I put in a call again to my doctor friend and said I had someone snooping around about the stuff the King got."

"Who did you call?"

"Doctor Saul Silverman. He's the guy that set me up with these people."

"Are you fucking sure?" asked Lee as he made his way behind the seated doctor.

"Yes," answered the doctor looking nervously over his shoulder.

"Good job," said Lee patting the doctor on the shoulder and grabbing a photo off the desk. "This your family?" asked Lee while showing the doctor the photo of his own wife and son and daughter.

"Yes," answered the doctor fearfully.

"You like them alive?" asked Lee looking the doctor square in the face.

The doctor didn't have a response.

"You like your wife and daughter unharmed?" Lee asked as he pressed the picture up against the doctor's bleeding face.

The doctor started to cry.

"Get yourself together. If you play this right, everyone lives. If you don't, your son is gonna watch his mother and sister get dismembered while he bleeds to death from missing his fingers and toes. You with me?"

The slumping doctor nodded through his tears.

"Good. The reason I don't cut your balls off and stuff them down your throat is that I don't think you knew calling Doctor Silverman was going to put a hit out on my life. But if I even think you called anyone, if I even sense it, I'm going to kill your family . . . and your friends, too." Lee put the photo in his other front jacket pocket. Patting the picture from the outside, "I'm gonna take this just so I know what they look like. We got a deal?"

The doctor nodded and as Lee walked out the door, he slumped and cried some more—a rare cry from the relief of the realization you aren't going to die mixed with the fear of continuing to live.

The doctor wondered if, from one of his palaces, that fucking King of Bahrain's brother had a little cry like that, too.

CHAPTER 8

The 1980s

Del Rio, Texas

Every mom has a secret hope her son will grow up to be a man. Unfortunately, depending on who you ask, there's a fine line between the words "man" and "monster." After all she sacrificed for her boys, staying in that piece-of-shit town with that piece-of-shit husband, Grace would've been mortified if she knew half the shit those Cain boys pulled.

Whether you think him a man or monster, Lee Cain was a product of his environment. The makeup of kids from those days would often result from the lessons inside his or her school followed by more lessons inside his or her home. For young Lee, his most impactful lessons came from two different places. In particular, those two places that had the most influence over his future self didn't come from the inside but from behind. One was from behind the bar at the VFW, and the other was behind the ranch where grew up on 6th street.

After a day of school, Lee would walk over to the VFW. Behind the bar was where he could always find his mother working her second job of the day. Up at 4 a.m., Grace would first work at the milk company and then head straight over to the Veterans of Foreign Wars facility. This job allowed her to tend bar for the sixty-and-over crowd of patrons as well as keep an eye on her boys, Lee and Chris. Chris wasn't the kind of kid you could coop up for long, but Lee didn't seem to mind hanging around the crowd of hexa- and septuagenarians. And boy, the men and women of the VFW sure liked that good-looking young boy with the blond hair and blue eyes.

One responsibility of being an older man is to pass on the wisdom you've learned to the next generation of men. Although that wisdom or advice could have to do with what car to drive or what political party was best to support, the most important lessons an older man often feels obliged to enlighten the youth of the day about (and this is way easier after a bourbon or two) is about how to handle the opposite sex. And by handle, he is usually talking about how to best fuck them. And so it was that Lee Cain learned about the "birds and the bees"—tall tales of conquests from old men who were three old-fashioneds deep. "Pay it forward" was their overriding philosophy of sexual philanthropy.

In addition to learning critical information like, "If she's red on the head, she's got fire in the hole," and "Remember son, it's always safer to stick it than lick it," Lee learned most of the lines he would successfully use to score chicks later in life in that bar. In fact, Lee later asking women if they had ever seen the "one-eared elephant" (while pulling out an empty pants pocket and then unzipping his fly) would always get him at least a blow job, just like Mr. Kern promised.

And the old men were happy even when their budding student finally taught them a lesson. Sixteen-year-old Lee came back to the bar occasionally to shoot the shit with the old codgers, and one day gave them some new vernacular. Lee told them he wasn't allowed to see a certain Aimee Kent anymore because Lee had cost her dad over $1,500.

"Fifteen hundred dollars?" The old men asked in shock, "Did you wreck the guy's car?"

"Worse," Lee said with a smile. "I've been nailin' old Aimee for weeks now just about every day after school. And as a result, all the drywall and ceiling damage is going to cost them a bunch."

"What do you mean?" asked the geezers in unison.

"Well, after each time I would finish getting a piece of her ass, ol' Aimee girl would flush the rubber down the toilet to hide it. Fuck and flush, fuck and flush. But yesterday the toilet backed up. The water overflowed everywhere upstairs and wrecked the floor and walls."

"I don't get it," said one of the old men with a smile.

"Hold your horses, I was gettin' to that," said Lee in his glory telling the story. "Since a plunger didn't work, her old man brought in a plumber. And when that sum bitch opened that pipe and got covered with a pile of used rubbers, Dad knew I broke his pipes and his daughter's cherry too! I guess I won't be back over there any time soon." The old boys were proud of that youngblood. "Better get the plumber" became a new line when they would see Lee after that. Seems you can teach old dogs new tricks.

If his skill with the ladies started from the wisdom of old men, his skill for fighting could be traced to the wisdom of old books. Lee and his brother Chris had a solid collection of boxing and karate books they had gotten from the town library. And since having an older brother meant you had a full-time sparring partner, Lee and his brother turned their backyard into part gym/part ring. The brothers would push each other physically with countless push-ups and squats followed by practicing their fighting techniques. They started off raw, but with the help of the books, their punches got straighter and both their bodies and their fighting philosophy began to take shape: Everyone is a threat. Land the first punch. Don't stop 'til you've won. Be brutal to send a message. Never get bitched.

On that training ground, the boys developed their own set of rules. And rule #1? *There are no muthafuckin' rules in a street fight.*

As you can expect with two competitive brothers throwing punches, things didn't stay civilized—with the Cain boys things could get downright ugly. When the scratches, cuts, and bite marks got too much for their grandmother, she even sewed them hand, foot, and face pads to minimize the damage. It was behind that ranch that Lee started lowering his tolerance for bullshit and raising his tolerance for pain. But no matter how tough they got—no matter if you could take a straight cross to the face or ignore some blood—Lee knew he would never be as tough as his old man. Shit, if removing a cap from a beer bottle with the bony ridge around your eye socket wasn't enough, Lee would never forget the day he saw the bastard skipping the dentist's bill by pulling a couple of his own teeth.

Lee Cain was born and bred to spend time in bars or rings. Girls wanted to be with him, guys wanted to be like him. Tough as fucking nails is attractive to both sexes.

CHAPTER 9

Thursday, January 12, 2023. 10:59 p.m.

Somewhere in South America

When a person has two cell phones, you can be sure he's leading separate lives. The first phone usually connects the man back to his known life—family, old and new friends, and current work associates. The digits of a second phone are held by more recent people, particularly women, whom he probably doesn't want the owners of the first cell's numbers to know about. But a third phone? That means you are one up-to-no-good motherfucker. That's the phone none of the holders of either of the first numbers should ever know about—because it would both confuse and scare the shit out of them.

It could only be his third "burner" phone lighting up with a text message that could spark the man's interest enough to check it so late at night. People who possessed this number only used it if they wanted someone dead. And people with the power to end someone's life were obviously unconcerned with the concept of time. Although the people who had his other two numbers might not agree with his current career choice, they might change their tune if they saw the pay grade. Text messages to the burner led straight to stacks of dollars—and dead-as-fuck ducks.

Ghost had had a long day at the beach. Ever since leaving Blackwater for the private sector, he had to find distractions. Twenty-four hours is a long fucking time to have nothing to do. The beer had worked for a while to calm the demons, but lately the surfing was a lower-calorie way to keep him in the zone and fit enough for his "day job." But compared to surfing, drinking, working out, or fucking, killing was the thing that cleared his mind the most. Maybe the best way to beat PTSD is to just keep adding new trauma on top. Why stop the violence anyway? Ghost hadn't ever been good at much else. A fuck-up in his Oklahoma high school, he was consistently told it was either gonna be jail or the military. He chose the latter and, with Uncle Sam footing the bill, he promptly moved up the ladder.

Now, a dishonorable discharge and couple sleeves of tattoos later, there wasn't exactly a bunch of job recruiters knocking down his door. After a get-together with a merc he'd met in Albania, he found the perfect gig. Lots of money with the occasional assignment. He laughed at those fuckers who dumped their lives into some shit job for no pay. A handful of hits a year and the rest of the year at the beach. Who's the dumbass now?

The locale of the hit got Ghost's attention.

"New York City?" He texted back to the number on the screen. "That's not my area. Why not send Diablo?"

"We already sent him." responded the number. "No communication leads us to believe he's dead."

"Who is the target?" typed Ghost, genuinely intrigued by the news.

"Seems we didn't do our research on this guy. He is a little better than we thought." was the response.

"You want it?" asked the number. Ghost knew they would not ask twice.

"Yah, I want it. Will take me a couple days to get there."

"We have begun the travel arrangements. Be at the airstrip Sunday at 6 a.m., and we will have the file on board."

"Copy that." typed Ghost as he stared that the phone before placing it down. Hit men didn't get killed—especially not Diablo. They did the killing—and if you didn't confirm the kill, you didn't get paid. There had to be some mistake—and there was only one way to find out.

"I guess I don't have to worry about the wave report tomorrow," said Ghost as he rolled out of the bed and banged out sixty straight push-ups.

Just to burn off a little nervous energy—and to try to clear that fucked-up head.

CHAPTER 10

Friday, January 13, 2023. 8:05 a.m.

Gregory's Coffee, New York City

Depending on what you're looking for, the internet can take you where you want to go—and for a guy as physically wiped out as radiation- and poison-filled Lee Cain, it was a good thing he didn't have to leave his seat at the coffee shop. Whether it's buying a book, booking a trip, tripping over gossip, gossiping about jerks, or jerking to porn, it just takes a search bar and a couple of keywords and you are headed down a rabbit hole without having to take a single step. The rabbit hole Lee dove down this morning all started with a simple question that had been bugging him all night: How much money is spent on cancer a year?

Although there were different sites and figures that immediately popped up to help, even a cancer victim like Lee was surprised by the size of the numbers. After checking the pages (and most of the sites seemed pretty reliable), Lee could be fairly confident that the US government alone was spending about 200 billion a year on cancer. "Give or take a couple of billion . . . with a fucking B," thought Lee to himself. Lee gained some clarity that the "200 bill" was to support oncology research, particularly at two agencies: the National Institutes of Health (NIH) and, by extension, the National Cancer Institute (NCI), but he was pretty sure politicians were taking their cut. Like his dad used to rant, "How the fuck does a person with a job making 75K a year for thirty years retire with a hundred million in the bank?"

And the billions didn't stop with the suspicious government funding. When you type in the words "cancer" and "money," two words that Google will surely spit back are "Big" and "Pharma." Lee read studies confirming that cancer drugs were big business and the same big business names popped up over and over: Roche, Bristol Myers Squibb, J&J, Pfizer, and Merck. One of those studies casually mentioned cumulative annual revenue generated from cancer drugs had increased in a three-year span by 70 percent, from $55 to $95 billion. That involved the insurance companies and people who would have to meet their ever-growing deductibles. He also read that doctors commonly ran their practices like a wine bar: there was a heavy markup. Most docs, it seemed, prescribed many of the cancer-treating drugs at a 6–10 percent increase in price for up to an additional $10,000 a month. Lee surmised that "First, do no harm," didn't apply to his wallet.

And that wallet was always the target of an ever-growing stream of charities for the ever-increasing number of cancers that created their own "walk of life" and color of ribbon. Hell, Lee had already been hit up by many of them just because he *had* cancer! The American Cancer Society (ACS) was the largest nongovernmental funder of cancer research and billions (with a B!) had been given in grants over the last sixty years. Lee was again surprised that only 80 percent of the resources available to the ACS were used for research. That left a fat 20 percent for "management and fundraising."

"Yeah," smirked Lee. "Only with his almost a million-a-year salary could that CEO of the ACS have the right tux for all the black-tie affairs." With more digging, he discovered the average researcher only made 75K a year. Seemed the money was going to the wrong places, and would attract the wrong people for the job. And wasn't that job supposed to be a fucking cure?

In Lee's lifetime, it seemed like science was working. They knocked out polio and smallpox, and even AIDS seemed to have gotten its ass kicked. But if the flu and COVID were proving as elusive as cancer, seemed that all Lee had to do was trace it back to the almighty dollar. Lee was well aware there were no cures for any kinds of cancer. Not a single fucking one. But when you do get the bad news that you have it, doctors are fast to tell you there are treatments that *may* cure you . . . with a smile on their fucking face. Treatments they will make an extra $10,000 a month on. Treatments that could last for money-sucking decades. Treatments the government is dropping billions on annually. Treatments for which the drug companies are raising the prices so high, patients can now barely afford them. Well, except maybe for kings.

And like it had been sitting there right in front of him the whole time, the light bulb in Lee's head turned on.

"Holy fuck," Lee thought. "This is a half-a-trillion business at the low end. No one wants a cure for this motherfucker. For these companies and governments, cancer isn't the end of the world, it's a cog that makes the world go round! What would happen to the drug companies, and charities and doctors and insurance companies if we had a cure for this shit? They would fucking collapse."

Lee Cain was no conspiracy theorist, but this was a rare case where he discovered a conspiracy all on his own. A Nobel prize for finding a cure would get you a gold medal, a diploma, and about 1.4 million bucks—chump change in comparison to what you could make over a lifetime of hiding it. Fuck, finding a cure wouldn't save lives, it would be your personal death sentence! There's no money in curing people. Half a trillion dollars a year was more than the gross GDP of about all but twenty countries in the world. If cancer was a country, it would generate almost as much as Spain. And Spain isn't planning on finding a way to have people stop buying their fucking tapas and fridge magnets.

While sipping his second black coffee of the morning, one last bit of connecting the dots had Lee sure he had stumbled onto something big. Charities like the American Cancer Society were primarily funded from personal donations. Last year alone, just that organization brought in a quarter billion from private donors. These groups weren't looking for the five- and ten-dollar contributions—these pigs were too big for that nickel-and-dime kind of feed. No, those groups needed whales and the money that came with them. Maybe that's what happened behind the scenes of those black-tie affairs—you sold the King of Bahrain the greatest insurance policy the world currently had to offer, and you did it to the tune of $40 or $50 million. "Yeah," thought Lee as he got up and readied himself for the oncologist visit he had after his chemo. "I want a bag of that shit the King of Bahrain got. It came from somewhere. That means there has to be more."

CHAPTER 11

October 13, 1989

Del Rio High School, Texas

Lee Cain didn't grow up hating Mexicans, but life on the border had a way of pushing certain feelings to the surface, especially in Del Rio. A town where, though the population was 90 percent Mexican, it often felt like 99 percent. The kids at school had their cliques, their groups, and Lee—white, blond-haired Lee—always stood out. He was a minority in his own town, and that meant something.

The taunting had started when he was young. At first, it was subtle, just small comments that he didn't fully understand. But by the time he was twelve, it wasn't subtle anymore. The Mexican kids, especially the ones who thought they were tough, took every chance they could to remind him that it was their time now. "Gringo," "white trash," "gabacho." They spat the words at him like venom, cutting deep into his young mind. They wanted him to feel it—wanted him to understand that the tables had turned.

And he did. He felt it every day, every time he walked into school.

If you thought being white at Del Rio High was tough, try being the new Asian kid who barely speaks English. Military brats got shipped in all the time because of the Air Force base, but this kid was different. His story floated through the halls like whispers of some urban legend: his mom married an American GI while he was stationed in Thailand, and they all ended up here—this dusty border town where 98 percent of the student body was Mexican and 100 percent of them carried a chip on their shoulder.

Wanchai arrived in the fall of Lee Cain's tenth-grade year. He was short, but with dark hair and tan skin, he hoped his features would help make him invisible. But in Del Rio High's jungle of slow tolerance and fast fists, he might as well have walked in with a neon target on his back.

Lee first saw Wanchai in the courtyard during lunch, the poor kid nervously clutching a tray of food while scanning the tables for a safe place to sit. A group of four Mexican boys noticed him, too. In less than a minute, that same group had turned into a pack of bullies who cornered Wanchai near the vending machines.

"Hey, Chinito," one of them sneered, stepping up and making Wanchai step back to the wall.

"What you got there? Gato?" The others laughed like jackals.

Wanchai kept his eyes on the leader, clutching his tray tighter. Another boy from the side pointed at him. "Hey, Chino, we're talking to you. You deaf or just stupid?"

The pack closed in, cackling. Lee leaned against the bleachers, watching with disinterest. This wasn't anything new. Bullies always went after the ones who seemed least likely to fight back. Wanchai looked like an easy target—small, quiet, and clearly out of his element. Lee wasn't about to play hero. Life at Del Rio taught you to stay out of someone else's fight unless you wanted your teeth knocked out. Lee figured the kid would take his beating and move on. That's just how it worked here.

Wanchai looked doomed—until he wasn't.

When the first boy reached out to smack him, as Wanchai's tray dropped from his hands, his leg simultaneously snapped forward in a blur. As his shin slammed into the bully's thigh with a sound like wood cracking, Wanchai also screamed a powerful "HEEYA" that echoed through the courtyard. The bully's face twisted in shock as his leg buckled, and he dropped to one knee from the pain.

The courtyard went silent. Even Lee straightened up, his eyebrows raised. The remaining bullies stared, dumbfounded, as Wanchai took a step forward, his fists raised in a stance that showed them he knew what he was doing.

"Come on! Want more?" Wanchai said, his accent thick but his tone deadly serious. The bullies hesitated, looked at each other, then decided it wasn't worth it. One thug pulled up his downed friend, who limped away with the others, leaving Wanchai standing alone while staring them down, defiant.

"Holy shit," Lee muttered with a smile.

He wasn't the only one impressed.

Over the next few days, Wanchai became the school's most unlikely celebrity. He took on other challengers, and each time, it ended with someone's pride—or shins—bruised. Most important, he never backed down. By the end of the week, no one was dumb enough to fuck with him. He wasn't just the new kid anymore; he was the Asian kid who knew martial arts. And to Lee, that was cool as hell.

A week later, Wanchai approached Lee after school. He'd seen Lee getting into his own fair share of scraps and apparently was impressed with Lee's toughness. But what he saw during Lee's altercations made Wanchai think he was worth talking to. Wanchai's English was broken, but his meaning was clear.

"I see you fight," he said. "I can help you."

Lee tilted his head, intrigued. "Help me? With what?"

Wanchai nodded solemnly. "Muay Thai."

The words meant nothing to Lee, but the way Wanchai said them sent a ripple of curiosity through him. That weekend, Wanchai showed up at Lee's house carrying a battered VHS tape. He handed it to Lee with an excited grin.

"Ramon Dekkers," Wanchai said, pointing at the handwritten label. "The Diamond."

Lee popped the tape into the VCR, and the screen exploded with violence. Dekkers's highlight reel was a whirlwind of fists, elbows, knees, and shins. There he was, this white Dutch guy with a smashed-in face beating native Thais at their own game. His lightning-fast strikes landed with brutal precision, leaving his opponents crumpled. Lee's jaw hung open.

"Goddamn," Lee muttered. "I gotta learn this shit."

Wanchai beamed. "This is Muay Thai."

Wanchai started coming over after school, bringing his bad English and an arsenal of techniques. They began in Lee's backyard. At first, it was simple stuff: learning to get up on the balls of the feet, basic stances, punches, elbows, and kicks. Wanchai's instructions were simple but effective. "Kick with this," he said, tapping Lee's shin. "Not foot. Foot break. Shin strong."

The first time Lee tried kicking Wanchai's shin, pain shot up his leg and a goose egg bruise formed immediately. Wanchai just absorbed the strike, shook it off, laughed, and handed him a broomstick. "Hit and roll the shin," he said, demonstrating how to roll the stick over his own shins with unnerving calm. "Make bone strong. Nerve weak."

"This is crazy," Lee grunted, but he did it anyway. As time went on, the pain dulled, and his strikes grew sharper.

Then there were the knees. "Knee is knife," Wanchai explained. "Sharp. Kill close." He grabbed Lee behind the neck with both hands and lightly speared his knee into Lee's abdomen. It kicked the wind out of him, and he felt his organs bash into the side of his ribs. It almost dropped him.

By summer, they'd moved their training to a dingy gym in town, a room with a single punching bag hanging from the ceiling. Wanchai drilled him relentlessly, holding pads as Lee honed his skills. Every session had new moves, but only after the most common were repeated for hundreds of reps. Lee pounded the bag until the skin on his knuckles, elbows, and knees split.

"First thousand," Wanchai said, holding the bag for Lee's kicks. "Brain learn. Second thousand, body learn. After that . . ." he pointed to Lee's chest. "Heart know."

Lee loved the training. He didn't get bored hanging from that bag and logging thousands of knees. Lee's strikes became automatic. He learned to hold the pads for Wanchai and felt his power. Wanchai sparred with him, showing no mercy. When Lee threw sloppy punches, Wanchai punished him with slaps to the ears. And Wanchai was always good for a thudding kick to the legs.

"Why do you kick the legs so much?" Lee had asked once, obviously preferring to use a punch to the face.

Wanchai grinned. "Kick legs, they cannot stand. Cannot fight."

It wasn't long before Lee learned to respect that lesson firsthand. Wanchai's low kicks sent him stumbling more than once, and his bruised thighs made every staircase a nightmare. Where others would have either given up or moved on to some less painful hobby, Lee kept coming back, driven by the thrill of learning something new and lethal.

By the next fall, Wanchai and Lee's backyard training sessions had gained a reputation. Neighborhood kids started showing up, curious to test themselves. These sessions turned into full-blown fight nights. Lee's backyard became an arena. They passed around mismatched boxing gloves, and kids from the block squared off. Wanchai stood on the sidelines, shouting instructions in his thick accent. "Elbow! Close! Like this!" he yelled, miming the motion.

Lee loved those backyard brawls, using everything Wanchai had taught him. During the next year, Lee not only put on height, but also weight. As he got bigger, his kicks and punches were even more devastating. One by one, he took down every challenger in the neighborhood until they all stopped showing up.

Then it was up to just him and Wanchai to keep the backyard sparring going. After a couple years of dedicated training, Lee's skills began to rival Wanchai's. One sparring session, Lee kicked Wanchai with such force he gave him a rare smile. "Good," he said as he limped slightly. "You fight smart now."

Despite their cultural differences, a bond formed. They weren't best friends, and they rarely talked about anything other than fighting. But in the gym, sweating and bleeding together, they found mutual respect. Wanchai's quiet discipline balanced Lee's wild aggression. As they trained for the next year, they rubbed off on one another while always pushing each other forward.

During Lee's senior year, Wanchai's family got stationed in South Carolina. But his influence on Lee remained, etched into every strike, every movement. Years later, when Lee won his first professional fight in Oklahoma, he looked out into the crowd and saw his old friend Wanchai, clapping and nodding with a smile.

Afterward, they shared a moment in the locker room. "You fight like the Diamond," Wanchai said with pride.

That was the best compliment Lee ever got.

CHAPTER 12

Monday, January 16, 2023. 10:30 a.m.

Merrill Center for Oncology

Over his lifetime, Lee Cain had learned the fear of death will make you do unspeakable things. Over the last half a year, he discovered hope of survival will make you do even more. Half a year starving; half a year with death haunting him; half a year feeling like total shit. But when there's no alternative, you suffer that suffering with a smile on your face. When death is the only other option, you would be amazed at the shit you can tolerate.

Chemotherapy was a tough teacher. Lee learned what it was to be ill the hard way—with a deep exhausted sickness all the way to the bone. By the end of the treatments, Lee worried his flesh couldn't take much more. He didn't sleep well, not because of the pain, but because of the fear he would die in his sleep. Because when he was asleep his spirit couldn't give his daily pep talk to his body—*Come on, you weak fucker, time to fight. Fight, damn you. We are going to live.*

This was actually Lee's second stint in New York City. When he learned of his diagnosis, he came to the city for his first round of treatment. Those eight weeks involved more radiation than anything, with daily bursts of rays shot directly into his tumor. During that time, he cleaned up his diet and researched additional measures like fasting and anticarcinogenic supplements. He went home to "recover" for the next eight weeks while choking down daily chemo pills. There he started his fasting and his daily exercise regimen. These last eight weeks in the city were his last shot to kill as much of the tumor as he could before surgery. The image of a hole in his side becoming his new asshole was his motivation to leave no stone unturned—including the intravenous vitamin C. Thoughts of wearing a colostomy bag full of shit like a fanny pack was not the future fashion statement he wanted to make—even if shit brown did match his boots.

Just how much of the tumor Lee had erased would determine just how much of his colon would have to be removed. Just how much colon would be removed would determine whether he would spend the rest of his life shitting sitting or standing up. Today was the day Lee would finally learn if all his hard work over the last twenty-three weeks had paid off. The CT scan results were in, and it would be the first time they checked the tumor since the initial diagnosis. The doctor wanted to give it as much time as they could to see how the tumor responded. When he walked in, Dr. Mulholland had a look on her face that was difficult for Lee to read. Was it suspicion? Disappointment?

"You know, Mr. Cain," she began, "I really don't like when people make me look stupid."

Lee was shifting in his seat, unsure of where this was about to go. He sure hoped he wouldn't have to hit this bitch before he got to ask her a few questions.

"I'm not sure what you mean, Doc," answered Lee sitting up straight.

"Well," she continued, "I have your results here, and let's just say they are not what I expected. Definitely not what I would have predicted, either."

"Well, lay it on me, Doc," Lee said nervously. "I can take it."

Then the doctor smiled and said, "You really made me eat my words, Lee. Before I got your results, I was discussing your case with a colleague and said I was hoping that you would bring the tumor back a few centimeters. As inflamed as it was, I'll be honest that I really wasn't all that hopeful how much treatment would help. That's why I gave the treatment such a long course before checking again."

"Okay," said Lee, about to puke from the nerves that come with a life-or-death prognosis. "So did I knock it back a bit?"

"A bit?!?" she exclaimed and put her hand on Lee's. "From this scan, it looks like you may have killed the tumor completely! What I can't tell is how much of what I see is scar tissue from the cancer retreating or if some of the colon is cancerous."

"YESSS!" Lee said and pumped his hand in the air. He took a deep nasal breath and exhaled hard. "You had me going there, Doc. This is better news than I'd hoped."

"This is as good of a response as I've ever personally seen in anyone," said Dr. Mullholland. "But we still aren't out of the woods yet. I want to get a biopsy just to see if there is any cancer left in either the colon or lymph nodes."

"For sure," answered Lee. "Can we get that done today?"

"Yes," responded the doctor. "And I'm hoping you will share with me again everything you have been doing. I'm afraid not all doctors are open to alternative treatments—me included. But after seeing your results, I can't ignore other options anymore."

"I'm glad to broaden your horizons," smirked Lee. And now it was his opening to cover things just as he had rehearsed. "Hey, Doc, I have a question about those treatments. . . . Do you get a cut of the chemo you are prescribing for me? I heard some docs get a cut."

"Well . . ." began the doctor, looking left and right as if searching for the correct answer.

"I can't say I never got a cut from some of the meds in my career, but I don't do it now. Just doesn't feel right to me. And as you know, those pills you are on are the generic version, so there's no cut for that. But yes, there are some crooked doctors out there. Hell, I have friends who prescribe shit just to sleep with drug reps on fishing charters."

Cain wanted to believe what he was hearing—that she was one of the innocent. But the big question was up next. Lee had already decided how the doctor answered would maybe decide her fate and surely decide her face.

"You think there could be a cure out there and the medical community is hiding it?"

He watched her eyes. She didn't waver. Didn't hesitate.

"I get this question more than you might think Lee. Not as much from patients like yourself, but a lot at get-togethers and parties. Seems there are a lot of people who buy into that idea."

"Do you buy into it?" asked Lee.

"Not at all," said the doctor with conviction. "A single cure? Come on. There are over two hundred types of cancer, and each one acts differently on both a genetic and molecular level. As you've probably learned, cancer is a DNA mutation that continues to mutate. Even the cells inside a tumor like yours can have different mutations, too. So even if a treatment kills some of the cells, some may survive, which is why we are going to biopsy you again to be sure. And these mutations can spread in the bloodstream and crop up somewhere else, like in your lymph nodes. Not to mention even when someone responds to a treatment, the cells can change and mutate and it can stop working."

Lee absorbed what she said and thought about Julia on that last point.

"So," sighed the doctor, "with all of that, I don't think there will ever be a single cure that cures them all. And if the cure was out there, how could you cover up the research? There are world conferences—and it's the medical Holy Grail. How could someone hold that back? Besides AI and immortality, there isn't much of a bigger prize . . . and hell, if you nailed the cure, you would be immortal."

Now Lee thought, *Is that what they tell them in school, or is that the research talking?*

"A great book you might want to look into is *The Emperor of All Maladies*. It covers the complete history of the disease including treatment leading all the way up to the present day. This one might help you dispel the myths out there."

Cain had to admit he was buying what the doctor was selling. Maybe this was a wild-goose chase. And the best news was Lee had kicked cancer's ass.

"Lee, if there was a cure out there, I damn sure promise you I would have it," the doctor said and paused. "Last year, I lost my mom . . . to lung cancer. Imagine the irony of when the kid you put through fifteen years of school who specialized in the disease you have can't save you."

Lee was convinced of two things: One, if there was a conspiracy, she wasn't part of it. And two, if there was a cure, she didn't know about it.

"I'm so sorry to hear about your mother. I know you did your best to help her, and I know she had to be proud."

"Thank you, Lee," she said. "Again, today is about you and not me, and as your doctor, I am telling you that you are doing great. I'll be in touch in a few days when we have the results of the biopsy and figure out next steps."

"Got it. Oh, Doc, one last question. Have you ever heard of a Doctor Saul Silverman?"

"Ha," the doctor laughed. "Everyone involved with cancer knows Doctor Silverman."

CHAPTER 13

May 2004

Forward Operating Base Shank, Afghanistan

On a combat outpost in the desert, certain people stand out among the rest. Although he was tall and built like a linebacker, it wasn't his size that distinguished him from the others—it was his gear. No, it wasn't how big he was, it was how he looked that struck fear in the hearts of the men of FOB Shank.

Yeah, among the moving sea of clean-shaven high-and-tight soldiers who couldn't take a piss without permission, the big man with the long hair and beard made men nervous. They couldn't see his eyes through those black Oakley sunglasses, but they could sure as hell see that M-4 556 rifle slung around him. That was his weapon of choice from a distance—but the Glock 9mm you couldn't see on his hip was the piece he preferred for close encounters. The other hip sheath hooked to the belt holding up his khaki tactical pants housed a Fairbairn-Sykes knife—for the less than likely, but often-wished-for chance things got really nasty.

The college team cap, Columbia plaid shirt, and Merrill boots made him resemble an American civilian—but this wasn't the Land of the Free, this was Af-fucking-Ghanistan. A fashion statement like that over here was only allowed for dangerous operators who killed to protect the Home of the Brave.

Operator. Such a docile title for an apex predator who hunts people for a living. In America, the word might bring a vision of a woman in India somehow connecting your call around the block. In Afghanistan, an operator is someone who disconnects your head with a high-caliber bullet from a mile away.

But even broadcasting who he was with the outfit, they still don't know what he was—and that was on fucking purpose. Maybe from some branch of Special Forces—Marine Raiders, Army Rangers, or Navy SEALs—fuck, he could be CIA or some other government three-letter agency you never heard of. Whatever he was, they didn't know and you can be damn sure he wouldn't tell anyone—unless you were the unlucky fool he was assigned to eliminate.

As the men watched how he moved throughout the base, they did know this dude did what he wanted. Unlike the other soldiers operating as a unit, this guy followed a different set of orders—he operated from a different playbook. And the men of FOB Shank got out of the way when they saw him coming. His modus operandi wasn't hard to decipher—everyone knew if you fucked up, he was "punch you in the face first, ask questions later." That's why no one did a goddamn thing the day this crazy mofo with the Southern drawl punched the new team leader right in the fucking nose.

The operator knew the route was a "no-go"—he'd been in theater longer than any other team members—and the new part of that particular road was called IED Alley. But his new fucktard team leader made a classic error of men in power—he was determined to show off his big dick and do it "his way"—and planned the route right through IED Alley because it would "save time" and for Ghost to trust the route would be cleared ahead.

Since the operator already had trust issues, he was not at all surprised earlier that day when soon after rounding a corner, an explosion incapacitated the lead vehicle and he and his men became part of a complex ambush. As his team started receiving rounds from machine guns all around their vehicles, the operator worried a lot less about "saving time," and way more about whether anyone was gonna make it back to base for the meat surprise with sweet potato tater tots.

Lucky for the team, this was not the operator's first rodeo. With a grin on his face, he turned into the teeth of the ambush and led his men straight toward the wadi and after some nifty play calls, neutralized the enemy with some grenades, 5.56 rounds, and a whole lotta of what the suits sitting at a desk in Washington refer to as "violence of action." In order to win enough battles to win the war, people gotta die. Lucky for the operator, that original IED only blew out both of his eardrums. His best buddy from the first car wasn't as fortunate. As the operator held his dying comrade in his arms and blood streaming out of both ears, sadness was quickly replaced with rage.

When the operator and his team limped back to "the Shank," the team leader had plenty of time to rehearse an explanation that would be weakly disguised as an apology. Before the team leader could exhale his first word, the operator punched him in his face with a right cross he had plenty of time to rehearse on the drive back. The team leader, now lying unconscious in the dirt, would have plenty of time to think about the lesson. The operator wasn't sticking around—he wanted some chow and was certain the tater tots would be running low.

After that episode, the operator didn't even get a slap on the wrist—fuck, saving all those men probably put him in line for his next medal. The operator would never have it pinned to his fifty-inch chest because killing people is fine when you are following orders—it's only a problem when you don't.

A few days after the team leader's jaw started opening and closing without excruciating pain, the buzz was the base had a few new inhabitants. Patrols had brought in a couple of insurgents who were thought to be responsible for making all the IEDs for IED Alley. To hold these suspects, they were placed in a cell with other captives. Most were younger military-aged males—some boys who weren't probably was a day over fourteen.

Since these men almost took his life, the operator reserved a front-row seat to listen in on the interrogation. His goal should have been to gather any actionable intel for his team to go after where the bombs were being made—cut the head off the snake. But the operator had another idea: revenge. Most soldiers did not attend interrogations—protocol was to wait for the intel officers to brief them on what information they extracted—but the operator knew things could easily get lost in translation coming down the chain of command. He preferred to be there and watch the words spill from the proverbial horse's mouth.

On the way to the interrogation, he saw a group of soldiers outside the holding cells—something was obviously up. He pushed through and when he got inside, he was unprepared for what he saw—a young boy curled up in the corner of the holding cell crying with blood streaming down both legs. The operator called outside for a medic to check the boy out, but he had been around long enough to know exactly what happened—no examination necessary. Before the medic even arrived, the operator, with the thought of holding his dead buddy in his arms flashing in his mind, immediately went to his default setting . . . violence.

As the interrogator was questioning the roughly forty-year-old bomb maker and getting nowhere, the operator burst into the room screaming in broken Pashto, "Is that how you treat little boys?" The bomb maker locked eyes with the operator and cracked a grin displaying his missing front tooth and said back in his native tongue, "Well, it was either him or the goat, but the goat has value." The bomb maker should have known to be far enough away when you detonate a bomb. The one he had ignited inside of the operator was way too close for anyone or anything to protect him. It didn't matter what the scumbag said, the operator's ears still weren't working, so he couldn't hear him. Before the bomb maker had barely finished the Pashto "ue" in "value" the operator had closed the distance across the room and impaled the bomb maker's genitalia with his Fairbairn-Sykes. As the bomb maker, now skewered to the wooden chair by his balls, howled in pain, the operator just kept looking him in the eyes and twisted the knife like he was revving a motorcycle.

"I don't see you smiling anymore, you fucking rapist raghead!" screamed the operator as he pulled his knife out of the man's testicles, and plunged it into his right groin, surely severing the man's right femoral artery. The operator punched four hard stabs into his guts with the sounds just like a hoe hitting fresh soil. The operator screamed with his face inches away, "You think it was funny now?"

By the time the shocked interrogator and military police officers in the room realized what was happening, it took all three of them to pry the operator off the fatally wounded captive. The bomb maker would bleed out before they could get him unstrapped from the chair.

That's how in just a few days the operator went from hero to kicked out of the military. Kill all you want for them, and they'll pin medals to your chest. Kill for what you believe in and they'll strip you of them and kick your ass out. Honorable to Dishonored discharge in four child-rapist stabs flat. Thankfully his command slipped him out quietly. He received an article 15 for actions, and although he could have been court-martialed and sent to Leavenworth, his command discreetly kicked him out of the Army as way to respect his otherwise exemplary service. Since it allowed him to return as a contractor unencumbered by the military's "rules of engagement," this was honestly a blessing and a curse.

Word spread around FOB Shank about what the big man had done. Everyone knew the horror stories how anyone under eighteen in a cell was not safe. They all said they woulda done the same thing—but they knew deep down they lacked the balls to put a knife in someone else's sack. That's why they thought he was so cool—why they wanted to be like him. But be careful what you wish for. To be like him, you had to sacrifice everything. To be like him, you accepted missions, no questions asked. To be like him you wouldn't have talked to your family in years. For the Special Forces unit he was part of, friends and family were things you gave up. To sign on to be like him, part of your job was to disappear.

That's another reason it was appropriate to refer to him as Ghost.

CHAPTER 14

Monday, January 16, 2023

Hope Lodge, New York City

Radiation was a different experience than the chemo injections that burned out your veins and the pills that ripped out your guts. During his daily treatment, Lee was strapped into a cast that had been made of his body to put him in the proper position for maximum tumor radiation line. The nurses carefully taped his dick and balls into the safest position—or at least Lee hoped. Usually it would be a young cute nurse that did the tape job, so Lee would hope for a warm day and play a little pocket pool before he left the change room. Last thing he needed was the nurse doing was chuckling at an Irish curse. Then with his sack properly taped, a huge machine circled around his body making loud honking, tapping, and ticking noises. Lee can't forget the smell of his own burning flesh. This whole mindfuck took about fifteen minutes and then it was back on the bus to the Hope Lodge.

He couldn't make it to his room without seeing the orange hair. He was a sucker for women of the redheaded variety, and Julia had properly planned on that. As Lee approached her at their usual table, he decided to stick to his plan, too—he would not tell her about his positive results. Few things could be worse than hearing about people improving when you aren't.

"Well, if it isn't Mr. Tall Dark and Handsome," Julia said with a slow seductive look that was enhanced by the appearance of some makeup today. With the hair and the cosmetics, Lee had to admit she was looking good.

"That's me," smiled Lee actually a little embarrassed. Julia had a way of making him feel better than he looked—a good skill to have.

"Where you coming in from today? Tanning bed again?" she asked.

"Yup," responded Lee as he sat down. "And the rays were strong today. Complete with a good dose of humiliation."

"Ha!" laughed Julia. "That reminds me, did you hear what the deaf, blind orphan got for Christmas?"

"No, what?" asked Lee suspiciously.

"Cancer!" laughed Julia.

"What?" laughed Lee after a few seconds. "Why?"

"Cause fuck that kid, that's why!" smiled Julia. "Life is tough," she said as she put her hand up for a high five.

"Damn right," said Lee as he delivered the high five and held it there as their fingers intertwined and eyes met. The hands stayed connected on the table for a second and then released.

"So, being a little more serious," Lee started, "is there anything you ever dream about?"

"What do you mean?" responded Julia. "Like is there anything I want to be when I grow up?" she said and followed it with a sad laugh.

"Yeah, I guess," answered Lee. "You could start there."

"Well, it may sound silly but," started Julia, "I would have liked to work at a Club Med."

"What?" asked Lee surprised.

"Yeah," said Julia, "you ever hear of those? They have these resorts all over the world. In the beginning when I got sick, my parents started trying to make up for all the time they thought they were going to lose with me. After we hit Disneyland and Walt Disney World, we started on the Caribbean next. The Club Meds were always a blast, and we would chat up the workers. One lady I met said it was the best job ever. She got to hang with people on vacation, eat amazing foods, and every six months end up in another place others could only dream of. She had learned and taught scuba and trapeze, and she sang and danced almost every night."

"Wow," said Lee, "I never thought about that. Sounds like a cushy gig to me."

"And," continued Julia, "she told me that the resort also wanted them to fuck the single guests if they wanted to. Good for repeat business, I guess."

"What?" laughed Lee. "Sounds more like a skilled escort service to me."

"Nah," laughed Julia with a sly look, "remember this girl was alone on an island. Just like if she was out at a bar at home, why shouldn't she be able to pick out a guy she likes on an island?"

"Can't argue with that logic or that career choice, I guess," smiled Lee. "So you ever have a boyfriend or anything?"

"Umm," thought Julia, "I can't really say I had someone I really ever dated or anything. As you can imagine, just like having dreams, it is hard to have a boyfriend when you are always focused on not dying that day."

"Yeah, I get it."

"But I have had a few guys interested in me over the years. Sometimes I would be in remission and get to go to high school. I want to believe some of the guys liked me because of who I was and not the disease I had. I wouldn't have wanted them just to be charity fucks," said Julia.

"Damn," laughed Lee. "And I'm sure it wasn't easy to kiss a girl with that potty mouth."

"I call it like I see it," smiled Julia. "And you think I'm fucked up to say that? You'd have to be pretty fucked up to try to pick up a girl whose sign is *terminal*."

"Ha," chuckled Lee. "I guess after a lifetime of cancer, you know all the jokes."

"Yup," nodded Julia. "Heard them all, ol' son. Now, speaking of jokes . . . you ever have any serious girls?"

"Come on," Lee said as he pushed his chin up with his index finger and thumb, "you think the ladies could escape these good looks?"

"Yeah," agreed Julia, "you got me there. Well, you are pretty damn old looking. You got any kids?"

"Actually I do . . . a daughter."

"Oooh," cooed Julia as she leaned forward. "Tell me all about her."

"Not much to tell, since I don't really know much about her."

"How come?" asked Julia.

"Well, when I was eighteen, I got the girl I was dating pregnant. I thought in my head no matter what, I would be that baby's daddy forever. But I was wrong. Two of the hardest things I ever had to do. Standing alongside that girl and telling her dad she was pregnant and then later signing that kid away on the dotted line to the dad who adopted her."

"Damn," said Julia. "What was it like to be married?"

"I didn't marry her. We knew we were too young to get married—we didn't have any crazy visions like that. But I was married to another girl for almost a day once."

"Oh shit," smiled Julia, "You know I gotta hear this."

"Well put your seat belt on, girl, 'cause this ride is a classic."

Lee took a deep breath and started the story.

"I got married on the beach in Mexico," he began. "Family and friends flew in from all over to stay at this five-star all-inclusive resort. Absolutely gorgeous place. The night before the wedding we had the rehearsal dinner—after which my fiancée and I went for a drink with my buddy Jimmy and his girlfriend at the time. It was at a little bar on the property, like a dance club, indoor/outdoor kinda thing. We originally sat down near the dance floor and ordered some drinks, and I noticed a couple big guys on the dance floor—one of which was wearing a leather vest. Nothing under it and from all the muscles and stretched skin, he was clearly juiced to the gills. The two girls they were dancing with were acting slutty and grinding on the guys. I knew this was trouble and told the group we needed to change seats, so we moved to the ones farthest away from the dance floor.

"Well, a couple hours pass and we're all laughing and having fun. Then here come the two juice-head guys and their hoes walking out the exit. As they pass our table, one of the girls says, 'Sorry about us, we're just drunk,' and my buddy's dumb loudmouth girlfriend says, 'Yeah you are.' The juice girl got all pissy, turned around and said, 'Fuck you, bitch!' My pal's girlfriend jumped up and now the two girls got in each other's face. Up walks the steroid boyfriend and says, 'Is there a problem?' so I did the right thing and punched him directly in the mouth. It didn't drop him, and we start fighting. After I blasted him with a leg kick, he goes down, and I laid him out with a beautiful punch. My fiancée is screaming the entire time in complete shock. The other meathead was in shock, too—Jimmy never even had to light him up. We are escorted out of the club by the waiters and security. Then to flee the scene before any cops come, we walk-run back to the hotel room. The entire way back my fiancée is telling me how trashy and low-class I am. She said that all of her relatives flew in and this is how I behave? We got to the room and she got some things and immediately left for her sister's room to sleep. I didn't see her until the wedding."

"Wow," said Julia genuinely intrigued. "So you still got married?"

"I guess you could say, 'yes' and 'no.' The next day my hand was so fucked up from that punch, I knew the ring was going to be an issue—but I thought I might be able to force it on. So we have the ceremony and the guy leading it gets to the part where he told us to put the rings on. Mine didn't budge over the knuckle. After trying to use all my strength to force it on I finally pulled it off and put it on my pinky. The new bride is giving me the death stare. That was the moment when I knew it wasn't going to work out," Lee said, and they both started laughing together.

"Ha!" exclaimed Julia, "so you were married about a minute and it was already over."

"More like a second," replied Lee. "But she knew it was over when I took all my shit and never came back. Peace out, you country bitch."

They were both laughing out loud. Lee was doubled over getting a true sense of how screwed up that day was. Julia was cracking up, and, whether it was laughing at him or herself or how screwed up her life had been, laughter really was good medicine.

Lee was laughing after Julia had abruptly stopped. As he was wiping tears from his eyes, he saw hers were staring at his forehead, but her expression had gone totally blank.

"What is it?" asked Lee.

"I don't know," responded Julia. "But there's a laser on your forehead!"

"Dead center?" asked Lee, relatively calm for a sighted target.

"No," said Julia quickly and looking at the static green spot on Lee. "It is up and slightly to the right."

Lee quickly turned to the left and looked out the window. He could track the beam across the street and up a few floors to a window. Lee knew then the hit man had probably told his bosses what happened without telling them. He also knew he was dead where he sat. So he just stared at where the laser came from with fearless eyes. It was like he was looking back at himself—with a look that said he was welcoming death.

Dogs of the same breed recognize each other instantly.

Ghost clicked off the laser.

CHAPTER 15

Friday, May 7, 1990

Pancho's Bar, Acuña, Mexico

You can tell when it's gonna be a good night in Mexico. The bars on the strip are packed with a bunch of out-of-towners who've come across the border in search of the "experience." That experience usually was less about buying Mexican tchotchkes and taking a taste of the local cuisine than it was about buying some weed and taking advantage of the below-twenty-one drinking age. Needless to say, when you cross an invisible line, are governed by new laws, and don't know the local rules, there's also a higher chance of trouble. Seventeen, yet looking more like twenty-five, Lee Cain and his friends usually came to town in search of that.

And most days they didn't have to look hard to find it.

This night, Lee and his buddies had come to town to "check the traps." Instead of a visit to one of the local whorehouses that had been a rite of passage when the boys were younger, they had graduated to actually picking up real women. It was the hunt that excited Lee. As he had learned over the years, if you could assess the situation correctly and say the right thing at the right time, girls could be convinced to do almost anything. And actually working to score a piece of ass was more fun than paying for a five-dollar whore.

What made this night even more special was that Chris was with them. Lee and his brother had lost touch since Chris left for the military, but when he made the occasional visit, like brothers do, they picked right up where they left off. Their blood brother, Jimmy Vale—*Slick Jimmy Bones* to everyone in Del Rio—made the trip over to Acuña, too, and like the Cain family did, they were measuring each other's manhood by the number of cheap draft beers each could stomach.

What happened next all started with a simple line: "Hey, any of you boys wanna get laid?" said the dark-haired girl with a shy girlfriend tagging behind.

"Sure," answered Chris over the noise of the ever-growing and smoke-covered crowd.

But the girl had already picked out her target. She turned to Lee and removed the Hawaiian lei from around her neck and placed it over Lee's head. Chris and Jimmy smiled and erupted with a combination of dog barks and fist bumps. Gotta recognize a smooth move when you see one. Lee reached his arm around the girl and she almost disappeared under his large frame. At six foot, three inches and almost 225 pounds, Lee had filled out. Being half-a-head taller than most of the people in a bar and having blond hair and good looks made him easier for girls to pick out, too.

"Hello, darlin'," smiled Lee as he and the girl made direct eye contact. "I think I been waiting for you all my life. I'm Lee, and this is my brother Chris and buddy Jimmy."

"I'm Jennifer, and this is my girlfriend Steph. So what are you boys drinking?"

"Whatever you are, Jennifer," said Lee. "And if that line about getting laid has any truth to it, I just might be buying!"

The five of them were having a good time getting acquainted. Jennifer and Steph were off on spring break and were visiting with a bunch of students from their college. Lee and Jennifer were hitting it off so well Lee had already begun telling Chris and Jimmy to stay away from his future wife. That line always worked like a charm on the girls. Jennifer was snuggling up to Lee and now Lee's biggest dilemma was figuring out where he could take her to let things get a little more private. The way Jennifer kept brushing her hands across his crotch was more than enough notice that Lee needed to know the getting laid fantasy was about to become a reality. Chris and Jimmy were having a hard time with Steph. She was playing cockblocker tonight, and with far fewer drinks in her system, her job was to have far less fun.

Jennifer gave Lee a kiss and let her palm spend a little more time on the zipper of his jeans. "Oooh," said a buzzing Jennifer with a smile on her face, "feels like what they say about having big feet is true." She had obviously noticed Lee's size-thirteen shoes.

"Nah," bantered Lee back at Jennifer. "It may be short, but don't worry. It sure is skinny!" And they both started laughing due to Lee's perfect delivery. "It might poke your damn eye out if you ain't careful!"

A couple more rounds of beers and the quintuplet was having a ball. Even Steph had loosened up a little to the Cain family. They were nice, had some funny lines, and this was supposed to be a vacation. Why can't she finally have a little fun too?

Too bad not everyone thinks that way when they go out to bars in strange places.

When you scan a crowded bar late in the evening, there are people who are easy to identify. There's the harmless loner-drunk stumbling around who you are just waiting for him or her to fall on their face. There are the creepy older dudes who are just staring at women, never with the intent to say something. There is the gang of girls who got all dolled up but shoot down every guy courageous enough to approach them. And then there are the few people causing a racket laughing and smiling because they are obviously having a better time than you are.

This was what seemed to piss off another person easy to identify: the guy who thinks it's his job to protect girls from a situation in which they don't need or want protection.

Lee and Jennifer's fast-moving romance had drawn the attention of some of the other students from her college. And since these guys had no girls, it was only natural to try to make sure no one else got any, either. Because it was getting late and the group was thinking about heading out soon, a few of the guys approached Lee and Jennifer.

"Is this guy bothering you?" asked the first student without ever introducing himself. "Because if he is, I'll kick his ass."

Funny how some people are so socially inept at reading an obvious situation. The only thing bothering Jennifer was how she was going to shake her friends and fuck this guy tonight, but Lee was also obviously bigger than the frat boy, who was nothing more than a mix of chronic blue balls and liquid courage. He had surely never been in a fight in his life, either. Unfortunately for him, where he now stood within a three-foot range of Lee Cain, he had just mistakenly thrown down a gauntlet in an arena where he didn't know the rules.

"Hey, hey, buddy," said Lee with a smile to the student with his arms crossed. "Why don't you just have a good time tonight? Go get yourself another Zima with your boys over there." This was actually a rare attempt at doing his best to save this poor asshole. Not because he was being kind, but he really wanted to fuck this chick.

"Who said I'm not having a good time?" responded the student in a tone that Lee just could not accept. Chris must have read Lee's change in expression and knew immediately the night was about to be ruined. He also knew it was time for another drink order.

"It's time for shots," said Chris, in what appeared to be an attempt to defuse the situation. He nodded to Jimmy to place the order. He put his arm around Jennifer and said to the student, "Come on, man, there's nothing to worry about, we got the ladies safe here."

"Who said I was worried about anything?" the student spat back just a little too quickly for Chris's taste. A few more of the student's polo-wearing and chickless friends were beginning to migrate over to investigate the situation that seemed to be developing. Most people are pretty good at reading body language. Lee already knew from the way Chris's smile disappeared that his chances of getting laid tonight were almost as small as this guy escaping without getting the brakes beat off him.

"Why don't you come on back over with the group, Jennifer," ordered the student.

"Don't tell me what to do, Mike," answered Jennifer. "I'm fine right here." And she wrapped her arms around Lee and Chris.

"Shots!" exclaimed Jimmy with a smile.

"Nice," said Chris as he took one of the shots and handed the other to Lee with a nod. "Look at this, ladies," Chris said like a carnival barker holding up the shot glass to make the burning blue flame at the top of the glass visible. "This is the famous Leatherneck Shot, also known as a Flaming 151. Bacardi 151 and Tabasco. It takes skill and years of practice to drink it without hurting yourself. Go too slow and you burn off your eyebrows—go too fast and you burn out your throat. But if there is one person who has mastered this death-defying trick, it's my little bro."

Lee raised his glass for all of Pancho's to see. He lowered the shot and in one quick motion, put his mouth completely over the rim of the glass. Not only did this seal give Lee the position to quickly fire the liquor down his throat, but it also extinguished the alcohol so he didn't get burned.

As all eyes were distracted by Lee pounding the shot, no one saw Chris throw the other burning shot right in the student's face. But no one could miss the huge ball of fire that burst all over him from the concoction of flame, Axe body spray, and hair gel.

Before anyone could react to what was happening, Lee blew him backward by hammering lefts and rights into the burning mass. As the student erupted in a horrified scream that usually accompanies ones recognition that one is on fire with eyeballs full of Tabasco, the scream was quickly extinguished by the fact the student got dropped and was now unconscious from the blows. Chris and Jimmy had already picked off the student's friends who had gathered and three more bodies hit the floor.

Lee delivered a couple well-placed kicks to the dome of the now-smoldering student. Since there was little hair or skin left to burn, the fire was all about out.

"You fucking clown," yelled Lee as Chris and Jimmy were assessing if there would be any more people ready to join the fight. "You coulda come out tonight and had a good time. But you had to be a dick. You thought you were tough. Well you know who I am, you fuck? I AM THE GUY WHO SHOWS YOU YOU ARE NOT SO TOUGH." And with the lesson came one more head stomp into the dirty cement floor of Pancho's. For good measure, Lee tore out a handful of the groaning student's hair in a final insult to injury. With both the sound and feel of undoing a Velcro shoe-fastener, the lock of hair came out surprisingly easy and would go in his pocket for later.

All of this took less than sixty seconds. Definitely not enough time to absorb this kind of vicious action for someone like Jennifer, who didn't know the rules. In that minute, however, most of the patrons at Pancho's were taught a few things they would never forget: one, don't try to act tough, 'cause you never know you're fucking with. Two, if you're gonna go out, go and have fun—don't act like a dick. And finally, three, if you're going to start some shit in Mexico, make sure it isn't with guys with the last name of Cain.

An open-mouthed Jennifer looked back and forth from her now-crispy friend to Lee—the man who moments ago had transformed from fun-loving to ferocious. Before he and his brother and Jimmy ran out the front door to escape the soon soon-to-be-arriving *federales*, as the boys called them, Lee looked at her, smiled and shrugged his shoulders, and took off.

Jennifer definitely had a night in Mexico she would never forget. So did the char-grilled frat punk—he'd be reminded every time he'd look in the mirror for the rest of his life.

CHAPTER 16

Tuesday, January 17, 2023. 1:35 p.m.

Madison Park, New York City

As Lee sat there looking at the Flatiron Building, he wondered if the architect was a genius or an idiot. Either the guy was a pioneer and wanted to create something that would make people stop and stare, or he could be a simple-minded kinda guy who just filled every inch of the space he had the only way he could. Well, either way, Lee agreed the guy was probably long dead and at least he left something behind—something iconic. He would have to agree with history—the guy was a genius.

The dog park, along with Gregory's, the Merrill Clinic, and the Hope Lodge, had become one of the places Lee spent some time each day in New York City. Each one, like the spaces of each person's life, served a particular purpose. Gregory's set the tone for the day—he laid out the plan, watered it with some caffeine, and got going. The clinic was where he fought the fight. With poison in his veins and gamma rays in his guts, he expanded his ability to get comfortable being extremely uncomfortable. The Hope Lodge was all about resetting—whether it was a conversation with Julia or just to sleep, that space got him ready to do it all over again. The dog park was his sanctuary—his place to quiet his mind and meditate. Lee would focus on his breathing (he'd read that could help beat cancer too) as he people-watched the humans passing by—some in a rush to get somewhere, others stopping to pick up their dog's shit. He did his best to let thoughts drift in and let them slide by. Definitely wasn't as easy as it sounds—especially when you had as much shit going through your head as Lee.

As he stared off into the dog park, he wasn't surprised when the guy sat down next to him. Actually it was quite the opposite—he was expecting him.

Without turning to even check him out, Lee said, "I was wondering when we were going to get to meet. Thanks for not letting the last thing go through my mind be a high-caliber bullet."

"You're welcome," said Ghost in a familiar drawl as he also stared forward into the distance. "Didn't seem right to have that girl watch the back of your head explode."

There was a long pause in the conversation. Neither man really knew what to say next.

"Where you from?" Lee asked. "I hear a little South in there somewhere."

"Grew up in Oklahoma," responded Ghost.

"Well, shit," laughed Lee, "My dad woulda been pissed if he knew I got shot by an Oklahomo."

Ghost smiled. "I could expect as much. Last night I violated a rule of the trade."

"Oh yeah? What's that?"

"I looked up a little about you. Kinda against the grain to start finding out shit about the people you are hired to kill. I guess they don't want you getting all personal."

"Makes sense," said Lee, still looking straight forward.

"But maybe it made my job easier—you being from Texas and all."

"Lone Star State, baby," said Lee.

"Yeah, but that's outta five stars," quipped Ghost.

Lee smirked as he stared at a woman walking her dog.

"So cancer, huh? I bet that's been fun?" asked Ghost, also staring off.

"Oh yeah," agreed Lee, "people don't know what they're missing. And fucked up part of it all is why we are having this chat right now. Seems I stumbled on to some shit about it that I shouldn't have. Trying to save myself might get me killed."

Ghost didn't want to hear about that shit. He'd already crossed so far over the line, last thing he needed to do was fall for some bullshit lies. Whatever it was, the job was the job—and he was still going to do it. But he still found himself interested in this guy. From what he'd read, he was living up to the hype so far.

"So you come here a lot?" he asked changing the subject.

"Hey buddy," Lee answered. "You mighta heard fags come here to pick each other up, but I ain't one of them."

Ghost smiled again—he was enjoying the banter. Reminded him of his days at Ranger Regiment.

"But yeah," continued Lee, "I come here . . . to watch the order of things."

Ghost didn't respond, which told Lee he was listening.

"When I was seventeen," started Lee, "My dad got this bright-ass idea to get a dog. Named him Dutch. Was supposed to be some sort of Lab, but he got some mutt. Maybe he felt sorry for it, but I never understood why the old man tolerated that fucker. My dad would beat our asses for even looking at him cross, but he let ol' Dutch growl at him and bite him. Bastard bit my brother and my mom, too. But I wasn't letting that stupid motherfucker bite me."

Ghost liked where this was going. He hadn't actually spoken with a real person in some time. "So what did you do?" he asked genuinely interested in the story.

"That fuck had to know the pecking order. Had to understand you can try to bite, but if you do, yer gonna get your ass beat on a regular basis. See, that damn dog was confused who the alpha was. He thought it was him, and he was fucking wrong. So me and my brother decide to teach Dutch a lesson. We wrapped our arms and legs up in bedsheets, got garbage can lids for shields and broomsticks."

"In your house?" asked Ghost.

"Yup, right in the living room. Now we gave Dutch a chance. When he started growling we said, 'Hey you shut up, you shit bag. This is our house.' He had a chance to back down. But we knew what he would do. He started barking and jumped at us all nasty and shit—baring his teeth and snarling. Then he took a broomstick to the head . . . about fifteen fucking times. Dutch put up a good fight—he was snapping and attacking. We kept him off with lids, but it wasn't funny. Not when yer worried about getting bit. When dogs turn it on, they are popping them jaws. You could lose a finger or worse. My brother slipped and twisted his knee. Wasn't never the same after that."

Ghost nodded with a half-sneer, half-smirk.

"Ol' Dutch would turn on my brother, and I would beat on him. Then he would turn on me. and my brother would give him some licks. Finally, after enough of this, Dutch tried to hide.

"That's when we told him, 'You fuck with us and every time this is what you're gonna get.' After that, he growled sometimes, but he never bit us again. Broke one of his teeth on one of the sticks. Dad later was trying to figure out how he broke his tooth. Me and my brother said, 'We don't got a fucking clue, Dad.'"

Both Lee and Ghost were laughing. Maybe they were laughing at the story and maybe they were laughing at their current situation.

"Yeah, Dutch was different after that. That was what he needed to get in line. Dog had to learn he wasn't the alpha and that betas don't get to be bullies. . . . So are you ex-military?"

"Yeah," answered Ghost. "Found out that killing in the private sector pays way better. And you don't have to deal with anyone's bullshit. I guess the problem with the Army is you gotta take orders from people you don't trust to do shit you don't wanna do."

"I get it," nodded Lee. "My old man and brother served. Fucked both of them up forever."

"Yeah," said Ghost, "I read that, too. And a little bit about your football days."

"Well, before we get all warm and cuddly," said Lee turning a little serious, "how is this all gonna work out? I don't think you came just for a talk."

"No," answered Ghost. "I didn't. Still wanted to meet you and kinda explain myself. Show you some respect or some shit like that."

"So am I supposed to just expect a bullet? If so, I think I am gonna cancel my shitty chemo and radiation treatments for the week—they kinda suck."

"No," sighed Ghost. "I think we're beyond that. But when I was reading up on you, I got a little idea. If what I read was true, I think you might like it."

"I'm all ears," responded Lee.

"To be honest, putting a bullet in someone from a thousand yards is an act of cowardice. Anyone could do it. You could be some paralyzed fuck in a wheelchair and still pull a trigger. I trained my entire career for something else—worked on skills I never got to use."

"So what are we talking here?" asked Lee. He liked where the conversation was going, especially the part about not getting his brains blown out.

"An old-fashioned throwdown." said Ghost.

"No rules—no weapons?"

"Yes," nodded Ghost.

"Place?" asked Lee.

"Central Park, Strawberry Fields."

"Time?"

"Tomorrow night, 2300."

"Roger that," confirmed Lee and he continued to impress Ghost. "Now, to be clear, we are all friendly now and all, but when it's on—it's on. Just giving you the same respect."

"Appreciate it," smiled Ghost.

"I had a brother who learned that one the hard way," started Lee. Since they were swapping stories, might as well share another he thought Ghost might like. "You already know I had an older brother. One summer he worked for my dad when he was about seventeen years old, and, man, he was spending all of his paycheck each Friday night. One of those Fridays, we're all sitting at dinner, and my dad told him to save some of that money.

"My brother popped off that it was his money, and he could do what he wanted with it.

"They went back and forth and then my dad told him to be careful the way he was speaking or he would kick his ass and take his check. My brother said, 'I bet you won't.' My dad told him to go get the check and find out. My brother got up, went up and came back down with the check in his hand, and walked up and threw the check down on the kitchen table. My dad exploded out of his seat and hit him with a jumping right hand. My brother went to sleep and my dad picked up the check and walked out the door. When my brother came limping back down for breakfast the next morning, he mumbled to my dad that he sucker punched him. My dad said, 'You knew we was fighting when you went up to get your check. What did you want me to say? Ready. Set. Go?'" Lee paused. "Yeah, that was a good lesson for me that day."

"So you won't be ringing a bell to start, huh?" asked Ghost.

"Nope," said Lee dead serious. "Just letting you know since you flashed that laser in my face, we are fighting now. Next time we get together, be ready."

"Roger that," answered Ghost.

Now they were past introductions. The fight was set, and the gravity of the situation was sinking in. They sat in silence starting forward for a few more minutes—neither man moved a muscle. Sitting next to the guy you had just agreed to kill tomorrow—kinda fucked up. Finally, Lee spoke.

"With this cancer shit, I spend a lot of time here thinking about my life—back to the beginning. I have come to realize the worst part is regret about the past. I'm sure you've been through some sick shit. Guess it comes with the territory when your job is killing people. Got any regrets?" asked Lee.

"Well," started Ghost, "since you brought up that dog and bullies, you got me thinking. One regret I have is about this one jerk-off I grew up with. This guy was older than me and for some reason just terrorized me. Beyond just the verbal humiliation and occasional punches and breaking my toys and shit. This fucker was sadistic. He'd spit goobers in my hair and one time pissed in my face."

Lee was the one listening now.

"I'm sure looking back that fucker was being raped by an uncle or some shit, but there still ain't no excuse. And yeah, you could say without bullies we probably wouldn't be who we are today. But if I had to say my greatest regret, that pussy went and got himself killed before I got a chance to do it. I wish I coulda been there to snatch the life out of him and right before I did, let him know I was the toughest kid on the block."

The two men continued to stare forward. The dog park had done its job for both of them. The conversation was cathartic.

"Well," said Ghost as he stood up and the men finally made eye contact. "Now I guess tomorrow night we are gonna find out."

"Yup," answered Lee with a smile, sizing Ghost up and hopefully psyching him out. "Never caught your name."

"That's cause I never offered it. Another thing probably better that way."

"Prolly," agreed Lee. "Before we get down to business tomorrow, one more joke my old man used to tell. . . . So a man from Oklahoma takes his daughter to the gynecologist and he tells the doctor he wants her on birth-control pills. The doctor asks him how old she is, and the man says, 'She's thirteen.' The doc is surprised and says, 'That's seems a bit young.

Is she sexually active?' The man replies, 'Naw . . . she jus' lays there like 'er mother.'"

Ghost smiled as turned and walked away. In another life, he and Lee coulda been friends. Too bad tomorrow he was going to kill him.

CHAPTER 17

Saturday, May 14, 1992. 10:30 p.m.

Acuña, Mexico

Lee Cain had been going to Acuña since he was barely a teenager, crossing the border for cheap beers, rough women, and the kind of violence that couldn't be found in Del Rio. His older brother taught him the ropes: how to drink until the world blurred, how to bed a woman without a word of English or Spanish, and most of all, how to fight.

It was a rite of passage, and Lee, being the youngest, had always felt he had something to prove. As the years passed, he came into his own. Now, just having finished his freshman year of college and doing well in football, he was a force to be reckoned with. That year, something inside him snapped, like a dam finally breaking. The rage he'd bottled up from years of feeling like he wasn't enough was ready to spill out.

Lee and Slick Jimmy had a favorite haunt just outside town—a grungy, run-down bar that seemed to thrive on chaos. It reeked of spilled beer and cheap tequila, the air always thick with cigarette smoke and the scent of sweat. But the real draw was out back—a chicken wire cage.

The cage was legendary. If you had a problem with someone in the bar, you could challenge them to a fight. Bare-knuckle. No rules. The only way to settle things was with blood. And Lee had seen plenty of it spill inside that cage. His brother had fought in there, taking his lumps, dishing out some, but always walking out the better man. Lee had watched him, soaking in the lessons. The way the cage seemed to strip everything down to its rawest, most primal state.

There was no bullshit in the cage. No fake smiles. No pretending to be tough. You either were or you weren't, and if you weren't, the cage would chew you up and spit you out.

It was the law of the jungle.

And everyone remembers their first time in the jungle.

Lee's first time wasn't about honor, though. It wasn't some grand act of bravery. It was about a girl—a girl with one fucking leg.

It had been a typical night, beers flowing, people grinding on the sticky dance floor, and Lee was feeling mean. The one-legged girl had caught his eye, hopping around the bar, her skirt barely hanging on. He'd had enough to drink that he didn't give a damn about the consequences. So, in a voice louder than it should've been, he called her "Stubby."

The bar went quiet for a second, like the collective gasp of an audience waiting for the action to start. The girl shot him a look, her face flushed with embarrassment, but it wasn't her he had to worry about.

Her boyfriend—a beefy local with arms like tree trunks—turned toward Lee with murder in his eyes.

"You got a problem, gringo?" he growled.

And there it was. The moment Lee had been waiting for. Maybe he hadn't meant to insult the girl, maybe he had. But deep down, he knew it didn't matter. He *wanted* this. The chance to step into that cage and see if all his training over the last couple years would pay off.

The beefy local wasted no time. He pointed to the door leading to the cage, and the crowd erupted. This was what they lived for—watching blood spill, bones break. Jimmy was already grinning, knowing damn well that his brother from another mother was about to get his baptism by fire.

Lee didn't hesitate. He drained the last of his beer, slammed the bottle on the table, and followed the guy outside. The cool night air hit him like a slap, but it wasn't sobering.

As they stepped into the cage, Lee felt that first thrill of danger seep into his veins. The cage door clanged shut behind him with a heavy, final sound. The crowd pressed in around the wire, their faces wild with anticipation.

Lee could feel his adrenaline spiking. His heart was pounding, but he wasn't scared. He was alive. His training with Wanchai and those backyard brawls had prepared him for this.

The guy across from him—Stubby's protector—was already bouncing on his toes, ready to kill Lee where he stood. But Lee had been paying attention. He knew this man wasn't a fighter. He was just pissed off, looking to impress his girl. His stance was sloppy, his fists low, leaving his face wide open.

The crowd roared as the fight began. Lee didn't wait. He moved forward like a predator, fists flying. The first jab landed squarely on the guy's nose, a sickening crunch that made the crowd wince. The guy stumbled back, but Lee wasn't done. He drove a knee into the man's gut, doubling him over, then brought an elbow down on the back of his neck. The guy hit the dirt, gasping for air, but Lee didn't stop. He couldn't stop. Not with that crowd screaming his name, chanting for more blood.

And it felt good. Too good. The rush of violence, the way his fists connected with bone, the sick thud of flesh hitting flesh—it was all so pure. So clean. The noise of the world faded, leaving only the sound of his breathing and the pounding in his ears.

There was no guilt, no remorse. When the cage closed, it was business, not personal. Just like his brother had taught him.

The guy tried to crawl away, but Lee grabbed him by the back of his shirt, hauling him up onto his knees. He cocked his right arm and drove his elbow into the man's jaw, sending him sprawling into the chicken wire, blood dripping from his split lip. The guy was done. But for Lee, it wasn't enough.

He leaned down, grabbed the man by the hair, and whispered, "This is what happens when you fuck with me."

With one final straight deep kick to the head, the guy went limp. The crowd erupted in cheers, some of them banging against the wire, rattling the cage like wild animals. Lee stood there, his chest heaving, but he didn't feel tired. He felt invincible.

That's what the cage did to you. It stripped away all the bullshit, leaving only the raw, primal truth. And the truth was that Lee Cain was a fucking monster.

As the cage door creaked open, Lee glanced down at his right elbow. He picked a tooth out of his flesh, noting he would have to throw some antibiotic on that. Jimmy was waiting, grinning like a wolf. Lee stepped out of the cage, and for the first time in his life, he felt truly untouchable.

From that night on, he wasn't just Lee. He was *the guy* no one wanted to fuck with. He wasn't some white boy from Del Rio anymore. He was a fighter. A survivor.

And the streets of Acuña learned to fear him.

There were more fights after that night. Some of them over stupid shit, others because someone thought they could take him down. But it was always the same. That cage door would slam shut, and Lee would feel that same thrill. The same rush of knowing that in here, it was kill or be killed. No laws. No rules. Just the law of the jungle.

The more he fought, the more he honed that killer instinct. He could see the fear in his opponents before they even threw a punch. The way their eyes widened, their breathing quickened, their fists trembled. They weren't ready for this. They thought they were tough, but they didn't know what tough was. Not until they stepped into the cage with Lee Cain.

He'd been there so many times, it had become normal. The cage was his home, the only place he truly felt at peace. Outside, the world was chaos. But inside the cage, everything made sense.

He always got out of trouble. And he always bet on himself.

Getting in the cage was like diving into the deep end of the pool. And in that cage in Acuña, Lee Cain was a shark, while the other fuckers didn't even know how to swim.

CHAPTER 18

Tuesday, January 17, 2023. 10:00 p.m.

Rocco's Steakhouse, New York City

What would you have for your last meal? Unless you do something horrible enough to get the chair, and your state gets the balls to finally fry your ass instead of dragging it out and feeding you on taxpayers' money, you probably won't ever have to worry about that question.

But for Lee Cain, tonight this was a legitimate question and he knew what he'd get. Since this could be his last meal and he was literally fucking starving, he was sure-as-shit having a fat steak—a bone-in tomahawk rib eye and an ice-cold beer . . . or two. Keep your fucking wine list to yourself, garçon.

Who would you invite to your last meal? Would it be a parent, spouse, or family member? Maybe this would be a chance to say what you needed to say or get a few things off your chest. You could use the dinner conversation to finally tell the truth or continue to let past lies protect the ones you love.

Cain knew who he'd bring. Since this might be his last meal and he literally told fucking no one he was dying, he was sure-as-shit bringing Julia. He had a pocket full of cash fresh from the ATM and told her to surprise him with the color wig she would be wearing that night. She had extra time to get dolled up, because the only way you get a last-minute reservation at a steakhouse like this is when a ten o'clock luckily cancels.

Lee knew he was in trouble when he saw her—with some makeup and that black dress, she looked great.

"Damn girl," complimented Lee, "you are looking hot."

Julia blushed and said, "Thanks, but I am swimming in this dress. It used to fit me better."

"Ahh, don't worry," answered Lee, "That heroin-thin look is what other women only wish they had."

They got to Rocco's ten minutes before their reservation and were seated right away. The place was a classic upscale New York steakhouse—low lighting and spread-out tables with a few bottles of wine on each. As he sat there, Lee imagined all of the Italian-looking men around them were mafia heads or owners of sanitation businesses. Whoever they were, he was right when he thought, *this ain't Del Rio.*

The service was first class, the bread and oil were on the table, and the orders were in. Lee's stomach, which had shrunk to the size of a lemon, was growling. The smells in Rocco's only made it worse. But even with the hum of dinner conversations around them and the prospect of digging into a dry-aged steak for the first time in months, Lee was having a hard time focusing on anything other than Strawberry Fields.

Lee looked up and realized he had been leaving Julia out of the conversation. He brought her out for a nice night—it wasn't her problem he had a potential date with death tomorrow night—might as well talk to her, too. So like Lee had done his whole life, he shared what was on his mind.

"What you do think happens when you die?"

"Ha," laughed Julia. "So much for small talk, huh, big guy? Well, I don't have to tell you what I think happens, I already know."

"What?"

"Come on man, ya can't be dying for over twenty years and not have found out the answer to that question." Julia said. "You see, you are new to the whole cancer thing. But I've been in the game just about as long as anybody."

"So if you have cancer long enough, you understand death?" asked Lee, really intrigued.

"No, it isn't about people with cancer who know," Julia replied. "All psychonauts know." She smiled and knew she had him. She waited for him to take the bait.

"Well? What the hell is a psychonaut?" he asked right on cue.

"Take a trip to Peru and find out," said Julia looking around like she couldn't be less interested.

"You went to Peru?"

"Yup."

"You never told me that." replied Lee.

"You never asked, Tex."

"Come on then. Gimme the scoop. What's that about?" asked Lee.

"It all kinda started when I got really sick a few years ago. My white cells were down and I was seeing a shrink," Julia began. "Yes, a shrink! And I suggest you try one sometime. Anyway, since I was dying, it was recommended to my family I go into alternative treatment. And by that I mean magic mushrooms."

Lee was listening and knew not to lighten up the mood with a poorly timed joke. After all, they were discussing death.

"Don't get me wrong, it isn't just some trip shit. The mushrooms were about preparing for my "end of life" journey, and it wasn't done in some crackhouse, either. It was performed at the shrink's office where he and a medical person acted as ground control."

"Ground control?"

"Yeah, cause when you're a psychonaut you always need your Houston." Julia gave him a look to stop interrupting when she was on a roll.

"Anyway, it was one of the most profound experiences I had. A lot of cancer patients at the time were getting a lot of good out of it. I did so well with the psilocybin, they recommended the trip to Peru to see Mother Ayahuasca."

"Who?" asked Lee.

"Not who, really . . . kinda what," Julia responded. "That's what the veterans who do this kind of shit call the all-knowing mother figure."

"So where was this place?" asked Lee.

"It was a pretty simple trip there," Julia answered. "You fly to Lima, Peru, and then take another plane to Iquitos. It was wild—no roads to the place—only get there by river or walking. Then from there you take a boat four hours up the Amazon River into an unmarked village into the jungle. No street signs—no laws, either. The real jungle, babe—the unknown."

"Doesn't sound that simple to me." laughed Lee. "Were you scared?"

"I'd be lying if I said I wasn't," answered Julia. "But there was a lot more to be scared about than just the jungle. This village wasn't a resort, but you stay at an interconnected group of grass huts. In the center is the maloca, think of it as the church of the Amazon. A big round room. That's where the ayahuasca ceremonies are held."

"Ceremonies?"

"Not some parade or trophy handout, no," laughed Julia, "this ceremony is different—totally fucked up. That's where the lead shaman is. Where you receive the medicine. They've got facilitators—like six people in there dressed in all white. Women wearing all white down to the wrist and ankles—men in the shirts and pants. They are in white so you can see them in the dark maloca and they are there to help people having trouble—off on fucking bad trips."

"So do they inject you?" asked Lee. "What is this stuff?"

"No, just let me tell the story would you?" said Julia. "First, you come in an hour early for quiet hour. You blow alcohol and smoke on yourself in a pattern to drive out the evil spirits for the coming journey. I thought it was stupid, but when you go in and see a bunch of vets all doing it, you follow the flow. These people were tense—you knew it was serious shit when you stepped in there. I bet like in a locker room and it's the big fucking game. You better believe I was blowing smoke all over my damn self."

Lee smiled and continued to be even more impressed with her.

"You asked about being scared? Fuck yeah," continued Julia. "In there it occurs to you everyone is afraid. They are gearing up for war, like an astronaut taking off and they don't know where the ship's gonna land—where it will end up. Good trip or bad trip? Better get your fucking mind right. Could be the best or the worst night of your life, and you don't know 'til it takes hold. Scary, scary shit."

"Damn . . ." said Lee under his breath, really feeling the story. "What did you do then?"

Julia kept center stage at the table. "How it works is the facilitators come in the room and blow out the candles and it's pitch black in the maloca—dark as fuck in the jungle. And when that darkness hits, you hear it come alive. The shaman walks in all in white too and goes to center of the room and calls out a name—first person up to take the "medicina"—a shot of purple-black liquid. Now everyone is laid around the edge of the maloca—heads to the wall, feet to the center—all around, shaman in the middle. That first person called steps up and sits Indian style. The shaman pours it into something like a shot glass and hands it to you—depends on how much you take, the studs take more. Before you pound it down, you breathe your intentions into the glass— tell that shit what you are there for—then fire it back like a tequila."

"What was it like?" asked Lee.

Julia's face crinkled up as she recalled the taste. "Tasted like charcoal and battery acid with a splash of gasoline. Fucking horrible. You choke it down and you go back and sit on your mat. Takes about fifteen minutes for the whole group to get the drink. Then you lay back in the pitch black—crickets and frogs and howler monkeys screaming. Then like clockwork, the first person who took it starts to dry heave. Then they throw up into a plastic bucket. Then it goes down the line in order of when they drank it, one by one, like perfect timing."

"You puke it up?" asked Lee.

Julia was nodding. "Yeah, that's how it works. Since I was the newest, I was last to drink the first night. The chain reaction of puke came around to my turn. It hit me like a massive wave—you have no pre-sickness—like zero to a hundred in a millisecond, and then I was violently pissing out my mouth. Then as fast as it hit, it was over."

"What the fuck is that stuff?" asked Lee.

"Ayahuasca, as I understand it, is a leaf and root. There's like 150,000 species of plants in the jungle and there are only two that give you the DMT. One prevents the stomach acids from killing the DMT—so the combo is the only way to get into your bloodstream orally. So short version, you gotta puke it out to get it in you."

"Fuck . . ." whispered Lee.

"Once you puke," Julia continued, "the DMT is in your bloodstream. That's the ignition for the psychonaut. That's when the fucking curtain gets pulled back—and then you go for a ride."

"What did you see?" asked Lee.

"Mother Ayahuasca shows herself in different forms. Thousands of people have taken this journey and weird that almost all say she is a serpent or a jaguar. They all see it—I saw her, too. Mine was the serpent and she was crawling down the walls. I was like 'Oh shit, here we go.' Looked like the top of the maloca was rotating and disappeared. I could see the stars. Then the shaman started to sing the icaro—the medicine song—singing this thousand-year-old song to send you on the way. I saw shit and heard shit. I started hearing the om frequency. Started like humming and got louder and louder like a thousand monks in a church singing '*ommmmm*.' Then the room was shimmering as if you're watching a movie screen, and the movie changed, and I was in a different place—like I was transported—best I can describe it is another dimension or whatever it is they are trying to show you."

"What do you mean 'they'?"

"Well, when people smoke the raw DMT, they report they have spoken to an intelligent entity. Like little elves or gods that talk to you. There are actual studies using IV drips of the DMT and all the people come back with the same stories. And the fucked-up part? None know what's up going in! Then on future trips, they give these people questions to ask the gods. I don't know. . . . Amazon people think you are talking to your ancestors."

"Could it just be brain stuff?" asked Lee, skeptical of all of it.

"I don't think so; I did it. And like me, a lot of people claim the experience was more real than this reality. They were there. Not a blurry dream you kinda remember—you were fucking there. When you see heaven or speak to God, and he says not to worry, this is the beginning, they believe that to be true—so profound and real they can't be unconvinced. Because of the beauty of it, far more beautiful than anything they've seen on this earth, comes from a different plane. When you sleep, you dream about what you know. When you go to the other side, I saw shit that never occurred to me existed. I can't even describe it to you—there aren't words to do it justice."

"It sounds amazing," smiled Lee.

"It was," said Julia. "Such a realistic interaction, these people come back with true belief. Total certainty of something bigger. Faith there's a higher being in control of all this."

"Can't it be shit that happens to our brains? Just a drug-induced trip?"

Julia frowned a little. "That's what everyone says who hasn't done it. But I did. And I'm sure. If you go where I went, there is no doubt. Call it what you want, God, the universe, whatever. But because of what happened to me, I'm not worried. There is something else. And I have faith I will see you there."

"Shit," exhaled Lee as he ran his fingers over his head. "I don't know if I could do that."

"Maybe someday, I'll take you and show you the ropes," she smiled.

Julia was so direct it made her convincing. Lee saw her in an entirely different light. She was no longer that sick skinny girl—she was fearless and powerful. He had a total new level of respect for her—crazy he couldn't see it before. Lee still couldn't wrap his head around all of it, but she had given him a gift. Just a glimpse of something that put his worried mind more at ease.

When the food came, it was worth the wait. The steak was an absolute monster. Forty-six friggin' ounces of muscle and fat. Whether it was because he hadn't had much food in months or not, there were few steaks Lee had eaten that he would never forget—and this was one of them. Perfect combination with the mashed potatoes and although he couldn't eat much of it, it actually felt good to see them on the plate. For dessert he finished his beer and woulda licked the bottle clean if he could. If there were still starving kids in Africa or China, fuck 'em. Lee wasn't going to stuff himself and fuck with his fight just cause some bastards had chosen to keep living in a desert.

The dinner hit the spot. If it was going to be Lee's last supper, he did it with style. On the walk back to the Hope Lodge, Julia held on to Lee's arm, but she could feel Lee was obviously distracted. Whether it was the silence or the pace, she could tell he was somewhere else—that arm wasn't giving anything back to her.

They rode the elevator up the eighth floor—it was the moment of truth.

"Do you want to come to my room?" asked Julia.

"Do I want to, yes. Can I tonight, no."

Julia nodded but wasn't giving up that easy. "Does the chemo have you all fucked up? I won't judge you."

"Ha," smiled Lee. "Everything is still in working order."

"Is it me?" asked Julia.

"No, it's not that. You look great tonight, and after the story you shared with me, you are a superhero—a guy would be absolutely stupid not to take you up on it. I just gotta take care of something tomorrow, and I can't fuck it up. If I pull it off, I will be back for you."

"Promise?"

"I promise," Lee said knowing it wouldn't matter if he broke that promise, 'cause then he would be dead.

"Well, you better come back and see me," and she leaned forward and gave him a kiss on the cheek.

I hope so kid, I hope so, thought Lee as he turned back for his room. As good as she looked, he couldn't nail her tonight—had to keep his legs. Long ago Lee's brother told him blowing loads was never good the night before a fight. Stole your energy or your mojo or some shit. But however it worked, that advice hadn't failed him so far, and the last thing he was gonna do was take a chance and fuck with fate.

Lee slept better that night than he had in weeks. Julia had given him a sense of ease he never had before. He dreamed of shamans, serpents, and roadside bars.

CHAPTER 19

February 2, 1991. 11:35 p.m.

Southwest Texas State, San Marcos, Texas

As the beer started flowing, Lee and his brother were partying like it was the last time they'd ever see each other. When your brother is being shipped off to the first war that's happening in your lifetime, you make the trip to see him—and you buy the beers. Lee, Chris, and the boys were almost a case of Lone Stars deep when they decided to leave the apartment for some action. A sixer each was just an appetizer before the Cain boys really started to get loose.

Chris found out that it's impossible to live two dreams at one time. After he'd represented his country as a Marine, he took Lee's challenge and enrolled at Cisco College. This was his attempt to prove the lifelong Chris Cain naysayers wrong about two things—he could pass college classes and play college football. Even though he was a little light for the offensive line, what Chris lacked in weight he made up in toughness; it also didn't hurt he was now twenty-three years old competing with athletes who could be four or five years younger. His years as a leatherneck paid off, and Chris had a solid season. His coach made a call and found Chris a scholarship at Southwest Texas State, a Division 1-AA school. So much for those shit-talking, know-it-all haters from Del Rio.

Chris left after the season at Cisco and enrolled at Southwest Texas. Starting right after the Christmas holiday would let him acclimate and more importantly, get ready for spring ball. But just as Chris started this new dream, his old one got in the way. One aspect of being a Marine that Chris had missed was never having gone to war. Since he was still enlisted in the reserves, oil-mad Saddam Hussein made a call of his own and found Chris a spot on a boat headed for the Persian Gulf.

Hussein invading Kuwait started the Gulf War. The American and allied response began as something called Desert Shield, but with global tensions mounting and the Americans itching to lay some hate with their new Patriot missiles, the plan was to move to Desert Storm. Chris was told to pack his bags for Iraq because he would be part of that storm—that order effectively ending his big-time college football career before it started. Since he was in the infantry—just a frontline grunt—Chris was sure he'd be among the first ones heading into Iraq as potential human fodder for the slaughterhouse. What he couldn't be sure of was whether he would see his family and friends again, and that's why they were going to party hard on his final night as a college football player.

Lee and Jimmy rode up from Del Rio. Only seniors in high school and never having thrown a going-away party before, the boys didn't know to be happy or sad; nervous or excited; accepting or pissed. On the one hand, Chris would be back repping the two-time world champs and could come back a hero. On the other hand, he could come back dead. Even though violence was a normal part of their upbringing, the idea of war was something foreign. Fights were over and done with quick—case closed. But a war hung over your head like a dark cloud brewing. Even though everyone but Chris wasn't enlisted, as they walked out of the apartment in search of a good time, they got to feel what it was like to be a patriot—to fight for something you stand for. Because right in the apartment next door, some stupid fucks decided to start a war of their own.

As the boys spilled out of Chris's new apartment in search of a good time, Chris was frozen in his tracks. Of all the places someone could pick to have a Gulf War protest party, right next to the marine's door was about as poor a choice as possible. This son of a vet didn't know everything about his country, but Chris sure knew this: You don't fucking hang an American flag on a door . . . upside down! Instead of heading to the car, Chris made a beeline toward the guy guarding the door to see if he couldn't "talk" with the host. Semper Fi.

Some people are led to believe universities are safe havens for protests—like you can just rip your own fucking country and there won't be any consequences. Like it's cool to piss on your homeland, the place you get to put your soft-ass head on your pillow and sleep good at night. Well, those queefs are sadly mistaken. Yes, freedom of speech allows you to say what you want, but when you speak your mind, you better be ready to get confronted for your beliefs—'cause there just might be a bigger, tougher motherfucker that believes something quite the contrary. And often when people pop off at the mouth, those consequences could involve you having a couple teeth popped out. Short version according to Chris Cain—you fuck with the flag, you're gonna pay.

When Chris tried to get inside, the bouncer at the door told him it was invite only. Chris checked with the big black guy if a right to the chops was what he meant. As the melee immediately broke out, seems it was something else the now semiconscious bouncer was looking for. Lee and the boys hadn't made it far from the apartment when the fight erupted. Chris was screaming, "What's up, camel jockeys!" as he was stepping over the KO'ed bouncer trying to gain entry into the party. Before he could get inside, a mass of people poured out of the townhome, driving Chris back. As thirty or forty people emerged from the door, Lee knew it was either time to turn tail or start dropping fools. Since his marine brother didn't exactly look like he was ready for retreat, Lee clipped the closest partygoer to announce which side he was on. Jimmy put his half-empty bottle of Lone Star over the head of another combatant, and the three of them circled up like it was their own personal Battle of Thermopylae.

Street fights are equal-opportunity lenders of violence. One reason for this is because an experienced fighter knows every person in or near a fight scene is dangerous. An old man can knock you out and a woman can put a knife in you just as easily as a man. Hell, even a kid can crack you a good shot, kick your balls in, or choke you out if you're not careful. But people who aren't regularly violent don't understand this everyone-is-a-threat philosophy—and the inexperienced often announce themselves by being the loudest. That's what the girls from the protest party began to do by screaming and running up, poking at the Cain triumvirate. Like they were tough . . . or safe. That stupid-ass thinking's what got the whores dropped like the rest. Step into the ring, prepare to get hit, bitch. Throw first, throw straight and fast until the threat has ended. Male to female, old or young, fat or skinny—tall ones line up, short ones pair up. Be very hateful in your intentions and careful in your actions. When you fight for your life, all threats are met with sudden and maximum violence—zero chances taken. Every filthy fucking human being is dangerous in their own way—every perpetrator needs to be punished. Make a maximum show of force that leaves fear in the hearts of all the onlookers and they will remember and tell others what they saw.

Each time another person got put to sleep, there would be a gasp of horror from the onlookers too terrified to join the fight. In the defense of the onlookers, it's not easy to build up your courage as a kid to be able to strike someone as hard as you can in the mouth. You'd ask yourself things like *what if I miss* or *what if it just pisses this tough guy off* or *what if I lose?* But the Cain boys had a different mindset, a different mantra: "You don't know until you throw." If you never throw that punch, you can't learn what you're made of. But this night wasn't about the Cain boys finding out anything. They already knew who they were. And because of that knowledge, this battle was about dishonor. It's only when you truly believe in death before dishonor can you start letting go of your hands on the regular. If you choose honor above all else, it sets you free to choose maximum violence as fast as that violence can begin.

The gasps were because bottles over heads and heads slammed into the street are shocking tactics. Most aren't ready for it to have gotten so violent so soon into the fight. No part of them is ready for the stack of writhing bodies and the guttural groans the couple of girls spit out of their bloody faces—they haven't been conditioned beyond their movies and video games. The horror and severity of it is a complete shock to the way they grew up—the rules they thought the real world followed. If they weren't one of the completely unconscious, the time was increasing to allow them to realize they had the opponents outnumbered—and as the adrenaline was wearing off, the Cain boys were running out of steam.

As Lee screamed, begging another punk to toe the line, he was tackled hard from behind by the now-lucid bouncer. Before Lee could turn, the bouncer had a rear-naked choke set in on him—and it was deep—deep enough to produce an involuntary "death rattle" that sounds when the life is being choked out of you. Getting choked out actually isn't a bad way to die. Just like freezing to death, you hit a moment of euphoria. Maybe it's nature's way of letting you go peacefully, but Lee wouldn't know for sure since Chris saved his ass again. Right before things went black, Chris kicked the bouncer in the face putting his bottom teeth through his bottom lip. But you had to hand it to the guy—he still didn't completely let off the choke until Chris went for one of his signature moves—a face bite. Chris chomped in just above where the bouncer's left ear met his head and shook his head from side to side like a gator ripping off a piece of meat. When his ear released from his head, the bouncer released the choke from Lee's neck.

Chris pulled Lee to his feet and knew they were out of time. The crowd was growing, and the cops would surely be arriving soon. They ran to Lee's car, which was parked half a mile away. None of the partygoers decided to chase. Before Lee got into his car, he started throwing up. He had expended so much energy in that ten-minute brawl, he was gassed to the gills. His brother patted him on the back with a handful of bloody knuckles. He was familiar with how raw your hands get when you pound the faces and hair-filled heads of people. Tell you this much, the brains inside those hair-filled heads would think twice before they hang a flag upside down again.

They gave each other a quick and sweaty hug goodbye—they didn't have to say what they already knew. As Lee made his way home with a broken hand and a swollen right eye socket, he didn't know that abbreviated goodbye would be one of the last times he saw his brother alive.

CHAPTER 20

September 11, 2001

Altus, Oklahoma

People rarely remember days—they're much better at remembering moments. Most moments are personal and ownership is only experienced by a select few—the ones who "were there." But there is another type of moment—one with the power to etch itself in millions of minds—a global one owned by humanity. One that profoundly affects us all, drives us, inspires us, and/or shuts us down.

Everyone remembers where they were when the Twin Towers fell down. Scott Burch was working his half-ass job on a half-finished deck, watching the buildings burn with a hammer in his hand. The high school fuck-up had finally found his moment of purpose. While many others around the globe were consumed with fear, a new feeling had entered his body—one that would set his life on a new course: vengeance.

Ghost quit the roofing and siding business and was at the recruiting station the next morning and signed an 18X contract—he'd at least get a crack at Special Forces after basic. Special Forces Assessment and Selection (SFAS) was the hardest thing he'd done in his life. He entered into the service soft, but he was hardened up fast—he vividly remembered stopping to wring the blood out of his socks on the land navigation course. He was tired, hungry, and hurting . . . and he was proud of what he was becoming. The service had given him the thing he was missing—to be part of something bigger—to really contribute. As others dropped out during the suck-fest around him, vengeance only lifted him up—there was no fucking way they'd make him quit.

Once he passed the selection, Scott became a Weapons Sergeant on a team, and so he jumped at the first chance to go to the Special Forces Sniper Course at Fort Bragg. He was naturally a good shot from his time spent hunting and putting food on the table in Oklahoma, but this course took his technical marksmanship to another level and simultaneously mentally prepared him to hunt the ultimate wild game: human beings.

Scott loved all eight weeks of the training. Growing up, Scott hated math, but this was different—he fell in love with calculating ballistic algorithms based on the weather and immediately seeing the results of his "math" hit the targets at eight hundred meters.

Scott also loved the field craft, especially stalking and getting into his "FFB," or final firing position, unnoticed to take his shot. Many of the other students in his class struggled with this, but Scott was never detected. Even the instructors were amazed at how well Scott moved in the woods. So much so they said, "For a big boy from Oklahoma, Burch, you sure do move like a ghost in the woods." The nickname would follow him for the rest of his career.

Everyone remembers their "first." First fuck—first kill . . . hard to say which one is more impactful. In Ghost's case, it was the kill. Sorry, Jackie, you weren't that great in the sack.

In Iraq, outside Sadr City, Ghost sat in the hide site with his spotter and best friend, Red, in a bombed-out building looking for targets. Ghost and Red had been inserted in this location three nights ago. It was hot as fuck, and the blazing sun pushed the temperature over 100. Seemed even the bad guys could be affected by the weather. Ghost and Red had done a textbook nighttime insertion, and besides surprising some kids playing soccer in the alley next to their building, they'd gone undetected. Red had given the kids a chocolate bar along with the universal sign for "be quiet" as they slipped down the alley to their hide site. The kids happily ate the chocolate and returned to their soccer game while watching the Americans walk down the alley.

Red was a good spotter, and his laid-back personality balanced out the intense no-nonsense demeanor of Ghost. The team had built trust with one another. Red was on the spotter scope when all of a sudden he started blinking profusely and cussing. Ghost asked, "You got something?"

Red responded, "No, I'm just getting some reflection of a mirror or something in my scope."

Ghost's honed instincts immediately alerted him and asked, "Where?"

Red responded, "Ten o'clock, four hundred meters in brown building. Why? It is noth—" As Red was forming his sentence Ghost had quickly moved his SR-25 sniper rifle into action, putting his scope right where he saw the light reflection, and fired. The reflection vanished. A stunned Red asked, "Why the hell did you do that? What did that poor mirror do to you?"

Ghost coldly responded with a smirk, "It wasn't a mirror, dumbass. Wait until nightfall. I'll show you, and you'll owe me beer."

Red, now more confused, asked, "Why?"

Ghost checked his weapon and calmly replied, "For saving your miserable life."

After nightfall, Ghost and Red slipped through the city to the building with the mirror. They entered the room where they had seen the reflection and saw the silhouette of a body holding a rifle—dead as roadkill. Red, looked at Ghost and said, "How the hell did you kno—" Ghost cut him off again, "The sun was reflecting off his scope, so for you to be able to see that reflection, means his scope was aimed directly at you." Red felt a little nauseous realizing for the first time how close he came to dying in this godforsaken country.

When they approached the body, it was much smaller than expected. As they inspected what was left of the face minus the blown-out right eye and huge posterior exit wound, the left eye staring back at them looked familiar. He was one of the boys playing soccer—one of the chocolate kids.

Ghost stared into that dead left eye. Red saw an emotion in his friend he had yet to see him exhibit—sadness. Red said, "Hey man, it's them or us . . . so fuck 'em," slapping Ghost on the shoulder. Ghost just nodded but could not take his eyes off that one eye.

Ghost received a Bronze Star with valor for his actions—he had saved Red's life. It was the first of many awards that Ghost received for killing. The kills and medals would only continue to stack up, but so did the nightmares. Each night when he closed his eyes, regardless how many horrors he forget, Ghost would continue to see that kid's face for the rest of his life.

So many bad stories start off with good intentions. The military had given Ghost a community and a mission. The Army had pushed him to "be all that he could be," but that was in terms of killing. When he was expelled from service, Ghost was left high and dry with PTSD, a specialized set of skills, and a really bad taste in his fucking mouth.

Although he was bitter when he chucked his medals in the North Fork Red River, Ghost quickly landed another job as a contractor with Blackwater and found himself back in Iraq in a matter of months. This new role was better than the good old days—this time he didn't have to follow the military's rules. He had a license to kill—and kill he did.

In addition to stints in Iraq and Afghanistan, Ghost also supported some three-letter agencies in South America. It was on one of those trips that Ghost picked off some targets and picked up surfing. He couldn't say he enjoyed being a gun for hire—a mercenary paid to kill—but like most workers, like it or not, you do the job you know how to do. Ghost had been a contractor for Blackwater for years—long enough for the company's notorious name to change to the more neutral "Xe"—when he was approached about a new outfit that was offering way more money.

Ghost made the move, and the work got easier. Unlike his military days, the targets became mostly what seemed like untrained civilians. Ghost didn't know exactly who the new crop of targets were, but the ease of the kills had Ghost feeling like a fox in the henhouse. If the upside was more money and less complexity, the downside was the boredom and the time left alone—more time inside his own head. When one's mind isn't filled with tasks, negativity often fills the void. Instead of pouring himself into something, Ghost secluded himself and poured himself more drinks. His emerging drinking problem was hard to control but easy to mask—especially when every kill went right to plan. In the hit man game, he became known as a "sure shot," which earned him the reputation within the new organization as a valuable asset.

Over time, he developed enough pull with the organization to get his old buddy Red a gun-for-hire gig, too. Red's code name: Diablo.

CHAPTER 21

Wednesday, January 18, 2023. 8:30 a.m.

Gregory's Coffee, New York City

On the days when he had a big fight coming up, Lee was always nervous—and those were the days the odds were really low someone was gonna die. On this day, the weather report for Central Park was calling for a 100 percent chance of death at around 11 p.m. The butterflies were in his gut, and they were not flying in formation.

He slept fairly well in spite of the situation. A steak and a couple beers for a starving cancer patient were better than a handful of Ambien to get some sleep.

On fight days, Lee liked to surround himself with friends and family—people he had trusted for a long time. They weren't there to offer any last-minute advice; it was too late for that. They were there to distract him and keep him loose. Since he never told anyone about his diagnosis, however, he was going to have to fight for his life all alone.

But Lee knew regardless of who was there, when the fight started, you were always on your own. That was how it was for every brawl in which he had ever played a part. As he sipped his espresso and drew upon his past for a moment or memory that might help, he landed on a classic: the day he rode Little Tornado.

BLOODFEUD

When you grow up in the Texas town that held the first-ever bull-rider-only event, you think bull riding is a big deal. When your godfather is George Paul, known as the world's greatest bull rider, you think bull riding could be your deal, too. So, when Lee and Chris were kids growing up in Del Rio, they both dreamed they would be bull riders. By the time they were thirteen and fifteen, they had ridden some bulls in some local shows. In his defense, their dad didn't want them to do it. Being a big guy himself, he knew they were gonna be way too big; bull riders are commonly five foot two or four inches, and his boys were already past that. But it was their idea and if they had the balls to get on the back of a couple-thousand-pound animal in the exact way God had not intended, then so be it.

That was why they got up at the ass crack of dawn and drove the four hours to Mason, Texas. Today was going to be their first real rodeo.

This one in Mason was gonna have it all: Calf roping, steer roping, team roping, saddle bronc riding, barrel racing—all that shit, and of course, the king-daddy of them all—bull riding. Thousands would come out, pay the admission fee, and make a day of it eating oversalted meats to watch even saltier cowboys compete.

When they got there, aside from the venue being way bigger and there being way more competitors, things were run just like the local shows—you get there and you sign up to officially enter the event. Then, the bull riders all meet behind the chutes for bull selection. How that worked was someone placing each bull's number in a cowboy hat and the riders picking a number. That number pulled would match an ear tag of the bull you got. So when you got your number, you walked over to size up your bull. Lee and Chris drew theirs, and Lee had pulled B-19.

They walked over to the pen where the bulls were walking around. All the other bull riders were looking for their bull, too. Lee asked Chris, "Hey, do you see B-19?" and one of the other cowboy kids says, "Oh shit, you got 19? Oh shit, that's Little Tornado." He wasn't smiling—in fact he looked genuinely worried for Lee's future health. Not a good omen and definitely not good for one's nerves.

Then Lee nervously started scanning the ear tags and finally got a look at the beast. Little Tornado was a stocky gray Brahma bull. You know that from those big fucking ugly humps on their back and the absurdly big horns. Noah should have thought twice before he let this species on the Ark—they look particularly nasty.

Once all the numbers were drawn, then they start corralling the bulls into the chutes. What makes a rodeo interesting is when they load the bulls they don't do it in numerical order—they let the bulls decide. So, whatever order your bull runs in the chute, that will decide when you are up. Makes sense. Try telling a one-ton mass of muscle, snot, and piss to please wait its turn in line.

Lee was already having second thoughts when he saw his bull. Those second thoughts were seconded when Little Tornado raced into the pen as the third bull up. Before Lee could even think about backing out or faking a heart attack, he already found himself standing up on the rails of the chute over this fucking great horned monster.

Damn, he was bigger than he looked from the other side of the fence. It was pandemonium as Lee was getting coached with shouts of conflicting instructions from a half dozen cowboys around his chute about how to sit down on the bull's back. When Lee got his legs over the bull, he could feel that motherfucker breathing under him—and when his legs wrapped around, that breathing only got faster. Lee grabbed the bull rope and was trying to get as strong a grip on that bitch as possible. The bull was now twisting and trying to turn in the chute—there was nothing more he wanted to do than get this piece of meat off his back as soon as possible. Lee would never forget how Little Tornado twisted and tilted his head to one side trying to use his dead black eyes to look back at him—look right through him. The only thing stopping him from turning his head completely was that his goddamn horns were so long.

Lee felt from the moment he got on that bull's back that he was not supposed to be there. It was a paralyzing feeling of powerlessness. The twitching and breathing was terrifying—both were no doubt signals that Little Tornado wanted nothing more than to gore and stomp him to death.

Jack Cain could immediately tell his boy was scared shitless. Shit, as tough as Jack was, if he was nervous he did a great job hiding it.

"Are you ready?" screamed the cowboy controlling the chute (he would be the one to open the gates of hell only after he received confirmation that the rider was dumb or crazy enough to try it). The other cowboys were screaming to fire young Lee up. But Lee shook his head and said, "No. Gimme a seckint."

This wasn't unusual. A lot of cowboys won't go until they are absolutely ready. But the cowboy at the gate wanted to get the show on the road—throw it open and watch all hell break loose.

All those cowboys were in a frenzy now. "You got this!" "Switch it on!" they called, doing their best to pump up the young rider—or at least trick him into something he was now well aware was totally insane.

Lee was focused on his hand—punching it to get it tight around the bull rope.

"You ready?" screamed the gatekeeper.

"No. Gimme a seckint!" yelled Lee as he was coming up empty on ways to get the fuck out of this.

"Lee!" yelled his father from outside the chute. "You look at me, boy!" Lee always did as his father instructed. "You see the eyes on that bull?"

"Yessir," answered Lee.

"Well, I'll tell you somethin', those eyes are on the side of his head. And animals with their eyes on the sides are not predators, they are prey!" he screamed, staring right into Lee's eyes.

"A predator's eyes are on the front of his face, son! Those are the killers and the rulers of the earth! Eyes out front likes to hunt! Eyes on the side, run and hide! Now you tell me, where are your eyes, boy?"

"Out front, sir!" yelled Lee back into his father's face.

The smile that spread on Lee's face disarmed him—relaxed him. Made him feel what he was about to do was possible.

"Then do what you came here to do, boy! The man asked, *are you ready?*"

"Yessir! Let's go!"

And with those two words, the gatekeeper fired open the chute, and although the ride didn't last long, Lee's greatest lesson had nothing to do with the ride itself, but the attempt. He had overcome the demon of fear that day and would never be the same after that—the needle on his fear meter was forever changed. Even though he was terrified, he rode into that fear on the top of a bull's back, screaming at the top of his lungs. Courage wasn't the absence of fear; it was still moving forward in spite of it.

Lee smiled as he finished his coffee and looked down in front of him. On the table he had scribbled some notes on a napkin. He had heard if you wrote out your will on anything it was supposed to be legally binding. He stared at the list of who would get what and then stood up with the napkin in his hand.

On his way out of Gregory's, he crumpled up the napkin in his hand and dropped it in the garbage.

Lee thought to himself at the exit, "If fucking Little Tornado couldn't get me, this fucker won't, either. And if the sum bitch does, fuck them. They'll sort it out."

Lee pushed open the door and headed out into the street. It was getting closer to the time to pull the chute.

CHAPTER 22

Wednesday, January 18, 2023. 10:50 p.m.

Strawberry Fields, Central Park, New York City

Strength sticks around, but as you get older, you start losing the speed. Lee noticed his quickness had started to betray him a little at forty—and that was almost a decade ago. *Fuck it*, he thought as he walked toward the memorial in Central Park, *always heard even if you made it to your fifties the wheels fall off anyways.*

Speed or not, Lee knew the motor memory was there—always would be. You throw a few million punches and kicks, and your body would have to be stupid as hell to forget.

Lee was going through his little prefight assessment. Running checks on the machine.

Labrum in the shoulder's been torn for years. Gonna hurt, but it'll do. Fucking ankle's always snap, crackle, pop, but no pain. That's good, but I won't be sneaking up on this motherfucker tonight. I've lost muscle from the fasting, but my cardio is up thanks to the treadmill. I know this bag of bones has got ten minutes of hell left in it. Hope it will take a lot less than that to be sure.

His mind was sizing up his opponent, too.

Guy's gonna be a little shorter, which means I should have the reach. Keep him at a distance. Kick and jab his face off. Gonna be heavier and probably a little younger. But I'm banking my technique will outweigh any strength advantage. And he's no spring chicken—he's gonna gas out, too.

Ghost was already at the designated location—his father taught him if you're not early, you're already fucking late. Maybe this guy wasn't even gonna show, and deep in the recesses of what was left of Ghost's soul, part of him hoped he wouldn't. But just in case this fuck had the balls to step up, Ghost was performing a SWOT analysis of his own.

For strengths, Ghost knew he knew way more about Cain than Cain could possibly know about him. Yeah, he knew he was ex-military and a hit man, but there was nothing about tactics or past history. Shit, the guy didn't even know his goddamn name. Hard to prepare for that. Ghost listed his younger age and fact he wasn't dealing with cancer as definite strengths as well. Ghost was also like most men: he didn't see any weaknesses. As for opportunities, Ghost felt if he had a chance to take things to the ground, he could finish Cain off. A purple belt and years on the mat agreed. In the threats department, Ghost was wise enough to admit anyone could be knocked out in a flash—and aside from that, he had to hope the son of a bitch didn't bring a knife or gun.

After the analysis, Ghost felt he had the upper hand. He checked his watch. *Ten minutes to go. This guy better show up.*

After the prefight checks, Lee felt he had the upper hand. He was focused on deep inhalations through the nose—*focus on your breathing, then it's hard to focus on anything else.* Keeping the adrenaline at bay now was critical. A fight like this can be lost in the walk up. Lee kept breathing to stay relaxed—it wasn't time to waste any energy right now.

10:52

As Lee walked toward the site he had mapped out earlier, he was throwing the occasional air punch—ingrained into his nervous system over a lifetime of violence. His heart rate and temperature were increasing—his blood leaving his organs for his extremities. No need to worry about digesting food now.

Along with the breathing, Lee was now opening and closing his jaw maximally—like a lion roaring with no sound. His head was bent side to side as his walking pace quickened. He was getting close to ready to do this fucking thing.

Ghost was shaking out his feet as if he was kicking water off his combat boots. Left foot, shake, right foot, shake. After a few sets of those, he put his hands up and rotated his shoulders forward and back.

10:53

Then came the slaps. Lee felt them and he was now close enough that Ghost heard them.

As Lee walked, he pounded his chest through his hoodie with an open slap. Then the other side of his chest with the other hand—in rhythm with his steps. After a couple of those, he stopped in his tracks and gave both thighs a slap down and then smacked the back of his sweatpants and hamstrings again as his hands came back up. Slap up, slap down, slap up, slap down. The whaps of his hands were loud—but Central Park was both dark and deserted. He had announced his upcoming arrival, but the cracks weren't for intimidation—they were to feel that fucking hot blood rushing into the areas that had been hit—to let those regions wake the fuck up and be ready for more.

10:54

Then began the bouncing.

In place, Ghost started jumping up and down—like when you jump rope except there was no rope. Hands now defensively up by his chin, the hops began on both feet and then the bounces alternated one foot to the other. Head bobbing—heart speeding up.

10:55

Lee paused in place and reached both arms overhead while taking a deep breath and holding it. He then bent over at the waist and punched the top of both feet. Then he gave the laces of his sneakers another shot—igniting the skin on his knuckles—before using those same weathered hands to hammer-fist both of his shins. *Wish I had a little novocaine for them like we used to.*

No turning back. Never did before, ain't starting tonight. *Take this fucker out, Lebo. Take him out!*

When Lee reached the memorial at 10:56, Ghost was already there. Still a few minutes to go, and each nodded to acknowledge the other's presence. A little show of respect and also confirmation that neither one had pussed out and ducked and ran.

10:57

Each man gravitated to opposite sides of the circular John Lennon memorial, which was lined with a continuous row of benches and a mosaic of the word "Imagine" in the center. Lee started pacing his corner back and forth at five-step intervals, hood over his head, never taking his eyes off Ghost. The sweat was rolling now. Ghost was standing stationary in a brown military T-shirt and a pair of military khakis still shaking out his hands and boots. Weaponless as agreed.

10:58

While still pacing to stay warm, Lee pulled off his hoodie. There was a little bite from the cold air on his sweaty tank top, but the chill wouldn't matter in a minute. Better that than staying warm and getting choked out with your own clothes. Deep nose breath and letting it out with a hiss. Lee violently used the knuckle of his index finger to rub his top lip back and forth right under his nose. The taste of blood and pain it created was the final stimulation for battle.

The two men were staring right through one another. Then, like two magnets being pulled together, as the distance closed between both their bodies, there was absolute certainty the fight was on. As the men marched in, hands came up, stances were assumed, and information was given and gathered as they toed the mosaic and began to circle. The fight had begun—there was no "ready, set, go."

Ranges dictate everything about a fight. Where they were in range four, the two combatants were out of physical reach. Ghost had learned a gun works well here, but this was a bullet-free party. Range four lets you feel out your opponent with feints and movement. As the two men circled, they were testing each other—learning. Both bodies were giving off signals—subtle movements that could be an advantage or a trap—an opening or a set-up for disaster.

They weren't taking their time because no one was rushing in. They were stalemating each other with subtle movements even without touching. Though it resembled chess, this wasn't some bullshit board game—this was a fight to the death. Both men understood that.

11:01

Right before moving into range three, Lee switched to a southpaw stance—from left to right foot forward, from right to left hand back. Since both men had come out orthodox, this was an opening Lee was looking for. As he stepped forward with his right foot and entered the range, he blasted the inside of Ghost's left shin with a left-footed kick. If either had been remotely unsure, the crack of that kick let them both know this shit was real. The fight's cherry was popped, and Lee knew he had the upper hand—first guy to land often wins the fight.

Neither man immediately felt the pain that happens from a kick like that—that shows up later when you wonder why you can barely fucking walk. Only one man would get to enjoy that pain later anyway. By the time Ghost recovered his left foot back to the floor, he pressed forward in anger and immediately moved into range two with his fists flying. Ghost threw a fast three-strike combination and clipped Lee with a shot. He didn't press when Lee retreated with his hands up—but somehow he knew Cain would respect his hands more after that.

They stepped back toward one another and a second Muay Thai kick to the inside of Ghost's left knee had his attention. Lee was using his kicks to dictate the fight. Ghost wasn't in range to punch, so in order to get there he was going to have to pass through the range to get kicked.

Ghost sprinted forward throwing straight rights and lefts. Lee had his hands up absorbing some of the shots and circled out to his right throwing a counter left hook that landed. The adrenaline was peaking. Ghost already seemed to be breathing a little through his mouth. Lee's energy was depleting, but his confidence was growing—that palpable flow of momentum only frustrated Ghost into another attack.

11:02

Ghost again drove Lee back, but this time, like just about every street fight, the two entered range one—the position of the clinch. Both men locked up. Ghost grabbed the back of Lee's head with his right hand and dug in a few dirty uppercuts with his left. Lee pushed Ghost off and as Lee postured up, Ghost dropped down for a double-leg takedown. Lee had assessed correctly—Ghost was heavier and stronger. Because of Ghost's style of attack, Lee now knew must have some ground skills—the cement was not where Lee wanted this fight to go. This takedown could decide everything—*end up on bottom and it could end your life.*

Lee didn't have the strength to stop the takedown. He kicked back with all he had and strained to extend his legs into a sprawl, but Ghost overpowered him and sucked Lee's legs back to him with his arms and scooped Lee up and dumped him on his left hip and back. With the slamming sound of over four hundred pounds of meat hitting and skipping across the stone, the fight now was on the ground.

When one dissects the anatomy of a street fight, the progression through the four ranges of the fight had been predictable—almost expected. The punches and kicks, clinch, and takedown are as common in the UFC as they are in an elementary school playground. Things that can be taught and performed by anyone—things that are familiar. And it is this familiarity that can be a fighter's demise, for when one dissects the mentality of a street fighter, you can find things that can't be taught—and others some people can't even fathom. When the fight hit the ground and Lee bit off Ghost's pinkie finger, his scream wasn't from the pain—it was from the disbelief that this was possible to happen in a fight—to happen to him.

The mentality of a fighter is unfathomable. Some have just dived much deeper than others—and few have ever gone as deep into the ocean of violence as Lee Cain.

Lee spit the finger as far as he could to his left over the benches and into the grass. *Even if I lose, good luck finding that, fuckchop.* The bite allowed Lee the opening to kick Ghost off him and get back to his feet—back to the ranges where he was most comfortable.

11:03

Ghost tried to stay focused, but that is hard to do when you will only be able to count to nine for the rest of your life. He tried to channel his horror and worry into anger. *I'm gonna kill this motherfucker!*

Lee launched a crisp one-two. He knew the cross was solid, because it rocked the bones up his own arm. He was trying to keep his distance. *No takedowns—no mistakes. You got him.*

That shot jerked Ghost's head back and he reflexively rushed in for a tackle around Lee's waist—when your instincts kick in, you fall back on your most comfortable fighting techniques. Again he wrapped Lee up but higher this time, driving Lee backward on his heels. Lee looked back because by trying to stay on his feet, he knew he was running out of real estate—the metal park benches were rushing toward him. Lee's most comfortable answer to Ghost's takedown attempt was a tackle of his own. Like he had done thousands of times on the football field when being rushed at by a running back with his head down, Lee locked his hands over Ghost's back and belly, turned to his right, and lifted as he used Ghost's forward pressure against him and slammed him back first into the bench.

Lee's right hip and elbow crashed into the ground as the bottom half of Ghost's body, complete with a few fractured vertebrae, slid off the bench onto the floor. Before Ghost could move, Lee was on his knees with a fistful of Ghost's hair in each hand—holding his head like a small steering wheel. Lee deadlifted Ghost's upper body to the height of the bench and began slamming the back of Ghost's head—ringing it off the metal bars of the seat like a jackhammer. *Wham, wham, wham* and as Ghost's body went limp, it was as if all the fury had doubled inside of Lee—he was blind in a pure and primal state of rage. He kept smashing Ghost's skull into pieces and then feeling the giant slice that had been opened with his fingertips, Lee put his knee in Ghost's chest and tore his entire scalp forward from the front to the back—like peeling off a toupee with the sound of twisting a stalk of celery in half. He kept going, peeling half his face off forward until he ran out of leverage and then with Ghost's hair laying over his own face, Lee rammed elbow after elbow into Ghost's dead head, filling the soldier's mouth with his own hair and the cement with chunks of his brains. *Eat. That. Mother. Fucker. Eat. That. Mother. Fucker. Eat. That.*

11:04

Right elbow covered in blood and skin and fat, Lee came back to reality. He was breathing rapid fire through his mouth and couldn't calm himself down. He was slowly coming back to where he was and how he had just won the fight of his life—by making a man eat his own fucking face.

Lee checked the body for any identification. Ghost didn't have a thing on him. Lee didn't have the energy to do any more than drag his body to the center of the mosaic—right over the "Imagine." This was one loose end he wasn't going to worry about. Lee was banking on the idea that this John Doe didn't match any records—rarely do hit men exist.

CHAPTER 23

Friday, January 20, 2023. 5:00 p.m.

Franklin Lakes, New Jersey

Saul Silverman wasn't surprised to see the man holding the cardboard box at the door. Ever since the advent of online shopping, his third wife had been melting credit cards ordering more shit she didn't need to the house. *This bitch needs a hobby*, thought Saul. They were rich as hell, but Saul still understood the value of a couple hundred dollars. He still got agitated every time the doorbell rang and a new box of shit was handed off by some delivery person using their piece-of-shit car to make another couple extra bucks off him. *Damn bitch can't even go to the store to pick it up.* The traffic on their long and winding driveway had increased so much, they didn't even use the front gate security system anymore. *Just let them in Saul, it's just the UPS or Amazon guy.* Even on a Friday, the doorbell ringing at this time wasn't out of the ordinary.

Lee Cain was banking on Saul's desensitization to strangers on his front porch—and as he waved to the approaching older man and sensed no state of alarm, he knew he wouldn't have to kick in the front door like he originally planned.

"Hello," said Lee as Saul opened the door.

Saul nodded and just looked down at the package wondering what it was this time. Fucking prick couldn't be bothered with small talk.

"Are you Mister Silverman?" asked Lee—but he already knew he was—he had seen the fifty-nine-year-old's photos when he looked up he address in the high-income New Jersey town.

"Doctor Silverman," he said in a snobby tone with his eyes on the box and his hands out. The fucker was so unsocial it took a few seconds for him to even notice the gun now pointed in his face. When he did, he was frozen.

"Don't fucking move. Don't make a fucking sound," Lee said with a calm authority as he pressed the barrel into Saul's Botox-smooth forehead with some force. "Understand, Saul?" Silverman nodded. With the gun still pressed right between Saul's eyes, Lee ordered "Take two steps back, and if you do anything I will shoot you in the fucking face."

As Saul stepped back in shock, Lee dropped the box and reached into his back pocket—never once taking his eyes off the doctor. Lee quickly assessed the situation. He hadn't seen any cars in the driveway, and from the lack of any noises coming down the hall, Lee knew the Silverman's weren't entertaining tonight—at least not yet—and that was good. Fewer people were going to die.

"What's this about?" asked Saul. He was already quivering.

"Did I say you could speak?" fired Lee back aggressively as he snapped Saul's head back harder with the point of the gun. "I'll be asking the questions here. And if you get the answers right, you may just live."

Saul shut his mouth.

"Is anyone else in the fucking house?" asked Lee.

"No," whimpered Saul as if he was going to start to cry.

"Is anyone coming here today?"

"My wife should be back, but I don't know when."

"Well, we better get cracking and pray I'm not still here before she gets back. Now turn around slowly and put your hands behind your back."

Saul did as ordered and Lee zip-tied the older man's manicured hands behind his back. *Nails like mirrors, this rich fuck*, thought Lee as he finished securing his prisoner. With the gun barrel pressed in the back of Saul's neck, Lee walked the old man down the hall to begin his recon tour on the Silverman estate. Art filled the walls, and the place seemed more museum than mansion—way more comfortable to look at than to touch anything. Lee couldn't imagine someone calling it "home."

As Lee and Saul passed through the kitchen area, Lee used his left empty hand and pulled a big blade from the knife block, an Enso Hammered Damascus, and kept moving to the great room—a huge room of luxurious leather couches, a monster TV system, and a bar area that was larger than ones Lee remembered from the Acuña strip. As Lee ordered Saul to sit in the big dark leather couch in the center, Lee put the gun on the glass table in front of the sofa and stared outside through the wall of picture windows out on the pool and tennis courts. *Lifestyles of the Rich and Famous* was one idea that kept flashing through Lee's mind—the other was he needed to know what role this doctor had played in trying to have him killed.

The backward right pimp slap really got the doctor's attention. It had knocked Saul off his ass and on his left side. Between the slap being so disorienting and the tender leather being so soft, the old man was stuck unable to sit back up. Lee yanked the man back by his shirt and pressed him hard back into the couch. If it had been in any question, complete dominance had been firmly established.

"Okay, Sauly boy," Lee began as he moved the knife in his left hand in front of Saul's face, "I need the answer to some questions. If I feel you've answered them to my liking, the odds are good you don't die today. If . . ." Lee put the tip of the knife right against Saul's Adam's apple, "I think you are lying, I'm going to fillet you alive. Starting with your fucking feet and working my way up."

Saul was too terrified to move a muscle with the knife on his neck. His eyes staring down at the blade so hard it made his face into a giant frown.

His cosmetic surgeon would not have been happy with the wrinkles it produced. With Saul completely transfixed on the knife, Lee moved the blade away and to the left—Saul's eyes and head turning to track it. He never saw the perfectly set-up second bitch slap coming.

"All right! All right!" yelled Saul through now bloody lips as Lee hauled him back to the seated position. Before Saul's ass was firmly sunk in the leather cushion, Lee had ripped a liver shot to Saul's stomach, the likes of which the doctor had never previously experienced. Saul's diaphragm locked up, and, as he choked from getting the "wind knocked out of him" for the first time since he was a kid, Lee was screaming in his gasping face, "Nothing is all right, you fucking shithead! You speak again and you bleed to fucking death right here!" and Lee put a three-inch slice across Saul's right shoulder. Saul didn't feel the incision, but he did feel the blood run down.

"Do you know who I am?" choked out Saul in disbelief from the knife wound.

Lee answered that question with an uppercut to the nose snapping Saul's head back like a Pez dispenser—a solid rip pressing Saul's nose horribly to the left. It took a few seconds, and the blood starting pouring.

"If you haven't figured it out, I don't give a fuck about you. But while we're on introductions, let's remove the suspense. My name is Lee Cain."

It took a moment to register, and then the look of fear in Saul's eyes was a combination of recognition and fear.

"That's right, Sauly baby," smiled Lee, "I'm the guy Dr. McCormack called you about . . ." and Lee leaned back and stomped Saul's nose even a little flatter. Saul was bloody and dazed, but still coherent—right where Lee wanted him.

"Now," Lee said as he sat on the table and placed the knife next to the gun, "why don't you tell me a little about yourself? And don't bore me with medical shit or your bio. Who the fuck do you work for and why did you try to have me killed?"

"They will kill me if I tell!" cried Saul.

"The way I see it, Saul," Lee said picking back up the knife, "talking to me gives you a chance to live. And better hurry up, too, 'cause we wouldn't want that pretty wife Kate of yours to die too would we? Now who do you work for?"

"Work for? You simpleton. We don't work for anyone. We run the world," sneered Saul.

"Who's 'we'?" said Lee, grabbing Saul's flattened nose and twisting it hard.

"Aggghhhh! Artemis! I work for Artemis." He screamed in pain.

There is a line of pain people have never reached. A threshold they think they can take and still be tough—still keep their constitution. The punches and slice weren't enough to get Saul chirping—he had stayed strong to honor his covenant with Artemis—but the crunching sounds in his ears of his own cartilage and nasal bones twisting off his face had him singing like a canary. Lee had his spot and wouldn't let go.

Saul was sobbing now. He had crossed his Rubicon. He knew he was dead now for sure. And if he had sealed his fate, he could at least extend what life he had left a little longer.

"And they are the people that tried to kill me?" Lee asked

"A division of theirs, called Security," Saul said in between mouth breaths—that was the only place air would enter him now.

"And what division do you work for?"

"Longevity."

"Does that division have a cure for cancer?" asked Lee lessening the nose hold.

"No," Saul answered tentatively. Lee instinctively twisted his nose harder.

"AHHHGGG! I mean they have it in another division! Disease control," screamed Saul, his face searing in pain.

"What the fuck is Artemis?"

"You've heard of secret societies? The Illuminati? The Freemasons? Skull and Bones? Bilderberg all the way back to the Knights Templar?"

"Yeah?"

"They are nothing. Some real and outdated, others legends we created . . . to keep people off our scent," Saul came clean through a face of snot and blood. "We are the rulers of society . . . of the world. We don't just move the markets, we control the economies. We control the political climate and the global climate. We dictate the information and entertainment. We decide on the wars overseas and who dies at home."

"Because you have a cure for cancer?"

"Cancer? Cancer? Ha!" laughed Saul. "That division has a cure for almost any affliction. Our cures are just goddamn fundraisers for the real objective."

"Fundraisers?" questioned Lee.

"Yes, you want a cure for your disease? It's a hundred million a pop."

Lee raised his eyebrows.

"Don't act surprised," spat Saul. "There are almost three thousand billionaires worldwide. A hundred million dollars to cure a loved one or yourself is an easy sale. And now people buy them like insurance policies if some disease does crop up. The trillions we generate fund the real project for my division."

"Longevity?"

"Immortality," answered Saul.

"What?"

Saul took a deep breath and tried to compose himself. "True wealth and power is not about money. History has shown us that the richest and poorest of us all leave the same behind—everything. But there is a most important currency. More important than silly money, gold, stocks, or real estate. None of them can buy an ounce of time. But we are closer than ever to Ambrosia."

"Ambrosia?"

"It was the food of the gods, the food of the immortals. This is our Holy Grail," sighed Saul.

"Is this what Longevity is working on?" Asked Lee.

"One of the divisions," replied Saul, "There is medical, particle physics, and space exploration."

"What?"

"Well, when you imagine living forever, you understand it won't be here. The earth will cool with ice ages, the sun will eventually burn out. If we create immortality through medicine or physics, we have to be ready. Artemis is planning ahead."

"But not for the human race," said Lee, absorbing the information.

"No. This isn't about preserving people. This is for the preservation of wealth."

"I thought you said this wasn't about money," said Lee.

"I said time is more valuable than money, but time really is money. Money gives you control over people's time. Money gives you control over your own time, which is true wealth. But with enough time, you can also have endless money and rule humanity. Instead of passing the money down from generation to generation and watch some drunk grandnephew blow it, there is another way. The rich aren't doing this because they want to cheat death or to see farther into the future, they seek immortality to experience the magical combination money and time can create—Compounding. This whole thing is what we have always been about—greed."

Lee knew the clock was ticking. He had the name of the company. He had enough leads to follow. The doctor had served his purpose.

Lee leaned over and grabbed the gun.

"What are you doing?" Saul whimpered.

"I'm gonna kill you."

"No . . . no! You said I would live," pleaded Saul.

"I lied. Don't you remember you tried to kill me, you stupid fuck?"

"But I have what you need!"

"What's that?"

"I have the cancer cure. Here!" bargained Saul.

"Are you fucking lying?"

"No, I promise. Take me upstairs. I'll show you."

Lee ripped him up with his gun-free hand, and Saul directed them up a massive, curving staircase and then down the hall to the master bedroom. They moved past the king-size bed into the walk-in closet. Packed with suits and shoes and bags. They made it to the back corner—to a five-foot black safe with a keypad on the front.

"Sit down and gimme the goddamn code."

CHAPTER 24

Friday January 20, 2023. 5:16 p.m.

Franklin Lakes, New Jersey

Saul sat down surrounded by an accumulation of the spoils of his career and spoke the numbers. With a turn of the giant handle, Lee opened what Saul had often referred to as his "infinity safe," and although he was unsure of what everything he was looking was at other than the $100-million IV bag on the top shelf, Lee knew everything inside had to be of great value. He also knew he would be filling the Bottega Venetta duffel with as much of it as he could carry. Lee grabbed the IV bag first.

"Is this the cure?"

"Yes," nodded Saul.

"And you just inject it?"

"Just like an IV," said the doctor.

Then Lee began opening the ten drawers inside the safe.

"What are these?" asked Lee holding up a stack of small rectangular objects.

"They are crypto cold wallets," answered Saul.

"How much is on them?"

"Billions."

"And these?"

"Hard drives."

"What's on them?"

"Things of greater value than on the wallets," Saul said and he slumped.

Lee unzipped the duffel and placed in the IV bag, the cold wallets, and hard drives. The gold and platinum bars did not need explaining, but they were heavy, so Lee stacked as much as he thought he could move. He filled the bag to what he estimated was about sixty pounds of precious metal. He grabbed some jewelry, a couple boxes, and a few six-inch stacks of manila folders filled with documents. The final quick grabs were boxes of ammo and a few guns and one suitcase on the bottom. Seems Saul really was ready for the future.

Lee carried the heavy bag from the shoulder strap and the suitcase in his left hand while keeping the gun trained on Saul and leading him back downstairs. The two bags were almost too heavy for Lee in his physical condition. He was still wrecked from his fight in Central Park, but when you know you have over a $100 million in loot, you'd be surprised what you can carry. Lee dropped the bag and suitcase in the hallway that led to the front door and sat Saul back down on the couch. Lee walked over to the bar.

"Any last things you can think of before you die?" asked Lee, still looking at bottles of spirits he had never seen before.

"But . . . but, I gave you everything! You don't have to kill me! Please!" pleaded Saul.

"If you gave me everything, then it is time for you to go," said Lee as he turned around with a bottle of Clase Azul tequila. "Man," smiled Lee looking at the bottle, "I've had my share of tequila, but this is one I've only ever heard about. Now I know in my condition I shouldn't be drinking, but maybe just this once . . ." and he took off the top and had a taste.

He heard her when he began walking back over toward Saul. . . .

"Saul?" called his thirty-nine-year-old trophy wife, Kate, "Are you home?"

"Say, 'in here,' or I shoot her," whispered Lee quickly.

"Over here," Saul called back as Lee rushed over and placed his left shoulder to the wall that bordered on the hallway.

When people list potential things that might cause their death, many list car crash, heart attack, or old age. Few ever list finishing up with their side-piece too early. But that's exactly what Kate did, and exactly why Kate was home thirty minutes earlier than usual—and got clotheslined by Lee as she rounded the corner in search of Saul. Kate was out before she hit the floor. She landed on her back with her legs spread eagle, G-string on full display.

While Lee admired Kate's assets, Saul pussied out and saw this as his last opportunity to run. He almost got past the kitchen, too, but it's hard to run when a bullet blasts through your left ass-cheek. As Saul writhed in pain facedown and bleeding on his shiny hardwood, Lee zip-tied Kate and dragged her to the couch by her bleached hair. Then he dragged Saul back over by his feet as his busted face slid through his own blood. With them both on the couch, this time he zip-tied their ankles, too. With his hostages secured, Lee went back to the bar and starting throwing bottles and smashing them against different walls of the room—shattering and splattering hundreds of thousands of dollars' worth of bottles with his quarterbacking arm. After he had chucked bottles into all four walls, he began selecting and carrying bottles over to the glass table in front of the couch—bottle service for a going-away party.

Lee wished he had time to look up the value of the different spirits— he had spent a lifetime in and out of bars, and most of these brands were totally unfamiliar. At least he recognized the Patrón, but man, even that was some fancy-ass bottle. He took a taste of that one, too—no self-respecting Texan wouldn't. He also scooped up some Macallan whisky, Glenfiddich scotch, Nolet's gin, Kors vodka, and Havana Club rum in his arms and placed them on the table. He realized he forgot the brandy to complete the set of six base liquors, but he could do some drinking later—it was time to get down to business. As Kate was grunting and drifting back into consciousness, Lee took a big slug of the Patrón and then to help her along, he spit it in her fucking face.

If you need a pick-me-up, a spray of tequila in your eyes and nose will restart your engine.

Kate woke up to the absolute horror of which she was now a part.

"Saul," she retched looking at her beaten, bleeding, and restrained husband. "What's happening?" She was wildly looking at the complete stranger in front of her.

"Stay calm, Kate," assured Saul, "Everything is going to be all right."

"The fuck it is, Saul," bellowed Lee as he turned toward them and held the bottle of Glenfiddich over Saul and the Nolet's over Kate and started dumping the expensive liquor on them in circles.

"You're both fucking dead. Yer about to burn. Yer about to feel pain like your little brains can't imagine. You ready for this?" screamed wild-eyed Lee as the bottles ran empty and he fired both of them into the wall.

The common pleas of desperation that occur during the death struggle came out.

"Noooo!" whined Saul, "Not her, not her, please. . . . She had nothing to do with this!" Kate just screamed in utter panic.

Lee turned back around again with the now opened bottles of Kor's and Macallan. He took a taste of each, savoring it as if he were oblivious to their begging and pleading. Then he turned back toward them in rage.

As he dumped the next two bottles all over the weeping and begging victims, he shouted, "You think I'm letting anyone go? How did you get to be a doctor, you stupid fuck? You tried to have me killed, and you know who the fuck I am. You were dead the second I set foot in this fucking place. And now she's dead, too. Did nothing? Did nothing? You both live on a big pile of blood money, you fucking clown. All this wealth because you let millions of kids die. Just sat there. With a fucking cure? Cancer is small potatoes? You are gonna burn in hell for the pain and suffering you have allowed to happen. I am just giving you the fucking preview."

Saul was blubbering at this point. Kate was screaming over and over, "Not me! Not me! I am innocent. I am innocent!"

"No, you are fucking guilty!" Lee raged. "Where did you think this house came from? The cars? The money? From a doctor that doesn't fucking see patients? This is all built on blood money." Lee leaned right into her ear. She leaned away and he yanked her back by the fucking fake colored hair. "You hear that? That's the millions of parents wailing after watching their kids shrivel up and die." Lee threw her head back and as she tried to respond Lee knocked her silly with an open-handed slap. "Shut the fuck up." Slumped over, she did as she was told.

"A hundred and fifty years!" screamed Saul with his last bargaining chip, "We have that already. That time is worth more than anything you have in those bags!

"A hundred and fifty?" Lee asked with his demeanor changing, giving Saul a sense of hope.

"Yes, yes!" pleaded Saul, "I can get that for you."

Lee placed his right hand on his chin as if he were pondering the deal. Then he opened the top of the Patrón and poured it over Saul's screaming head. "If it's out there, then I don't need you to find it. Do I?"

Saul was out of options; he had reached the final stage of desperation—when you're backed in the corner with nowhere to go but forward. "You know how big this goes? No movie stars ever get sick. No politicians die. The big charities? They know! Don't you think it's interesting the boards of these places never die of disease? We rule the world, you country bastard. The most powerful people in the world will be after you! They are gonna kill you!"

The threat made Lee smile as he fired the Patrón bottle into the wall and put his hand in his front pocket. "Fuck you, Saul. They tried a few times already. Maybe I'll make them beg like an absolute pussy just like you. Remember that as the last great thing you did. You went out a coward—without a shred of fucking dignity. I'm not the bad guy here. You have killed millions."

As he pulled the matchbook from his pocket and struck a match, Saul started kicking, screaming, and convulsing. Kate lay there slumped in half-consciousness. Lee dropped the match and set them ablaze.

As Lee walked out of the house with the duffel and suitcase, he pondered just how much value was in the bags. Little did he know he had just set the most expensive liquor-based fire ever. Chris would be proud. Cost infinitely more than a Flaming 151. But, damn, it went up just as good.

CHAPTER 25

1992–1994

VFW Building, Del Rio, Texas

When Lee went off to college, his mom told everyone at the VFW who'd listen that she was the mother of a college football player. Lee did this and Lee did that. She was never one not to brag about her sons if there was something worth bragging about. And none of those grizzled war vets minded a bit. Hell, they all had a hand in raising that boy. The old ladies who taught him to dance with that jukebox knew all the girls at school would like him as much as they did. Lee had gone from that little towheaded kid at the end of the bar to a bit of a hometown hero. Not many people ever got out of Del Rio—and when they did, it was worth talking about.

Grace would often take a moment in between serving whiskey sours at the bar to wonder what her youngest was doing. She couldn't begin to imagine what it was he was learning in those schoolbooks, but there was one thing she was sure of—her boy was tearing up fools on the football field. Yeah, the one thing she missed most was watching her boy kick ass under the Friday night lights. When you are the mother of the starting quarterback and linebacker, you get special privileges. Grace enjoyed being a center of attention for two seasons compliments of her boy Lee.

When Lee went off to college, the toughest part for Grace was the distance. Besides the occasional phone call update (Lee and Grace sure as hell weren't gonna be writing letters) and a holiday and summer visit or two, her boy had moved on. She often thought if she had known how little time she would spend with Lee after about sixteen, she would have savored the time more when she had it. When you are a parent, hindsight is often twenty-twenty.

But there were two nights that Lee put his momma back in the limelight—center stage. Those were the two nights that his games were televised in Del Rio. And the biggest night of them all was when Lee's school played Texas A&M. Seemed like the entire damn town was in the VFW that night. The drinks were flying over the bar, but no one seemed to mind if Grace wasn't paying attention except to that TV when Lee's team was on defense. His sophomore year, he was a linebacker since his quarterbacking days were long gone—kinda what happens when you jack yourself up to 230 pounds and like punching people in the mug.

Every time Lee made a tackle, the whole VFW erupted in cheers. Everyone was pointing and telling each other, "You see him?" "There he is!" "I knew him when . . ." Cowbells were ringing, and all eyes were on Grace. She was smiling from ear to ear and cheering her boy on with the rest of them. The pours that night were more generous than usual, and so were the tips. That's what you do when your son helps his team win one of the biggest games in school history. That 35–34 victory was another gift Lee gave her from afar, but he wasn't done that night.

After the game was over, Lee called her at the VFW from the stadium. When Joe handed Grace the phone, he started shouting for everyone to quiet down so Grace could talk to her son. The whole crowd obediently quieted down and listened in to Grace's half of the conversation.

"Hey y'all," shouted Grace to the group, "It's Lee, and he said, 'those tackles today were for you!'"

The crowd burst into cheers, only to be quieted down by Grace using one arm to shush them while the other held the phone to her ear.

"I am proud of you, son," said Grace. "You done real good tonight. Real good. It was somethin' else to see you up there on the TV."

"Thanks Momma," replied Lee. "And don't tell all of them at the bar, but those tackles were really for you."

Grace died of cancer less than a year after that phone call.

The funeral service was why Lee found himself back in Del Rio driving with his older brother Chris. Chris had returned a little fucked up after Desert Storm. The town respected who he was, and every person he was around was afraid of him. Everybody.

With his dreams of college football behind him, Chris found himself back in trouble. He felt most natural when he was living most dangerously. Perfect fit for the Cain house. While Lee was now wreaking havoc on the sports field, Chris began to excel in a much less desirable arena. First, it was collecting money. Then it was dealing drugs. Then it was shit no one wanted to even think about. Chris did the dirty jobs few wanted to do. Money was money.

As bad as he was, Lee always knew Chris was different than just a drug dealer. To those on the outside, Chris was a bad dude. With a capital B. A different echelon of evil. Everything he did had a constant element of risk and danger. But Chris was still Lee's big brother. His mentor and friend.

Sharing blood or not, Lee became less and less comfortable around Chris.

Visits home from college only led to places littered with shady-ass creeps and hookers. Lee would be sitting outside realizing there were people on the fringe into some wacked-out shit. Finally having escaped Del Rio, Lee had too much to risk.

Lee knew better than to try and talk to him about it. Chris was so far gone, it woulda been a colossal waste of words. There was never a question he was not going to do it. You couldn't have that conversation.

He knew it and knew you knew it. So you just kept your mouth shut and hoped he came out of a crackhouse not shot up.

When Lee found himself back in the car with Chris after his mom's service, he actually couldn't believe he was fucking stupid enough to be there. It's so easy to fall back into bad habits. After some small talk, Chris pulled off into some neighborhood and pulled the old, "I gotta pick up somethin' real quick."

When the car came to a stop outside a shitbox trailer, Lee said, "Hey man, I don't wanna be here."

Chris quickly turned to him and said, "And I don't want you here, neither!" Then Chris got out of the car, hustled inside and came out in less than a couple minutes. As he walked to the car, he looked left and right like something was obviously bothering him.

When Chris sat down and placed the brown paper bag under the seat, he turned to Lee and said, "Shitbird, you think I want you here? Hell nah. I wish you never came back here and sure as hell never had to see me. I always told you you are smarter than the rest of us. Didn't I always say, 'don't fuck with this shit'? You got talent, and you gotta be the one that gets outta here. Dad said yer the one to break the cycle."

He turned back to the steering wheel and started up the car.

"You got some talent, too, ya know," Lee snapped back. "Now that you are out, you could still take a crack at playing ball."

"We will see, little brother," Chris said with a smile as he patted Lee's leg. "Just keep your fucking head down, and keep doin' what yer doin'. When we're all dead here there won't be no reason to ever come back," said Chris, looking straight forward. "No one like me to fuck things up for you. That will be when you are finally safe."

As many lives as Chris had probably ruined, he promised himself to damn sure not add Lee's to the list. When Lee returned years later for Chris's services following his unsolved murder, he broke that promise big time.

CHAPTER 26

Saturday, January 21, 2023. 2:00 a.m.

Eighth Floor, Hope Lodge

Lee felt the fatigue in the marrow of his fucking bones. What was left of his once hulking frame was sore as hell, and he thanked it for coming through for him just one more time. He had finally reached a mythical state he was never able to achieve in the athletic arena: complete fatigue. Yeah, he thought, *I squeezed all the juice out of this fucking orange*. No matter how many years Lee had ahead, few people's bodies could rack up the same mileage.

As fucking physically dead tired as he was, he couldn't close his eyes. With the mixture of adrenaline, caffeine, and chemo coursing through his veins, he just laid there on the bed—the bed where he had offed a hit man only days earlier—his body incapable of motion, but his mind racing. His eyes bored holes in the ceiling of his room as if they would uncover an answer. Were more hit men coming? Did he cover all his tracks? How far up did this friggin' conspiracy go?

But there was one question that kept jumping up to the front of the line in his mind over and over. Raising its hand and yelling louder over the rest. Call it selfish or call it self-serving. Whatever it was, old habits die hard—he still had a little of the young man still trapped inside of him. Since shut-eye was impossible, and he was gonna disappear in a few hours, he was faced with a dilemma—what was he gonna do when he said goodbye to that girl?

He couldn't take it. In a few minutes he was going over there and he was either gonna do it or he wasn't.

The debate raged inside his head so loud, he groaned as his used his pulled ab muscles to sit up. With his head throbbing, he was looking left and right on the floor for answers as if the devil on one shoulder and angel on the other were offering choices.

Should he do it? Or shouldn't he? The angel and devil offered up their evidence. Right or wrong, wrong or right.

There was the age thing for sure. Fuck, he was twice her age. Some people might commend him, and others would say he was completely insane. But, Lee remembered, he'd stopped worrying long ago about what other people thought about him—fuck them.

And what about her? Would it fuck her up worse? Shit, she was so sick at this point, what the fuck did it matter? He wasn't going to be sticking around to find out anyway. Ethics were completely out the window.

Would he be doing her a favor or would it be a disaster? He wanted to, but then he didn't. He had his share already; he didn't need it this time, did he? Right or wrong, wrong or right?

Morals and values are shit you're told when you're young—be nice, say thank you, respect your elders, tell the truth. But when the rubber hits the road, those are usually things you figure out over a lifetime for yourself. What you stand for and what you don't, what you'll put up with and what you sure as fuck won't tolerate. Unfortunately, most people's values are created from their behaviors instead of the other way around. For most of Lee's life this had been true. He'd broken half the Ten Commandments before he knew who he really was—and learned to be okay with it.

But this was a decision he wished he didn't have to make. A strange case where neither one was the best choice. No matter how it went in her room, someone was going to lose—and for sure both people were gonna get hurt.

Lee mustered all his strength and used his battered hands to help minimize the cracks in his knees as he stood up. He arched his back and got a solid couple of audible spinal pops. He left the room and forced himself down the hall. He thought to himself, *If you are a fucking man, stop being a little bitch and go.*

When he knocked on the door, he still didn't know how this was gonna go.

She answered the door and looked so unsurprised to see Lee, as if she knew he would be knocking. Like she was expecting him.

"I'm so glad to see you, Tex-ass," said Julia rubbing her eyes. "I was getting worried you weren't coming back."

She saw the bruises and the cuts.

He saw she wasn't wearing much, and she didn't hide it.

All it took for Lee was to see her like this—he wasn't going to stop now. He knew what he had to do. The decision was made.

"Nah, no worries, kid. You knew I would be back. What are you doing up so late?" Lee asked.

"Waiting for you . . ." she said seductively and before her courage gave out, she grabbed his wrist and pulled him inside.

Less than an hour later, Lee Cain snuck back out of the room. Even though he hadn't been there as long as he would have liked, he wanted to believe he gave her the night of her life.

Some would not agree with what he did. Some would go as far to say he was crazy.

Fuck them. Now he needed to get the fuck out of Dodge.

CHAPTER 27

Saturday, January 21, 2023. 6:00 a.m.

Atrium, Hope Lodge

"Aren't you supposed to be here another week?" asked the doorman as Lee handed in his room key.

"Nah, Donny," smiled Lee, "I am feeling so much better, I thought I would get outta here a little early and enjoy that sunshine."

"Glad to hear it," replied Donny as he noticed the stuffed hockey bag on the dolly Lee was using to move his things. Looked like country guy had picked up a lot of stuff during his stay in the Big Apple.

That duffel bag would be tossed in a dumpster in a quiet town still too far behind to have video cameras. Buried in some burg like a lot of Lee's other skeletons.

It was time to move. He had covered his tracks, but there was still one loose end. Whoever the fuck was at the controls for the hit men knew who he was—and what he could do.

Lee's only hope was they only came after people at the time they received an order. Since he was pretty sure no one else was going to be placing one of those in the near future, he felt he had bought himself some time.

Time—until he had cancer, he never realized it was the thing of greatest value. Only when you come to the harsh reality that it's running out do you really appreciate it—only when you realize it is coming to an end will you fight for it.

The money behind the conspiracy wasn't about cancer treatments, drugs, charities, or crooked docs. The billions was all about selling time. And for even a few extra months with a loved one chewed to the bone and withered to shit, a person would squeeze out every last nickel. And if it was you with the cancer in your ass, you would spend all your money and time killing yourself just to have a little more.

Talk about a vicious cycle.

As Lee pulled the hit man's car out of the garage, his shredded knuckles were testament he had spent his life fighting for time in different ways. Sometimes it cost him time in a jail cell. Recently, he fought like hell just to extend it—to pay himself back with a few more years. But either way, Lee knew he would never give up fighting for time. When the reaper came for him, Lee Cain knew he wouldn't roll over—he would go down in a swinging fury of lefts and rights like he just might be the first one to get out of this shit alive.

As he crossed over the George Washington Bridge headed into New Jersey, Lee let the call go to voicemail. When you are driving a stolen vehicle of a dead hit man with said dead hit man in the trunk in a duffel bag, you pay a little more attention to the rules of the road. When he would play that message at his first piss break in Pennsylvania, he was frozen by the good news that the cancer was gone. Doctor Mulholland read him his report and even she couldn't believe it—the biopsy came back clean. She was proud to say the words she rarely used: He was "medically now considered cancer-free."

After Doctor Mulholland hung up the phone, she sat back, smiled, and said to no one in the room, "Son of a bitch. The guy discovered the cure for cancer." Little did she really fucking know.

Knowing he had completely killed the tumor was liberating, and as he sat in that parking lot of an Exxon gas station, he started to laugh out loud. All that deliberating—all that mental turmoil—a few hours before was for nothing. Either way it woulda went, Lee Cain would have no regrets. But thank God he made the right choice on that one. Maybe it was the news, or thinking about last night with Julia—but for the first time in months, he was feeling better—people always had more energy when they had a sense of purpose.

As he popped the radio on to the only country station he could find, the compass read "south." He was going back to Del Rio to get the boys together. Maybe even hit up Pancho's for a drink. Then he had way bigger fish to fry. Artemis was supposed to be the goddess who had magical powers of healing and immortality. Lee was gonna need some time to figure out how he was going to make her die.

The soldier was right. Best gift you can give yourself is no regrets.

Lee regretted nothing—he was glad he gave the IV bag to the girl.

Now it was time for her to finally dream for once.

Eyes out front.

PART 2
BLOODFEUD

There's a man goin' 'round takin' names
And he decides who to free and who to blame
Everybody won't be treated all the same
There'll be a golden ladder reachin' down
When the man comes around
—Johnny Cash

The Bull

The bull is an impressive animal. It doesn't know fear. It knows only the instinct to charge and fight.

In the open field, the bull is king—its strength unrivaled, its ferocity unmatched. But the arena is not the open field. Here, the odds are skewed, the game fixed. In the trap of the arena, the bull's raw power is meant to be contained, its spirit tested, its body broken for the applause of the crowd.

Yet, the bull has no concept of surrender. It charges again and again, bleeding defiance. The matador wields a blade, but when the matador is careless, when the crowd underestimates the bull's ferocity, it does the unthinkable. It reminds the world that even when the rules are stacked, raw power can rewrite the script.

CHAPTER 28

Thursday, December 31, 1995. 10:15 p.m.

Acuña, Mexico

The city of Acuña had a pulse that beat harder on New Year's Eve. The air vibrated with anticipation, a frenetic energy spilling out into the streets. Music, laughter, and the sharp crackle of fireworks echoed through the night, painting the sky in fleeting flashes of light. The neon sign above Lando's, a grungy nightclub on the city's strip, buzzed as partygoers lined up below with the excitement of a fresh year only hours away. It was the kind of night that could go either way—wild celebration or chaotic disaster.

Lee Cain had never been much for quiet nights.

Before he even reached the front door of Lando's, Lee found himself in trouble. Across the street, a young white kid he knew was being tossed around by two Mexican guys. The kid, Jamie, was barely old enough to be in Mexico unsupervised, let alone handle a couple of grown men.

Lee's temper flared as soon as he saw it. There was nothing he hated more than a bully. He didn't care that it was New Year's Eve. He didn't care that he was supposed to be going out for a good time. Lee's night had just changed.

Without a second thought, he sprinted across the street, and like a hammer coming down hard, he was ready to jump into the fight. The two

Mexicans, Clown 1 and Clown 2 as Lee would later call them, were just a couple of posers. Like most street punks, they didn't know shit about fighting, but they sure knew how to swing at someone weaker.

Lee loved these moments. He loved the clarity of it all. The world made sense in a fight.

He made the first move, driving a hard teep kick straight into the first guy's jaw. The sole of his boot connected with a sickening crack, and Clown 1 crumpled to the ground like a marionette with its strings cut. His body hit the pavement in a heap, out cold before he even realized what happened.

Clown 2 was ten feet away, still pounding on Jamie, oblivious to his friend's downfall. That was his first mistake. Lee closed the distance, his adrenaline pumping as he grabbed Clown 2 by the shoulder and yanked him off the kid.

"Your turn," Lee muttered through clenched teeth.

Clown 2 tried to throw a punch, but Lee was faster. A left hook came swinging in, landing with a thud against Clown 2's temple. The guy's knees buckled as he swayed on his feet, stunned by the power behind the hit.

Lee was relentless. For good measure, he kicked the guy in the head as he went down, but his foot slipped on the slick pavement, and Lee tumbled to the ground.

He glanced down at his now scuffed pants and chuckled, feeling a little embarrassed. Two guys knocked out cold, and all he could think about was how he'd just decreased his chances of getting laid tonight. Still, KO'ing a couple of greasers was worth it.

The sounds of fireworks were still popping in the background as Lee wiped the dust off his jeans. He reached out a hand to Jamie, helping the kid to his feet.

"Get your shit together, man," Lee grumbled, shaking his head. "Don't go getting in fights you can't finish."

Jamie nodded, still in shock. "Thanks, man."

Lee didn't stick around to hear more. He had his own night to enjoy, and with the adrenaline still coursing through him, he was ready for whatever Lando's had to offer.

Lando's was packed, just as Lee had expected. The inside was a swirling sea of bodies, the air thick with sweat, booze, and anticipation for midnight. It was exactly the kind of chaos Lee loved. As he made his way through the crowd, he spotted his older brother, Chris, on the other side of the bar, cracking jokes with his best buddy Slick Jimmy.

The three of them had always been tight, ever since they were kids. Chris and Lee were a wild pair, constantly getting into fights, trouble, and whatever else came their way. Jimmy was no different, a hellraiser in his own right. The three of them together? It was a recipe for disaster, but in the best possible way.

Lee grabbed a beer and leaned against the bar, half listening to the music, half scoping out the girls nearby. The night was young, and the prospects were looking good. The crowd was getting drunker by the minute, and Lee could feel the tension building toward something bigger. Something crazier.

He didn't know how right he was.

Across town, one of the Salazar brothers was nursing a slow burn of anger. His younger brother, the same Clown 1 who Lee had just KO'd, had called him. The kid was whining about getting beat up, crying about how some white guy blindsided him.

The oldest, though, wasn't like his brother. He didn't cry. He didn't whine. He didn't talk. Salazar acted. And when he acted, people got hurt.

He tossed his phone down after the call, glancing at the kid slumped in his passenger seat. Pathetic. Salazar didn't care about most people, but his family? His blood? That was a different story.

"*Vamos,*" he muttered, shifting the car into gear and heading toward Lando's. He was about to teach someone a very painful lesson.

Back at the bar, Lee had just downed his second beer when the commotion started. The door to Lando's slammed shut with a loud bang. Someone yelled something in Spanish. It wasn't until the words fully registered that Lee realized what was happening.

"*Cierra la puerta!*" The door was locked. On New Year's Eve.

"Shut the gate?" Lee muttered under his breath. His eyes scanned the room, the hairs on the back of his neck standing on end. Something wasn't right. This wasn't just a bar fight brewing. This was something else. Something bigger.

And then it happened. Clown 1, still nursing the wounds Lee had given him earlier, pointed across the bar. Pointed straight at Chris and Jimmy.

A wave of recognition hit Lee as his stomach dropped. The fight from earlier. They weren't after him. They were after his brother.

Salazar, a hulking figure in the crowd, made his way through the packed room like a predator stalking prey. He didn't stop. He didn't hesitate. He just walked right up to Jimmy and blindsided him, brass knuckles flashing as he sucker punched him in the side of the head. Jimmy went down like a ton of bricks, crumpling to the floor.

Before anyone could react, the elder Salazar spun on his heel and clocked Chris with the same set of brass knuckles, knocking him out cold. Lee's world slowed to a halt. His brother—the toughest guy he knew—was down.

"Chris!" someone screamed.

Lee's eyes went red with fury. He grabbed the nearest bottle from the bar and launched it across the room, smashing it into the wall next to Salazar's head. The crowd gasped, parting like the Red Sea as the two men locked eyes.

"It isn't over, motherfuckin' greaser!" Lee roared, charging across the room.

The fight that followed wasn't like anything Lee had ever been in. It wasn't just a brawl. It was war.

Salazar was strong, his fists deadly with the added weight of the brass knuckles. But Lee was faster. He ducked under a wild swing, landing a vicious left hook that sent Salazar stumbling. But the man didn't go down. Instead, he grinned, blood dripping from his lip as he swung again, aiming for Lee's head.

Lee sidestepped and countered with a knee to the gut, then a savage elbow to the side of Salazar's head. The crowd roared as Salazar hit the floor.

But it wasn't over. Lee never had a shut-off switch. He stomped on Salazar's head, the heel of his cowboy boot grinding into the man's skull.

With each stomp, the wooden floor beneath them became slick with blood. When Salazar finally stopped moving, Lee wasn't satisfied. He kicked him one last time, hard enough to spin his limp body around, leaving a gruesome scar that spit a trail of blood in a circle around his lifeless form.

Lee's friends—the Piranhas, as they called themselves—were handling the rest of the thugs. It was a full-scale brawl now, bodies crashing into tables, fists flying, drinks spilling. Lando's had transformed into a battleground.

As the dust settled, Lee wiped the sweat and blood from his face. His hands were shaking, the adrenaline still pumping through him like a drug. It wasn't until someone grabbed his arm that he snapped out of it.

"Lee," a voice said urgently. "Your brother . . . he's hurt."

Chris was standing by the door with Jimmy, pale as a ghost, his white shirt stained a deep purple from the blood. His hands were jammed into his pockets, as if trying to hold everything together.

"Chris," Lee muttered, rushing over to him. "You okay?"

"No," Chris replied weakly. "I'm hurt. Bad."

Without wasting any more time, Lee threw his brother's arm over his shoulder and helped him to the car. As the three of them sped toward Del Rio, the night air whipping through the windows as Chris bled all over the seats.

The car, their dad's brand-new Cadillac, was completely ruined by the time they pulled into the emergency room. The seats were soaked in blood, but neither of them cared at that moment. They were just lucky to be alive.

The next morning, the hangover wasn't the worst of their problems.

Their father stood in the garage, staring at the ruined upholstery with his hands on his hips, rage building in his chest.

"What the fuck?" he yelled, his face turning red. "Why'd you ruin the fuckin' seats? You should've put him in the trunk!"

Lee shrugged, his own head pounding. "It was a long night, Dad."

Their father didn't look amused. "Who the hell did you fight?"

Lee sighed, running a hand through his hair. "The Salazar brothers."

The color drained from their dad's face. He started pacing back and forth, his brow furrowing in panic. "You just started a fucking war, Lee. You think they're gonna let this go?"

Lee swallowed hard, the reality of what he'd done settling in.

"This isn't over," his dad said, his voice low. "You better get the fuck back up to school, Lee. Those guys are damn good at making people disappear. Don't get it wrong son. This isn't just a vendetta, this is a goddamn *bloodfeud*!"

CHAPTER 29

Thursday, December 31, 1992. 11:55 p.m.

Dracula Club, Saint Moritz, Switzerland

The snow fell in heavy sheets outside the mansion, a thick blanket of silence settling over the cold, desolate night. The town of Saint Moritz, tucked away in the Swiss Alps, was known for its luxury, its opulence, and its power. But what lay hidden beneath the facade of extravagant hotels and picturesque ski lodges was something far darker. Something few would dare to whisper about, let alone acknowledge.

At the heart of it all was the Dracula Club, an ancient building, older than the village itself. Its facade was stark, with dark, looming towers and windows that seemed to gaze down like eyes. Inside, the cold stone walls muffled the sounds of laughter and music from the grand ballroom where the wealthy mingled, dancing away the last hours of 1992. But deeper within the mansion, beyond a heavy oak door that most would never know existed, was a gathering unlike any other.

The Dracula Club had secrets.

In a private chamber far from the warmth of the party, twelve men sat around an elaborate table. The room was dimly lit by the flicker of old candles, their flames casting eerie shadows that danced along the walls. These men wore masks—grotesque, ceremonial things that obscured their faces, making their expressions impossible to read. But their eyes, glinting from behind the masks, told the story. They were not here to celebrate the New Year. They were here for something far more sinister.

At the head of the table sat Olivier, the man who had orchestrated this gathering. His fingers tapped lightly on the edge of the table, his mind elsewhere, lost in the past.

1978

Europe

Olivier remembered it vividly, the way the sunlight filtered through the tall windows of his family's estate, casting a golden glow over everything. Outside, the world was beautiful—lush green fields, manicured gardens, and the dense, ancient forest that surrounded the estate like a protective barrier. But inside the mansion, the air was heavy with decay.

His father, once a towering figure in Olivier's life, lay in bed, his skin pale and taut over brittle bones. The disease had eaten him alive from the inside out, leaving behind a shell of the man Olivier had once worshipped.

He remembered sitting by his father's bedside, the air thick with the stench of sickness, the oppressive silence only broken by the old man's labored breathing. There was no hero left in that room, only the slow march toward death. Olivier hated it. Hated watching the man who had taught him so much wither away, powerless against the one thing no amount of money or knowledge could stop—time.

His father's voice was weak, a rasping whisper. "Do you know why I had you walk through the forest every day?" he asked.

Olivier shook his head, his young eyes wide, absorbing every word, every lesson. He had been a boy of ten when his father first brought him to the woods, teaching him about the patience of trees, the silent battles they fought among themselves—struggles no one else could see.

"Trees . . ." his father coughed, the sound rattling deep in his chest, ". . . are eternal. They grow where no one watches. They fight, and they endure, and long after we are gone, they remain. I've envied them, you know? The beech tree near the south gate—my father watched it grow, and now I've watched it grow. It has seen more than I ever will. And yet, here I am . . ."

His voice trailed off, eyes staring at the ceiling. Olivier could feel the weight of mortality pressing down on him, suffocating. His father, once so strong, was now fragile, a flickering flame about to be snuffed out.

On one of their final walks together, his father had stopped beneath that very beech tree. The branches stretched high above them, ancient and unmoving.

"I'm leaving you everything," his father had said, the words cold and distant, "but don't make the same mistake I did. Don't accept that this is all there is. There will be advancements in science, technology. You'll have the resources, the power, to go further. Don't let me down."

Olivier had promised. He hadn't realized then the depth of what his father was asking for, but he knew now. And every step he had taken since that day had been in service of that promise.

1992

Dracula Club, Saint Moritz

Olivier's gaze snapped back to the present, the heavy scent of candle wax and wine filling his nostrils. The men around the table watched him expectantly, their goblets held aloft, waiting for his signal.

The liquid inside those goblets was dark—thicker than wine, redder than anything natural. The blood shimmered in the dim light, adrenaline-infused, harvested from sources only Olivier and a select few knew of. This was not a ritual of superstition; Olivier had made that clear. This was a symbol. A declaration.

"This," Olivier began, his voice low and measured, "is not something we believe will grant us immortality. It is not the elixir of life. It is, instead, a reminder."

The men were silent, their eyes locked on him.

"A reminder," Olivier continued, "that like the trees my father spoke of, we must grow in ways the world does not see. We must advance where others remain stagnant. We must push past the limits of science and nature, because, if we don't, we will wither like the old and the weak."

He lifted his goblet, staring into the deep crimson liquid. "This blood, this symbol, is like the leeches used to bleed infection from a body. It is primitive. But it is a beginning. It marks the foundation of something greater."

The men, their masks hiding any trace of emotion, nodded in solemn agreement. They understood. This was about power. This was about the first step toward a goal so grand, so impossible, that only the boldest of men dared to dream it.

Immortality.

Olivier raised his goblet higher. "We, the founders of Artemis, do not seek immortality for science. We seek it for control. We seek it for dominance. The world will bend to us, and time itself will be our weapon."

With a nod from Olivier, the men tipped their goblets back, drinking deeply of the adrenalized blood. The ritual was grotesque, their eyes gleaming with manic fervor as they drank, their bodies trembling slightly with the rush of adrenaline. They were men of power, men who had built empires, and now they had gathered in this cold, hidden chamber to cement a pact that would transcend mortality itself.

The sound of goblets being set down on the table echoed in the silence that followed.

Olivier smiled beneath his mask. His father had been right. Time was the enemy. But Olivier had no intention of losing that battle. Artemis had been formed with one purpose, and tonight, they had taken the first step toward achieving it. The blood was a symbol, yes, but the real work—the science, the research—was already underway.

He leaned forward, hands clasped in front of him, and spoke the words that would seal their pact.

"This is the beginning," Olivier said. "From this moment, we are no longer bound by the rules of ordinary men. We will find the key to eternal life, and when we do, the world will be ours—until it comes time to leave it."

Outside, the wind howled, swirling the snow into thick, impenetrable flurries. Inside the Dracula Club, the festivities raged on, oblivious to the dark rituals being conducted behind closed doors. But in that cold, hidden room, a decision had been made. A pact sealed in blood. And as the men rose from their seats, they knew there was no turning back.

Olivier watched as each man signed the document that lay in front of them, a solemn agreement to commit their wealth, power, and resources to the quest for immortality. It was not a document of hope, but of conquest. They were not searching for eternal life for the sake of discovery. They were searching for it to seize control, to become gods among men.

The last signature was scrawled, and the paper passed back to Olivier. He stared at it for a long moment, the weight of what they had just done pressing down on him. But then, slowly, a smile curled his lips.

His father's words echoed in his mind.

"Promise me you will figure it out."

Olivier had kept his promise. And now, the game had begun.

As the men dispersed, their masks discarded, Olivier stood alone in the room, the cold stone walls closing in around him. The sound of the New Year's countdown drifted through the mansion, distant and faint.

But for Olivier, time was no longer a concern.

This was only the beginning.

The blood on the table glistened in the dim light, a symbol of what was to come. Artemis had been born, and soon the world would know its name.

But not yet. No, not yet.

The trees knew how to grow in secret. So would they.

CHAPTER 30

Saturday, January 21, 2023. 9:20 a.m.

Silverman Residence, Franklin Lakes, New Jersey

The Silverman mansion was still smoldering, the remnants of a life built on secrets and deception now nothing but twisted steel and charred wood. A man in all black stood among the ashes, the acrid scent of burned chemicals biting at his nose. His boots crushed bits of glass and debris as he crouched down by what was once the foyer. A slick, dark liquid pooled at his feet, glistening under the early morning sun. The man dipped two fingers in, brought it to his lips, and tasted it.

"Blood and booze," he muttered, shaking his head. "What the fuck happened here?"

A group of Artemis's top security contractors stood nearby, watching Anderson, the captain of the team, closely. They were tatted-up mercenaries, tough guys who knew better than to talk unless spoken to. One of them, a grizzled man named Vickers, squatted beside his boss, wiping sweat from his brow. His eyes scanned the wreckage, flicking nervously back and forth.

"This wasn't just a fire," the man said, standing up and dusting off his pants. "Silverman's house doesn't just burn down by accident. What did the fire department say?"

"They're calling it a possible electrical failure," Vickers said, rubbing his chin. "But we both know that's bullshit. Don't we, Cap?"

"Damn right it is," Anderson growled, looking at the scorched remains of what used to be the study. "This was intentional. The safe was left open, the fireproofing couldn't save anything inside. But where's the fucking bag?"

Vickers glanced over his shoulder at the other contractors, then back at Anderson. "No sign of it, boss. We've been through every inch of this place."

"That bag had shit worth more than this entire goddamn house," Anderson spat. He paused for a moment, letting the weight of it sink in. "And now it's gone. Someone wanted what was in that safe, and they knew exactly how to get it."

Anderson walked over to the spot where Silverman's office used to be, where the floor was stained with soot and ash. He crouched down, his fingers brushing over the remains of melted metal and plastic.

"No ordinary thief pulled this off," he said. "This was a professional job. Clean, precise . . . except for the fire. That was sloppy. That tells me one thing—this wasn't about money. They were covering something up."

Vickers stood, shifting uncomfortably on his feet. "You think it was an inside job?"

Anderson nodded slowly. "Has to be. Silverman was too careful. He had security protocols out the ass. No one gets in without someone on the inside pulling strings."

Before Vickers could respond, Anderson's phone buzzed in his pocket. He pulled it out, glanced at the caller ID, and immediately answered.

"Hello, Razor," he said, his voice lowering.

On the other end, Razor's voice came through, cold and calculating. "Is everything under control?"

"Not yet," Anderson replied, pacing through the wreckage. "We're still piecing it together. The fire's suspicious, but I don't think it was random. Someone got to Silverman before we did."

Razor's tone sharpened. "And the contents of the safe?"

"Gone. Someone took the bag, left the rest to burn."

A heavy silence hung between them, the weight of the situation pressing down. Razor's voice came back, clipped and decisive. "Find out who did this. I want answers, Anderson. No leaks, no loose ends. If this gets out, Artemis will be compromised."

"I've got my best guys on it," Anderson said. "But it'll take time. Whoever did this knew what they were doing."

"You don't have time," Razor snapped. "I don't care if you have to burn down the entire fucking city. Find that bag, find who the fuck did this, and end them."

Anderson clenched his jaw, the intensity of Razor's words firing him up. "Understood."

The line went dead. Anderson pocketed his phone and turned back to Vickers and the other contractors. His eyes burned with fury as he barked to his team, "I want names. I want leads. And when we find out who pulled this shit, we make them disappear. No fuck-ups, no excuses."

Vickers nodded and motioned for the rest of the team to get to work. As they dispersed, Anderson lingered a moment longer, his gaze fixed on the ruins of the Silverman mansion.

Whoever had taken the bag was playing with fire. And Artemis was about to burn them alive.

CHAPTER 31

Tuesday, December 20, 1979. 5:30 p.m.

Cain Residence, Del Rio, Texas

The late December air in Del Rio was unusually cold, biting through Lee's jacket as he and Chris trudged down the hallway of their small house. It was a week before Christmas, and the two brothers had been up to no good, as usual.

"You sure this is a good idea?" Lee whispered, glancing nervously over his shoulder.

Chris shot him a devilish grin. "Trust me, Lee. We're gonna find the presents. Mom and Dad think they're so slick hiding them, but we know better."

Lee wasn't so sure. They'd tried this last year and nearly got caught when their father, Jack, came home early. But Chris was always convincing. Always the one leading them into trouble.

"C'mon," Chris said, waving him forward. "They're up in the attic. I saw Dad putting something up there last week."

The two brothers climbed the stairs, their footsteps muffled by the creaky wooden floor. They reached the attic door and pushed it open, revealing the dark, dusty space filled with old furniture, boxes, and—hidden behind a stack of suitcases—their mother's poorly wrapped Christmas presents.

"There!" Chris whispered excitedly, pointing to the stash. "I told you."

Lee's eyes widened as he crouched down beside his brother. They quickly tore into the wrapping, finding a couple of cheap action figures and a baseball glove. But the excitement that had brought them up there vanished the moment they realized what they were looking at.

"This is it?" Lee asked, his voice tinged with disappointment. "Where's all the stuff Mom said we'd get? Where's the big presents?"

Chris sat back on his heels, a dark look crossing his face. "There aren't any big presents, Lee. This is it. No Santa, no surprises. It's all bullshit."

Lee felt a sinking feeling in his gut. He'd never questioned it before, never thought about how Christmas really worked. But here it was—proof that Santa was just a lie, that his parents had been playing him all along.

"Bullshit," Chris muttered again, shaking his head.

The next morning, they couldn't hide the guilt. And when their father found out what they'd done, the beatings came swift and harsh.

Jack's voice boomed through the small house, a belt in his hand. "You boys think you can ruin Christmas, huh? Think you can just break the rules and not pay the price?"

The sting of the belt cut across Lee's back, and he winced, tears brimming in his eyes. Chris stood silently beside him, fists clenched, refusing to cry.

"You want to know why you don't open your presents early?" Jack barked, delivering another lash. "Because life doesn't give you everything you want. You work for it. You wait for it. And if you think you can just take what you want without consequence, you're gonna learn the hard way."

When the beating was over, their father stormed out of the room, leaving Lee and Chris nursing their wounds. The lesson had been learned—delayed gratification, the understanding that nothing came without a cost.

Chris broke the silence, his voice low. "There's no Santa, Lee. It's all a lie. The world doesn't work the way you think it does."

That line stuck with Lee for years. It was the first time he realized how fucked up the world was. Just like there was no Santa, there was no such thing as fairness. It was all run by people behind the scenes. People like their dad. People like Artemis.

Now, decades later, as Lee drove down the dark Texas roads, the same bitter taste of deception returned. Artemis wasn't a fairy tale; it was the ugly truth. A secret society pulling strings, shaping the world in ways most people could never understand.

CHAPTER 32

Thursday, October 4, 2018. 3:50 p.m.

deCODE Genetics Lab, Reykjavik, Iceland

The sterile, white lights of the Icelandic research lab illuminated Dr. Natalie Bauer's focused face as she meticulously typed her observations into the terminal. The soft hum of the equipment created a soothing backdrop, but her thoughts were chaotic with excitement. The telomere research was finally bearing fruit—tangible results that could extend human life by decades. She knew the breakthrough was just within reach. Her fingers hesitated over the keys as she stared at the latest data, her heart racing.

"We did it . . ." she whispered under her breath. She understood the magnitude of what she had just uncovered.

"Long day?" Razor's deep voice cut through the sterile quiet, startling her. She turned, and there he was, leaning casually against the doorframe of her lab, his tattooed arms crossed over his chest. The head of Artemis security looked out of place in the pristine lab with his sleeved tattoos and rugged appearance. But he had a way of infiltrating every aspect of her life.

Natalie's lips curled into a smile. "You could say that," she replied, her excitement temporarily replaced with warmth. "We're on the cusp of something huge, Razor."

He pushed off the wall, slowly closing the distance between them. His smile didn't quite reach his eyes. "That's what I keep hearing," he said, his gaze locking onto hers with a mix of curiosity and something else—something darker. "Maybe it's time to celebrate?"

He reached into his leather jacket, pulling out a bottle of red wine, the label worn, but unmistakably expensive. Natalie's heart fluttered, not just from the progress in her research, but from the man in front of her. Razor Ramirez was everything she shouldn't want—dangerous, mysterious, emotionally distant—but their connection had been intense from the moment they met. He had this way of making her feel both safe and constantly on edge, and that mix of thrill and danger had drawn her in.

"You think it's time for that?" Natalie asked, half-smiling as she raised an eyebrow.

Razor placed the bottle on the counter beside her, his hand grazing her lower back. "I think you've earned it," he murmured, leaning in close, his breath hot against her neck. She felt a shiver run down her spine, caught between his intoxicating presence and exhaustion from the long hours she'd been working.

She glanced at the clock, realizing it was late—too late to still be working. "Maybe you're right," she whispered, feeling the weight of the day slip away as he kissed the nape of her neck softly. Natalie turned around, her body responding to his touch. Razor's hands slid over her hips, pulling her against him.

They had always kept their affair quiet, hidden behind closed doors and clandestine meetings. Razor wasn't just her lover—he was a shadow of Artemis itself, a reminder of how dangerous their world was. But in moments like these, when his lips were on hers, none of that seemed to matter.

They ended up in her private quarters, a small room adjacent to the lab where she could rest between long research sessions. Razor pulled her onto the bed, his hands rough against her skin as they stripped away the layers of clothing between them. There was no tenderness in his movements—just raw, animalistic need. Natalie didn't care. She wanted to lose herself in him.

Their bodies moved in sync, each kiss more fervent than the last, as if this moment was a temporary escape from the world around them. Razor's tattoos rippled under his skin as he gripped her waist tightly, pulling her beneath him with a primal hunger that matched the pace of their encounter.

Afterward, they lay in silence, the room filled only with the sound of their breathing. Natalie rolled over, her head resting on Razor's chest, tracing the lines of the tattoos that covered his skin. "You think we'll ever get out of this, Razor? Live normal lives?"

Razor's hand lazily stroked her hair. "I don't believe in normal," he replied, his tone detached. "But you and I—we're cut from different cloth than the rest of them."

Natalie smiled, closing her eyes. "I guess you're right."

They stayed like that for a while, her body tangled with his, until Razor quietly slipped out of bed. She barely stirred as he dressed, her mind half-asleep, exhausted from both her work and their time together. Razor moved with practiced stealth, gathering his things and retrieving a small vial from his jacket. The same vial he had slipped into his pocket earlier that day.

He hesitated at the doorway, looking back at her sleeping form one last time. A momentary flicker of something passed over his face—regret, maybe? Doubt? No. He crushed it before it could take root.

Natalie stirred, opening her eyes. "Leaving already?" she asked sleepily.

Razor turned to face her, smiling softly. "Yeah. I've got things to take care of."

She sat up, her body silhouetted against the pale light filtering through the window. "Come back tomorrow. We can . . . celebrate again."

Razor smiled, but it didn't reach his eyes. "Sure, Nat."

The next night, Razor returned to the lab, just as Natalie had asked. This time, however, he brought two glasses and a bottle of the finest wine he could find. They ate a small dinner together in her quarters, laughing and talking about the future—her future, mostly. Razor listened, nodding, playing the part of the attentive lover.

After dinner, he poured them each a glass of wine. Natalie took hers without question, sipping it while leaning back in her chair.

But it didn't take long for her to feel the effects.

At first, it was subtle—a slight dizziness, a faint tightening in her chest. She blinked, confused, setting the glass down.

"Razor. . . . I feel strange."

Razor didn't move, just watched her. His eyes were calm, detached.

Natalie's breathing became ragged, her chest heaving as she struggled to stay upright. "What . . . what did you—?"

She collapsed onto the floor, her body convulsing. Razor crouched down beside her, his expression cold and unreadable as she gasped for breath.

"Shh . . . it's okay," he whispered, brushing her hair back from her face, just like he had the night before. But this time, there was no affection in his touch. "You've done amazing work, Natalie. But this is the end of your chapter."

Her eyes widened with betrayal and fear, but she was too weak to respond. Razor leaned in closer, his voice barely above a whisper. "You were never going to see the finish line. You know that, don't you?"

Tears pooled in her eyes as her body spasmed one final time before going still.

Razor stood, looking down at her body, and sighed. He felt nothing—no remorse, no guilt. She had served her purpose, and now she was gone.

CHAPTER 33

Wednesday, August 14, 2001. 8:00 p.m.

Jiménez, Mexico

The sun had just dipped below the horizon, painting the Jiménez sky with hues of blood-red and gold, as Salvador Salazar followed his jefe, Braulio Enriquez, down the creaking staircase of the crumbling building. The scent of cheap cigarettes and sweat clung to the air, mingling with the smell of street food from the bustling marketplace below. Salvador's heart pounded in his chest—not from fear, but from a surge of excitement. The life he had been born into was one of poverty, but the life he was beginning to craft for himself was one of power, wealth, and danger.

Braulio's towering figure, casting long shadows on the cracked pavement, had been watching Salvador for months. The kid had something—grit, determination, and a mind sharp enough to navigate the violent streets of Jiménez without getting killed. Today had been another test, just one of many, to see how well Salvador could handle the pressure of the game. The drug deal had gone smoothly, and Braulio was pleased. That was good news for Salvador. Braulio wasn't the kind of man to hand out praise or second chances.

"You did good today, kid," Braulio grunted, his gravelly voice cutting through the sounds of the market as they reached the street. "You didn't ask any stupid questions, and you kept your mouth shut. That's the first rule of survival."

Salvador nodded, his eyes fixed ahead, though the compliment made his chest swell with pride. He had learned early on that asking too many questions got you killed, especially in La Sombra business. But he had questions—plenty of them. Why was Braulio giving him this opportunity? What did he have to do to rise up the ranks? How far could a kid with nothing make it in a world that swallowed the weak whole?

"I'm a quick learner," Salvador said quietly, his voice steady.

Braulio stopped walking and turned to face him, his dark eyes boring into Salvador's with an intensity that made the younger man's skin prickle. "You better be," he said, flicking his gaze down the narrow alleyways where young boys played soccer with a ragged ball, oblivious to the life of crime growing around them. "In this business, you don't get a second chance to fuck up. One mistake, and you're dead. You understand that?"

Salvador met Braulio's gaze, the weight of the words sinking in. "I understand."

Braulio studied him for a moment longer before grunting in approval. He reached into the pocket of his leather jacket and pulled out a small wad of cash. "Here's your cut," he said, handing it to Salvador. "It's not much, but you earned it."

Salvador took the money, feeling the weight of it in his hand. It was more than his mother had ever made in a year, more than he had ever dreamed of having at his age. But he wasn't in this for small bills. He had bigger dreams, bigger ambitions. He pocketed the cash without a word, knowing better than to show too much emotion.

"Stick with me, and you'll see more of that," Braulio said, his voice low and full of promises that Salvador knew came at a steep price. "But there's a lot more than money at stake in this world, kid. You want power? You want respect? You'll have to prove yourself again and again. You're going to need to do things that'll haunt you. You ready for that?"

Salvador didn't hesitate. He had grown up in the dirt, surrounded by the kind of despair that left boys broken or dead before they even hit adulthood. He wasn't going to let that be his fate.

"I'm ready," he said, his voice firm.

Braulio's lips curled into a dark smile. "Good."

Time passed, and Salvador's role within La Sombra shifted from a mere lookout to something more integral, more dangerous. He was given the job of a "watcher," tasked with observing the streets and reporting any movement by rival gangs or the police. It was tedious work, but Salvador took it seriously. Every night, he'd climb onto rooftops or slip into alleyways, his eyes sharp as he monitored the comings and goings of La Sombra's enemies.

But as the weeks went on, Braulio began giving Salvador more responsibility. He started sending him on minor drug runs, deliveries that didn't seem like much but were crucial to La Sombra's operations. Salvador handled them flawlessly, earning Braulio's trust more and more with each job.

And then came the night that would change everything.

It was just after midnight, the air thick with the sounds of the bustling nightlife and the scent of fried street food. Salvador had just finished a delivery when Braulio called him, his voice gruff and to the point.

"Get to the docks," Braulio had said. "There's a problem."

Salvador didn't ask questions. He just went.

When he arrived at the docks, the scene that greeted him was one of tension. A small group of La Sombra members stood in a circle, their faces shadowed by the dim streetlights. At the center of the group was a man tied to a chair, his face swollen and bloodied. His hands were bound, and his head lolled to the side, barely conscious.

Braulio stood in front of the man, a cigarette dangling from his lips as he puffed smoke into the air. He glanced up as Salvador approached.

"Took you long enough," Braulio muttered, flicking the cigarette onto the ground. He gestured to the man in the chair. "This piece of shit tried to skim from us. Took a cut of the money, thought we wouldn't notice."

Salvador's stomach tightened as he realized what was about to happen.

Braulio turned to him, his eyes hard. "You said you were ready to do whatever it takes, right? Time to prove it."

He handed Salvador a knife, the blade gleaming under the dim light.

Salvador's heart pounded in his chest as he took the knife. He had seen men killed before. He had seen blood spilled, lives taken. But he had never done it himself. He looked at the man in the chair, who was barely conscious, his breathing shallow and ragged.

La Sombra members around him watched in silence, waiting to see if Salvador had what it took. This was the moment—his initiation. If he hesitated, if he showed weakness, he'd never make it. He'd be stuck at the bottom, a nobody. Or worse, he'd end up dead.

Salvador's showed zero fear or emotion as he approached the man in the chair. He could feel the eyes of La Sombra on him, waiting, judging. He didn't have a choice. He had to do this.

He gripped the knife tighter, his knuckles white as he knelt in front of the man. The man's eyes fluttered open, dazed and filled with fear. He muttered something incoherent, blood dripping from his split lip.

Salvador raised the knife.

The blade sliced through the air, cutting deep into the man's throat. Blood sprayed across Salvador's hands, warm and thick, as the man gurgled his last breaths. Salvador's heart raced, his body trembling with a mixture of adrenaline and horror as he watched the life drain from the man's eyes.

The world around him felt distant, muted. He could hear Braulio's voice, but it was as if it were coming from far away.

"Welcome to the family, kid."

CHAPTER 34

2002

Jiménez, Mexico

In the months that followed, Salvador's reputation within La Sombra grew. The story of his first kill spread like wildfire among the ranks, and with each retelling, the details became more brutal, more exaggerated. To some, he was a ruthless killer, a rising star in La Sombra. To others, he was a young kid who had made the right connections. But to Braulio, he was a potential asset—a weapon that could be shaped and molded.

Braulio began giving Salvador more responsibilities, trusting him with larger shipments and more dangerous missions. Salvador excelled at every task, his hunger for power and respect driving him forward. He learned the art of negotiation, the nuances of La Sombra politics, and how to outsmart the police and rival gangs.

But with every step he took up the ladder, the dangers increased. Rivals wanted him dead. The police were always one step behind. And within La Sombra, enemies lurked in the shadows, waiting for him to slip up.

One night, as Salvador sat in a dimly lit cantina, nursing a bottle of tequila, Braulio slid into the seat across from him.

"You've done well," Braulio said, lighting a cigarette and taking a long drag. "But there's something you need to understand. In this life, loyalty is everything. And there are men above you who will want to test that loyalty."

Salvador nodded, his eyes focused on the older man. "I understand."

Braulio smirked. "Good. Because there's a promotion in your future, kid. But you need to prove yourself again. And this time, it's not about killing some low-level scumbag."

Salvador leaned forward, intrigued. "What do you need me to do?"

"There's been an . . . incident."

Salvador asked, "What kind of incident?"

"A shipment was intercepted. Veracruz. The locals are whispering that it was El Coyote." Braulio muttered a curse under his breath, turning back to Salvador. "You've heard of El Coyote, haven't you?"

Salvador nodded. "A loud fool."

"Exactly," Braulio said, leaning back in his chair. "He thinks he can make a name for himself by taking on La Sombra. He'll learn the hard way."

"How?" Salvador asked.

Braulio's grin returned, sharp and wolfish. "You'll remind him of the rules."

Braulio dragged on his cigarette. "You know why you're here?"

"To learn," Salvador said evenly. His gaze didn't waver, his hands resting on the table in a gesture of calm control. "About the rules."

Braulio chuckled. "You think there are rules in La Sombra?"

"I think without rules, there is no shadow," Salvador replied. "Only chaos."

Braulio's chuckle turned into a laugh, a dry, rasping sound. "You catch on quick. All right, Salazar. Listen close."

He set his glass down and leaned forward, his voice dropping to a near whisper. "La Sombra isn't just a cartel. It's a force of nature. An idea. You don't join La Sombra. You become it. You breathe it. You bleed for it."

Salvador didn't flinch. "And what keeps it together?"

Braulio's eyes narrowed. "Fear. Secrecy. Omnipresence. We don't just kill our enemies; we erase them. We don't just punish betrayal; we destroy the traitor's family, their legacy. No one crosses La Sombra and survives, not in body or memory."

Salvador leaned back, his mind absorbing every word. "And loyalty? How do you inspire that?"

"Loyalty comes when people believe," Braulio said. "When they think La Sombra isn't just men with guns and money. They need to see us as a shadow over their lives. Something eternal. Something they can't escape."

Braulio gestured to the bartender, who brought over another glass and filled it for Salvador. This time, Salvador accepted, lifting the glass to his lips and taking a slow sip. The burn was sharp but grounding, the taste of mezcal mingling with the heavy air.

"You want to rise in La Sombra, Salazar?" Braulio asked. "You need to understand our rules. And you need to enforce them."

"Tell me," Salvador said.

Braulio smiled faintly. "Rule one: secrecy above all. Speak about La Sombra to anyone outside, and you're dead. Speak too much even to someone inside, and you're dead. Betray us, and we don't just kill you— we erase you. Your family, your friends, anyone who knew you. By the time we're done, it's like you never existed."

Salvador nodded. He'd heard whispers of such punishments, rumors of entire households vanishing overnight, their names scrubbed from history. Now, he knew the truth.

"Rule two: the shadow over all," Braulio continued. "La Sombra isn't just a cartel. It's a religion. A way of life. To defy it is to defy nature itself. And like nature, La Sombra does not forgive."

Salvador's expression didn't change, but his mind raced. The structure of La Sombra was more complex than he'd realized. An invisible hand pulling strings, an organization so compartmentalized it was impossible to dismantle.

"Rule three: fear is our weapon," Braulio said, his voice lowering further. "Violence is never random. It's calculated, symbolic. When we kill, we leave a message. A body hanging from a bridge, its shadow stretching across the ground. A handprint burned into a wall. A whispered threat that makes a man too afraid to sleep. Fear is power, Salazar. And power is control."

"And the leaders?" Salvador asked. "Who are they?"

Braulio's smile widened, but it was colder now. "You think I know? You think anyone knows? The leaders are ghosts, faceless and nameless. Orders come down through intermediaries, whispers in the dark. You could be sitting next to one and never know. You shouldn't even trust me. Now, let's go."

The night was darker than usual, the moon shrouded by thick clouds. Salvador followed Braulio and a young man through the streets, their footsteps muffled against the dirt road. When they reached a clearing near the outskirts of town, Braulio stopped and turned to Salvador.

"Watch," Braulio said.

In the clearing, a group of La Sombra operatives surrounded a bound and gagged man. His face was bruised, his clothes torn. Salvador recognized him as one of El Coyote's lieutenants, a mid-level thug who had likely been caught during the shipment raid.

Braulio approached the man, crouching down so they were eye to eye. "You made a mistake," he said softly, almost kindly. "But you're not the only one who will pay for it."

The man's eyes widened in terror, muffled cries escaping through the gag. Braulio stood, motioning to the operatives. They hauled the man to his feet and tied him to a wooden pole, his shadow stretching long and grotesque in the light of a lantern.

Salvador watched in silence as Braulio gave the signal. One of the operatives raised a blade, carving the symbol of La Sombra—a shadowy handprint—into the man's chest. The lieutenant screamed, his voice raw and broken, before Braulio slit his throat with a single, precise motion.

As the blood pooled at their feet, Braulio turned to Salvador. "This is how we enforce the rules. This is how we remind them that the shadow sees all."

Salvador nodded, his expression calm. But inside, a fire burned. He wasn't just watching. He was learning. And one day, he would take everything he'd learned and make it his own.

"*La Sombra no duerme,*" Braulio said, his voice low. "*La Sombra no olvida.*"

Salvador repeated the words, his voice steady. "The Shadow does not sleep. The Shadow does not forget."

After his removal of El Coyote's lieutenant, Salvador's star continued to rise. But with every step up the ladder, he learned more about the brutal realities of La Sombra. Men who got too ambitious were cut down without hesitation. Rivals were tortured and executed in the most horrific ways. And even those within La Sombra weren't safe. Salvador watched as men he had once called friends were betrayed, their tongues cut out as a warning to others.

Salvador had no illusions about the life he had chosen. He knew that one day, it could be him in the chair, his life snuffed out for crossing the wrong person. But he didn't care. He was willing to risk everything for power, for respect, for a chance to escape the poverty and desperation that had defined his life.

As the years passed, Salvador became a force to be reckoned with. He rose through the ranks, earning the respect of La Sombra's leaders and the fear of its enemies. His reputation as a ruthless enforcer spread far beyond Jiménez, and soon, he was being called to handle business across the border, in the United States.

But with every step he took, he knew that the higher he climbed, the harder he would fall if he ever slipped.

And in La Sombra, no one was safe.

CHAPTER 35

Tuesday, January 24, 2023. 11:45 a.m.

Remote Gas Station, West Texas

Lee Cain coasted into the lone gas station on the edge of nowhere, his truck sputtering as it rolled to a stop next to the pump. Dust caked the windshield, and the sky above was a dull, slate gray, hinting at the long miles ahead. The neon sign for the gas station flickered erratically, casting a dim glow over the near-empty lot. Inside, the glow of fluorescent lights buzzed overhead, flickering like a distant memory of civilization.

Lee stepped out, his boots crunching on the gravel, and took in his surroundings. The place reeked of loneliness. No one would remember him here—exactly the way he wanted it. The guy behind the counter, a slouching figure with greasy hair and vacant eyes, was barely more than a shadow. He wouldn't give a second thought to the man who stopped in for gas and energy drinks.

Lee topped off the tank, watching as the numbers ticked by on the pump. The wind whispered through the desert, carrying a sense of emptiness with it. After filling up, he made his way into the small, dingy convenience store. The loser behind the counter barely acknowledged him, his eyes glued to a flickering TV in the corner playing some old sitcom rerun.

Lee grabbed a couple of energy drinks from the cooler. The burn in his chest reminded him that his body was still healing. He wasn't out of the woods yet, but that didn't matter right now. He had work to do.

After paying in cash and giving the cashier a nod, Lee stepped outside, cracked open one of the cans, and leaned against his truck. The bitter taste of the energy drink hit his tongue, waking him up just a bit more. He needed every ounce of energy for what was coming next. He took out his phone, scrolling through his contacts until he found the number he hadn't called in a year. It was time to reach out to *Slick Jimmy Bones*.

Jimmy was a Del Rio legend in his own right. The man could make anything happen, especially if it involved the cartels. Jimmy was the kind of guy everyone liked. Even the Mexicans. Especially the Mexicans. He was the link between the American and Mexican underworlds, fluent in both their languages and ways. Jimmy had this way of fitting in anywhere, talking to anyone, smoothing over tensions that could have erupted into something worse. He was the go-between, the bridge that connected the white kids to the Mexican cartel, a foot in both worlds. Lee and Jimmy grew up together and their history ran deep—fights, deals, and enough blood spilled to bind them forever. If there was anyone who could, and would, help him disappear, it was Slick Jimmy.

Lee tapped the number and brought the phone to his ear. The phone rang twice before a familiar, deep Texas drawl answered, "Well, look who the fuck finally decided to call. Thought you were dead, Hoss."

Lee chuckled. "Still might be, but not today, Slick."

The two of them fell into the easy rhythm of old friends, their connection unbroken by the years of silence. Jimmy laughed. "Hell, you sound like shit. Where you been?"

"I've been sick," Lee admitted, taking another swig from his drink. "But I'm better now."

"Good to hear, Hoss. Knew you'd bounce back. What the hell you want with me? Ain't no way this is just a friendly catch-up."

Lee glanced around the desolate stretch of road, knowing what he was about to ask was going to stir up some real trouble. But that's what Jimmy was good for—handling the shit no one else could.

"I need you to make me disappear," Lee said quietly, watching the horizon like an old gunslinger waiting for trouble.

There was a pause on the other end of the line, then Jimmy's voice came back, a little more serious. "Shit, man. What did you do this time?"

"It's not just me," Lee added. "I need you to make my dad disappear, too."

Jimmy let out a low whistle. "Now we're talkin' some serious shit. Where you headed?"

"Mexico," Lee said flatly. "We need to go south, and we need to go fast."

"You think someone's comin' for you?" Jimmy asked, his tone shifting into something darker, more urgent.

"They're already on their way," Lee replied. "I'm running out of places to hide, and the safest place to be right now might just be the most dangerous."

"Jesus Christ, you never do things easy, do you Hoss?" Jimmy muttered.

"You still in with the cartels?" Lee asked, his voice edged with urgency. He already knew the answer, but he needed confirmation.

Jimmy chuckled darkly. "Hell yeah, I am. What are you thinkin'?"

"I'm thinking you are gonna think I have lost my goddamn mind, Jimmy."

"Well, spill the beans son."

"I need you to set up a meeting with me and the Scar," answered Lee.

There was a pause over the line.

Then Jimmy finally answered after he absorbed what he had just heard, "Crossin' the border and meetin' up with *the Scar*? I do think you done lost your gaddamn mind!"

Lee's grip on the phone tightened. "I have to meet him. There's no other way."

"The Scar," Jimmy said, shaking his head over the phone. "That man's a goddamn nightmare. You're fuckin' crazy, Hoss."

"Set up a meeting," Lee ordered. "And make my dad disappear. This isn't some bullshit drill, Jimmy. I need you now, more than ever."

Jimmy was quiet for a moment, considering the gravity of the situation. "All right," he finally said. "I'll make the call. But you know once you're across that border, you ain't comin' back the same. The Scar ain't just a man, he's a force."

"I know," Lee replied. "But I have no other choice."

Jimmy sighed heavily. "All right, brother. I'll set it up. Just know that whatever happens next, it's on you. I ain't gonna pull your ass out of the fire this time."

Lee smiled faintly, the kind of smile that barely reached his lips. "Old habits die hard."

"Damn right they do," Jimmy drawled. "Get your shit together, Hoss. I'll call you back with the details. And for the love of God, don't get yourself killed before we even get there."

"I won't," Lee promised, though in the pit of his stomach, he knew this was just the beginning of something much darker.

The line went dead, and Lee pocketed his phone. He stared out into the vast desert, the horizon burning with the setting sun. Trouble was coming, and he had just set it all in motion. But if there was one thing Lee Cain knew how to do, it was survive.

He climbed back into his truck, engine roaring to life, and pointed the nose toward the border.

This time, disappearing meant facing something far more dangerous than anything he'd ever encountered before. And the thought of it made his blood simmer with anticipation.

The game had just begun.

CHAPTER 36

Tuesday, January 24, 2023. 9:30 p.m.

Russian Bathhouse, Midtown Manhattan

Dr. McCormack sat in the Russian banya, his body dripping with sweat, the heat inside the big wood and stone sauna like a living thing pressing against his skin. Every breath he took felt like inhaling molten air, but he loved it. In the heat, the fear and panic he had been battling since his encounter with Lee Cain seemed to melt away, if only temporarily. Bruises still marred his body, the aftereffects of the fight, a constant reminder of just how close he had come to death.

He knew Artemis was watching. He wasn't stupid. You didn't survive long in his line of work by being naive. After what had happened with Silverman, McCormack knew they would be looking for answers. They'd know by now that he had been involved. And he knew what that meant: his time was running out.

The fear was always there, lurking in the back of his mind, gnawing at him. He was a man on borrowed time, but right now, he was determined to live in the moment. Might as well go out in style, he thought to himself with a grim smirk. The fear was dulled by the drugs and the decadent distractions around him. The Russian bathhouse was one of his favorite escapes—real Russian vodka, pure blow, and the comforting presence of a voluptuous, blonde Russian hooker working on his prostate like she was tuning a fine instrument.

He'd always had expensive tastes. "Should've been a goddamn gynecologist, just like Mom wanted," McCormack muttered under his breath, laughing bitterly at his own reflection in the nearby steam-fogged mirror. He could have been elbows deep in Jewish pussy all day, living a quiet, boring, risk-free life. But no, he had to chase the money, had to get involved with Artemis. Had to feel important.

Now, his decisions were catching up to him, but at least the hooker rubbing him down wasn't half bad. Not bad at all.

The blow still buzzed through his veins, intensifying the pleasure as he took another shot of vodka. The heat of the sauna made everything blur—his thoughts, his regrets, his impending doom. For a moment, the pain and fear receded, replaced by a high that made him feel untouchable, invincible.

The wooden door to the banya creaked open as his first girl finished, leaving him with a wink. Now it was time for the real treat. The beater came in, a burly Russian man holding tree branches soaked in oils. McCormack relished this part. The branches would be spun in the air, capturing the heat, before being whipped across his naked, glistening body. The leaves would slap his skin with a satisfying crack, creating waves of intense heat and relief. The oils would seep into his pores, soothing his battered body.

WHAP! WHAP! WHAP! The branches danced across his back, shoulders, legs, creating a symphony of sensation. McCormack groaned with pleasure. After the beating, the beater left him, and McCormack pulled the rope that dumped a bucket of ice-cold water over his head. The shock made him gasp, the contrast of the heat and cold a drug in itself.

Another shot of vodka. Another line of blow.

This was how McCormack wanted to live. If it all ended today, he'd go out like a fucking king.

As he settled back in the cold tub, feeling the numbness from the icy water wash over him, a new girl approached. He recognized her—a favorite of his. She smiled seductively as she began massaging his shoulders, whispering something in Russian that McCormack didn't care to translate. His mind was drifting, a mix of drugs, heat, and pleasure taking him farther away from the cold, harsh reality waiting for him outside the walls of the bathhouse.

But then the door creaked open again.

McCormack tensed, his senses prickling despite the haze. He wasn't expecting anyone else.

Two figures walked in—men. Not the kind of men who were there for relaxation.

Before he could react, one of them snapped something to the hooker in Russian. She stopped massaging McCormack, her face going pale as she quickly grabbed her things and left the room, glancing at McCormack one last time with pity in her eyes.

McCormack's heart sank. The drugs that had been numbing his fear started to fail him, the high crashing down as cold, stark terror took its place. He knew what this was. His time had come.

"Gentlemen," McCormack started, trying to push himself up from the tub, his voice shaky. "Let's—let's talk about this."

The two men didn't say a word. One of them crouched beside McCormack, giving him a look that sent a chill through his bones. The other man, built like a brick wall, was holding a billy club in one hand, tapping it menacingly against his palm.

The man crouching down looked McCormack dead in the eyes. "Artemis sent us. You know why we're here."

McCormack's heart pounded in his chest. "Look, look, I can explain—"

But before he could finish, the man holding the billy club grabbed McCormack by the throat and yanked him out of the cold tub, slamming him onto the wet floor. The impact knocked the breath out of him, and before he could recover, the billy club was driven straight up into his ass with brutal force. McCormack screamed, his voice echoing through the empty banya.

The pain was excruciating, but it wasn't over. The man yanked the club back out and shoved it into McCormack's mouth, forcing his jaw open until his lips were torn. Blood trickled from the corners of his mouth as he choked on the taste of metal and his own shit.

"Now," said the man holding McCormack down, "you're going to tell us everything. Starting with Silverman. And if you lie, I'm going to make this a whole lot worse."

McCormack's mind raced as the drugs battled against the terror coursing through him. He knew he didn't have a choice. Artemis wasn't fucking around. He'd seen it happen too many times before—people disappeared without a trace, their existence wiped clean as if they'd never been born.

"I—" McCormack sputtered through the gag of the billy club, blood trickling down his throat. "I had this guy Cain beat the shit outta me. He broke my face and I broke down about Silverman! I—I fucked up, okay? I told him! I was trying to save my own skin, but—but I didn't think he'd—"

He couldn't finish. His words were swallowed by sobs as the fear overtook him. He was a coward, and now everyone in the room knew it.

The men exchanged a look. They had the name they were looking for. For a brief, fleeting moment, McCormack thought they might let him live. Maybe, just maybe, they'd spare him.

But the grin on the man's face said otherwise.

"Thanks for your honesty," he sneered. Then, without warning, he drove McCormack's head under the icy water of the cold tub, his hand pressing down with terrifying force. McCormack's arms flailed wildly, his eyes wide with panic as he tried to fight back, but he was no match for the strength holding him down.

The freezing water filled his lungs, cutting through the haze of drugs like a knife. His mind raced in desperation, flashes of his life blurring through his mind. The fear of death was all-consuming, a primal terror that clawed at his soul. But then, just as his strength began to fade, a strange sense of calm washed over him.

The panic subsided. The struggle ceased.

In those final moments, as his body went numb and the euphoria of oxygen deprivation set in, McCormack saw something like peace. It was fleeting, but it was there. A final release. Maybe it was the drugs, maybe it was something deeper—he couldn't tell.

But then it was gone. Everything was gone.

The men stood over the still body, watching as McCormack's lifeless form floated face down in the cold tub. The room was silent except for the drip of water from the ceiling and the faint echo of footsteps outside the door.

The man who had drowned him looked over to the other. "Clean enough. The blow and vodka will make this look like a classic rich man's drowning accident."

The other man nodded, wiping his hands on a towel before throwing it onto McCormack's limp body. "No loose ends."

"Well," said his partner, "There seems to still be one loose end, whoever this Cain fucker is. Time to call it in."

They left without another word. The Russian hookers would return in the morning to find McCormack dead, the scene perfectly set. Another casualty of the high life, they'd think. Another drowning in a cold tub.

But Artemis would know. And that was all that mattered.

CHAPTER 37

1982

The American School, Paris, France

Olivier Malraux awoke with a start. His chest heaved and his pulse pounded in his ears, every beat like a drum signaling impending doom. The room was dark, the heavy velvet curtains in his dorm room at the American high school in France blotting out the moonlight. In a cold sweat, he clutched his chest, struggling to breathe, the muscles in his body tense and trembling.

Am I dying?

The thought sent a surge of terror through him. For the first time in his seventeen years, Olivier became acutely aware of his own mortality. Death wasn't just a distant concept anymore—it was real, tangible, and waiting for him. And he was not fulfilling his promise to his father.

"You're not dying," he whispered, trying to calm himself. But the words rang hollow. He knew, deep down, that he had glimpsed something far worse: the truth. *You are going to die someday.*

"No, no, no," he whispered to himself, curling into a fetal position as if the act could protect him.

After several minutes, the crushing weight on his chest began to ease. His breathing slowed, though his body still trembled. He fumbled for the lamp on his bedside table, its harsh light casting long shadows across the room.

He stumbled to the mirror above the sink, gripping its edges to steady himself. His reflection stared back: sweat-matted hair, pale skin, and wide, fearful eyes. For the first time, he saw not the heir to the Malraux fortune, but a fragile, mortal boy.

"I'm going to die," he whispered to his reflection. The words were foreign and jarring.

It wasn't just fear he felt—it was rage. Rage at the unfairness of life, at the realization that no matter how much money or power his family had, it couldn't stop the march of time. He clenched his fists, his nails digging into his palms until the pain grounded him.

"This can't be it," he muttered with quiet defiance.

The next morning, Olivier sat alone at one end the communal breakfast table in the cafeteria. Other students laughed and chattered as they shoveled food into their mouths, but he stared at his tray, his appetite nonexistent. His eyes scanned the untouched breakfast: scrambled eggs, bacon, a croissant, and a glass of orange juice.

Will this kill me faster? What if the food was poisoning him in some unseen way? What if the bacon's grease clogged his arteries, shortening his life? What if the sugar in the orange juice fed some hidden cancer growing inside him?

He pushed the tray away, the mere thought of eating making his stomach churn. The noise of the cafeteria faded as his mind spiraled.

Returning to his dorm, Olivier began to research obsessively. He found a few medical journals and scientific papers, seeking answers on how to prolong life. He studied conflicting opinions on diet, exercise, and lifestyle. He read about diet and its impact on cellular health, about inflammation caused by processed foods, and about the risks of high cholesterol. One thing was clear: everything he consumed, every action he took, needed to be filtered through one question—*Will this help me live longer?*

On the following morning, he broke his fast with a glass of water, a handful of blueberries, and a boiled egg. Each bite felt calculated, deliberate, as though he were performing a sacred ritual; each bite felt like an act of defiance against the specter of death.

This simple act became his new mantra: Everything I consume must help me live longer. It was the first step in a lifelong journey.

Over the next few months, Olivier transformed. He stopped drinking alcohol, refused desserts, and began meticulously planning his meals. His diet became rigidly structured—lean proteins, fresh fruits and vegetables. He fasted for hours at a time, reading about how intermittent fasting triggered autophagy, the body's natural process of clearing out damaged cells. He was no longer a regular at the late-night parties.

He became a champion of sleep, ensuring he got precisely eight hours each night, no more, no less. He began exercising daily—not for enjoyment, but for longevity. His mornings started with long runs through the countryside, his lungs burning as he pushed his body to its limits. Weight lifting followed, not for aesthetics, but for the muscle mass he'd read would protect him in old age. He confused others around him as he practiced controlled breathing exercises.

His classmates noticed the change. They mocked him at first, laughing at his strict routines and refusal to join their parties.

"Come on, Malraux," one boy in the dorm jeered, holding out a beer. "You're no fun anymore. One won't kill you."

"That's exactly what someone who wants to die early would say," Olivier replied coldly, setting the beer down untouched.

"You're crazy, man," the boy laughed.

"No, I'm the only one here taking life seriously." said Olivier, brushing past him.

The teasing faded as his classmates realized Olivier was unshakable. His teachers noticed the change, too, praising his discipline but worrying about his intensity. Even the school doctor, whom he visited regularly for blood tests, pulled him aside one day.

"You're taking this too far," the doctor warned one day. "You're young," the doctor said. "You should be enjoying your life, not dissecting it."

"I *am* enjoying myself," Olivier replied, his tone sharp. "I'm enjoying living. And I'm going to enjoy it longer than anyone else."

One evening, alone in his room, Olivier came across a story in an old philosophy book. It told of a kingdom where the water had been tainted, causing everyone who drank it to go mad. The king, drinking from a separate well, remained sane. But the people, seeing their king as different, declared him mad. Unable to bear his isolation, the king eventually drank from the tainted well, joining his subjects in their madness.

Olivier closed the book, staring into the flickering flames. The story resonated deeply with him.

I am the king, he thought. His classmates drank and smoked, wasting their youth on pleasures that hastened their demise. The world outside was no better, filled with people who gorged themselves on sugar and stress, oblivious to the damage they inflicted on their bodies.

But unlike the king in the story, Olivier vowed he would never drink from the tainted well.

Despite his rigorous routines, Olivier couldn't escape the nagging realization that no matter how perfectly he lived, he would still die. Maybe at ninety, or even a hundred if he pushed the limits, but death would come.

Father Time always won.

But what if there was a way to change that?

His father had once told him about the ancient trees in France, oaks that had stood for hundreds of years. "Why do they live longer than us?" his father had asked, a wistful look in his eyes.

That question became Olivier's next obsession. He began studying trees, learning about their indeterminate growth, their ability to compartmentalize damage, and their resistance to aging.

"They never stop growing," he muttered to himself one evening, flipping through a botany textbook. "They heal themselves. They don't have organs to fail. And they don't grow old the way we do."

He began studying the world's longest-living trees, poring over scientific journals and ecological studies. He devoured books on the bristlecone pine, which lived for over five thousand years, and the giant sequoia, which resisted disease and fire with its thick bark.

"The answer is in the trees," he whispered, his heart racing. "Their biology is built for survival," Olivier muttered to himself late one night, his desk covered in notes and sketches. "Why isn't ours?"

But trees weren't enough.

The more he learned about trees, the more he realized their limits. Even the oldest trees could be felled by a storm or disease.

Olivier's research expanded to include other long-lived species: jellyfish that could revert to a juvenile state, effectively resetting their biological clocks. Hydras that appeared immune to aging—hydras appeared biologically immortal.

If cells can stop aging in other species, why not in humans?

This realization consumed him. He studied cellular senescence, telomere lengthening, epigenetic reprogramming, and mitochondrial function. He read about experimental drugs, stem cell therapies, and gene editing.

Olivier experimented on himself and began manipulating his own body. He paid for hyperbaric oxygen therapy, which claimed to rejuvenate cells. He injected himself with stem cells harvested from his own body. He tracked his bloodwork obsessively, adjusting his routines with every new piece of data. Every new treatment, every discovery, brought him closer to his ultimate goal: conquering death.

Doctors and scientists were amazed by his knowledge, marveling at the young man who spoke with the confidence of a seasoned researcher. But even they began to whisper about his obsession.

"He's going too far," one doctor said to another after a lecture Olivier attended.

"He doesn't care," the other replied.

And they were right. Olivier didn't.

One day, Olivier's financial adviser summoned him to a meeting.

"Olivier," the man said, sliding a ledger across the table. "You're burning through your inheritance at an alarming rate. You're running out of money," the man said bluntly.

Olivier stared at him, unblinking. "That's impossible. The Malraux fortune is endless."

"Endless for most," the adviser replied. "Not for what you're doing. The treatments, the research, the scientists you've hired—it's draining faster than we can replenish it. Even with the Malraux fortune, you can't sustain this forever. You'll need more money. A lot more."

Olivier leaned back in his chair, his mind racing. He couldn't stop now, not when he was so close.

That was when the idea for what would become Artemis was born.

He would build an empire, a corporation that fed off the very vices he despised. One that would profit from the world's obesity, addiction, stress, and disease. People wanted Band-Aids for their self-inflicted wounds, so Artemis would provide them—and charge them dearly.

The very behaviors Olivier scorned would become the foundation of his empire. And the profits would fund his ultimate mission: immortality.

"I'll make them pay for their madness," he thought, a cold smile forming on his lips.

CHAPTER 38

November 4, 2022. 1:17 p.m.

Artemis Headquarters, Geneva, Switzerland

Olivier leaned back in his leather chair, gazing out the floor-to-ceiling windows of his penthouse office overlooking the Alps. The sprawling city lay beneath him, its bustling life moving in rhythmic flow, oblivious to the man who sat plotting to outlive it all. His eyes, a cold and calculating gray, traced the line of the distant horizon as if measuring how much longer the world would last. To him, the city was a reminder of time—a ticking clock, a constant enemy.

He was fifty-seven years old, but his body had the biological markers of a thirty-one-year-old. His regimen was relentless: hyperbaric chamber sessions, daily vitamin drips, hormone injections, genetic modifications to erase the markers of aging. It was working—he was living proof that time could be delayed. But delaying wasn't enough. He wanted to stop it.

His father's words echoed in his mind: "The real wonder of the world is compounding interest." The old man had always preached about the value of time, not as a philosophical notion, but as a financial strategy. He would tell Olivier about it when he was young, with a glint in his eye, as if revealing the secrets of the universe. Compounding interest was the reason his father had amassed such wealth, the very thing that had provided Olivier with the privileges of his upbringing.

But Olivier had realized early on that his father's ambitions had been small-minded, his goals limited to earthly desires. The idea was to enjoy the wealth, yes—but what was the point if time ran out? His father had not lived long enough to see his wealth truly grow to its potential. It was like planting a tree and dying before you could sit in its shade.

No, Olivier was going to go further. He wasn't going to let anyone or anything—least of all time—outlive him.

In addition to developing his unusual passions at the American academy in France, he also became worldly at an age when most boys were still trying to figure out who they were.

At this institution, Olivier was surrounded by the sons and daughters of the ultra-wealthy—the children of sheiks, diplomats, and business tycoons. His network grew not by happenstance, but by design. He knew that achieving his true goal would require more than just his own inheritance; he would need the resources, minds, and loyalties of others.

As he continued his studies, his ambitions evolved. He pursued an undergraduate degree in genetics, obsessed with understanding the biological roots of aging. He followed it with an MBA from Harvard, where he sharpened his business acumen and continued building his network. Each person he met was a potential asset, each asset a potential opportunity to inch closer to his ultimate goal.

At Harvard, Olivier found his obsession crystallizing during a class on ancient mythology. The professor spoke about Artemis, the immortal goddess of the hunt. "Artemis had one condition for those who swore loyalty to her," the professor had said, "that they must forever renounce men. For if they broke this vow, Artemis would strip them of their immortality."

The idea struck a chord with Olivier. It was a noble hunt he was undertaking, but not for game or conquest. It was for time itself. He would reject everything that might distract him from his path. He would swear off friendships, deep relationships, even human comforts. Everything was secondary to his goal.

His obsessions grew to encompass more than just genetics and pharmacology. One day, while speaking with a scientist who was consulting on one of his projects, Olivier was asked, "Why do you want to live forever? The earth is a ticking time bomb. Someday, the sun will burn out, or we'll destroy the planet ourselves."

The conversation marked a shift in Olivier's thinking. It was no longer about defeating time on Earth. It was about escaping the planet altogether. Artemis's reach expanded, and so did its ambitions. Space colonization, astrophysics, even the development of technologies for constructing artificial habitats in orbit—all became part of the grand design.

Olivier's companies became labyrinthine entities, with legitimate fronts and secretive back channels. Some of these firms were designed to make money and then sell off for profit. But there were also projects hidden within them—research centers that worked on the fringe of ethical science. No one truly understood the full scope of what they were contributing to; each scientist or researcher only had a small piece of the puzzle. The master puzzle, the immortality machine, existed solely in Olivier's mind.

The secret labs around the world operated under shell corporations with innocuous names, while in reality, they were researching everything from genetic modification to nanotechnology, telomere extension, and even neurological downloads—attempts to transfer consciousness into a digital form. It wasn't just about stopping death; it was about achieving true immortality.

His ruthless ambition led him to develop cures as well as killers. On one hand, his companies created revolutionary drugs—new statins, treatments for Alzheimer's, advancements in surgical techniques. On the other hand, there were darker innovations—engineered viruses and pathogens. He knew that if cures were valuable, killers might be even more so. There was always a market for controlling life and death.

When he finally held the formula for the cancer cure, he could have gone public with it and earned a Nobel Prize. But he didn't. The cure was not a gift for humanity; it was a business model. At $100 million a dose, it was sold to the ultra-wealthy who wanted to live longer, who could afford to extend their lives without the limitations of morality or insurance companies. Why give it away and save the disease-riddled masses? They were only consuming resources, his valuable air, as they inched toward death—a fate Olivier intended to avoid at any cost.

As he perfected his techniques, Olivier became obsessed not only with his appearance but with his biological age. He tracked it religiously, charting each small victory over time. He performed daily blood tests, and continually searched for any indicators that might reveal his body's decline. Every minute detail was scrutinized, from advanced hydration techniques to the daily injections that kept his muscles from atrophying and his cells from breaking down.

He hadn't just learned to delay death; he had made death his sworn enemy.

CHAPTER 39

Wednesday January 25, 2023. 8:17 a.m.

Artemis Headquarters, Geneva, Switzerland

Juan Ramirez had once believed in the American Dream, but now he understood it was a myth. He'd grown up in Southern California, the son of Mexican immigrants who'd toiled long hours for meager pay, never quite fitting in. His parents had hoped their sacrifices would carve out a place for their children in a country that promised so much. But for Juan, the reality had been far less welcoming.

In the predominantly white neighborhood where he lived, his name marked him as different. No one saw him as just another kid. He was always "Juan," a boy from the wrong side of the cultural divide. Resentment built in him early, stoked by insults and exclusion. It didn't take long for him to find his way into trouble, rolling with local gangs to feel like he belonged somewhere, even if it was among the broken.

By the time he was eighteen, the path ahead was clear: jail or the military. Both offered discipline, daily meals, and a place to channel his anger. So, he chose the Navy. He wanted to prove something to himself and the world that had dismissed him, so when the chance to train for the Navy SEALs came, he jumped at it. He wasn't the biggest guy, but his drive more than made up for what he lacked in size. His instructors took note of his willingness to push beyond his limits. Ramirez made it through BUD/S, each day honing his body and mind into a weapon. The challenges didn't stop there. He continued east, earning a coveted spot on SEAL Team 6.

It was there, on the bleeding edge of combat, that Juan Ramirez transformed into Razor. He had a natural talent for knife work, combining speed, precision, and an understanding of human anatomy that was both intuitive and deeply studied. He had killed his share of men, often up close and personal, feeling the resistance of muscle and bone as his blade sliced through flesh. The name "Razor" fit him perfectly—it represented his cold efficiency, his lack of hesitation. It was a new identity, one he took pride in because it was forged in battle. But even the most finely crafted blades can dull, and Razor's body was beginning to show the wear and tear of years of warfare.

When the Navy washed him out due to combat-related injuries—damaged lungs from inhaling toxic chemicals in Iraq, a shredded shoulder from a parachute landing gone wrong—it felt like being discarded by the only family that had ever really mattered to him. He tried to find his place in the civilian world but felt lost, disconnected. The adrenaline that had fueled his existence was gone, and in its place were the dull aches and lingering injuries that no amount of painkillers seemed to alleviate.

It wasn't long before he found his way to Blackwater, where his skills and experience were more than enough to earn him a place in the world of private military contracting. There, he began building a reputation that rivaled what he'd achieved in the military. But even this felt like chasing ghosts—old battles with no real meaning behind them. What he craved wasn't just money; it was purpose. That's when Artemis came into his life.

It started with a contract to oversee security for a research lab in a remote location. Razor thought it would be just another job—protect the perimeter, control the access points, keep the eggheads safe from whatever threats lurked in the dark. But this lab was different. The work was too secretive, the scientists too nervous, the security protocols too extreme. It didn't take long for Razor to understand that the people funding the lab weren't interested in money—they were interested in something far more valuable: time.

Olivier had taken note of Razor's skills and his unwavering demeanor. Over the next several months, the two men formed a bond built on a mutual understanding: Olivier saw Razor as a weapon, a tool to be wielded; Razor saw Olivier as a doorway to a new world. And when the lab's research uncovered experimental treatments that could repair Razor's damaged lungs and restore his physical abilities beyond their original state, the bond between them strengthened.

The treatment worked. Razor was no longer just healed—he was enhanced. His lung capacity improved to that of a high-altitude athlete, his reflexes sharpened to a level he hadn't experienced even in his peak years as a SEAL. It was as if the injuries that had once defined him had never existed. The Artemis treatments had given him back his identity, but also something more—purpose. For Razor, that was worth more than any paycheck.

He began to see Olivier as not just an employer but as a kind of savior, someone who understood the value of second chances and what a man could do when he was unburdened by time. Olivier confided in Razor, sharing details about the Artemis mission—the quest for immortality, the idea of outlasting death itself. It wasn't just about living longer; it was about mastering time, bending it to their will. Olivier sold him on the mission, and Razor bought in with everything he had.

Over the years, Razor moved up the ranks, proving his loyalty and his effectiveness time and time again. He was no longer just a security contractor; he was head of Artemis's entire security apparatus. Under his leadership, the division grew into a military force that rivaled the capabilities of a small nation. Artemis Security had state-of-the-art weapons, cutting-edge technology, and a global network of operatives capable of operating in the shadows.

Weapons, tech, manpower—Artemis Security had it all. And Razor had shaped it into an organization with a singular purpose: protect the secrets of Artemis at all costs. They weren't merely guarding research facilities or VIPs; they were erasing threats and eliminating loose ends. Razor's team handled situations that governments wouldn't touch, operating above the law and beyond any official scrutiny.

Razor had recruited some of the deadliest operatives he'd encountered over his career. Men like Scott Burch and his best friend Red had been brought into the fold because they shared a certain ruthlessness that was necessary for the kind of work Artemis demanded. Razor had met both men at Fort Bragg, and he'd seen the kind of hunger they had—the need to prove themselves against the worst the world could throw at them.

"Exterminators gonna exterminate," he'd tell them before sending them off on assignments that usually ended in bodies being buried and secrets being kept. Razor had personally orchestrated the removal of scientists, field operatives, and even rival corporate executives when they had outlived their usefulness. He saw his role not as one of protection but of purging. He wasn't here to keep anyone safe—he was here to keep the mission pure.

January 25, 2023—8:17 a.m.
Razor's cold, dark eyes scanned the data on his tablet. The latest reports had come in, pointing toward a name that had surfaced in Artemis's security database: Lee Cain. Former college football player who never got his degree. But there was more to the man than met the eye—even though he was not ex-military, he had a background filled with violence. He had a handful of professional fights and run-ins with the law, the latter leading to the occasional jail that didn't hold him for long.

"Who are you, Lee, and why are you causing fucking problems for me?" Razor muttered as he stared at the tablet.

The information pointed to the Texas border town of Del Rio. Razor knew the area well enough to understand its significance—close to the border, the kind of place where men like Cain could slip through cracks and disappear. But no one stayed hidden forever. Razor knew how to hunt, and this was going to be his favorite kind of hunt: the kind where the prey thinks it's already escaped.

With Olivier's blessing, Razor began planning the offensive. The Artemis mission had always been about security and secrecy, but now it was time to shift gears. The hunt for Lee Cain was on, and Razor wasn't going to stop until he had his man. This wasn't just another job—this was personal. Artemis had given Razor a new life, a purpose, and a mission, and he would die before letting anyone threaten that.

CHAPTER 40

Wednesday, January 25, 2023. 2:30 p.m.

Hope Lodge, New York City

The cold fluorescent lights flickered as the door to Hope Lodge swung open. Two men, dressed in black tactical clothing that screamed military, stepped inside. They carried themselves with precision, every movement calculated. To the casual observer, they might have looked like ordinary security personnel, but anyone who had spent even a moment sizing them up would know better. These men were the real deal—professional, lethal, and dangerous.

The taller of the two, with a buzzcut and a scar slicing across his eyebrow, scanned the room like a predator. His eyes darted to every corner, every exit, every person, cataloging it all. His partner, a shorter but broader man with tattoos peeking out from under his collar, moved with the same purpose, his face expressionless.

"We'll start here," the taller one muttered, his voice low and gravelly.

They weren't here for a routine check. They were from Artemis, and they were hunting. Hunting for Lee Cain.

These men had worked their way from Donny at the front desk to questioning every patient they came across in the building. They were going to talk to everyone at the Hope Lodge before the day was out.

Julia sat in her room, her heart pounding against her ribs. She knew something was wrong the moment she heard from another patient about the "military guys" asking questions in the building. When she got a look at them coming down the hall—the way they moved, the way they avoided eye contact with anyone—they were predators. And predators always had prey.

Her hand trembled as she reached for the door, trying to close it before they could notice her. But she wasn't fast enough. The taller one spotted her in the hallway, his cold gaze locking onto hers like a snake about to strike.

"Hey," his voice cut through the tension like a blade. "You seen this guy?" He held up a photo of Lee Cain, the grainy image showing him at some previous checkpoint, looking as rugged and dangerous as ever.

Julia's heart skipped a beat. She had to think fast. The *bag*—the bag that Cain had left—was hanging in the other room, barely out of sight. If these guys got even a hint of it, she was dead.

She had to keep them out. She had to lie, and lie well.

"Oh, *that* asshole?" Julia rolled her eyes and forced a smile, leaning against the doorframe in what she hoped was a casual stance. "Yeah, I've seen him. Real piece of work, that one. Always kept to himself. Never talked to anyone. Acted like he was too good for the rest of us. What did he do? Did he die or something?"

The taller guy narrowed his eyes, clearly not buying her casual attitude. He stepped closer, towering over her. "What else do you know about him?"

"Not much," Julia shrugged, trying her best to seem indifferent. "He was just . . . there. Didn't say much. Seemed like a loner. Kind of a jerk, really."

The shorter guy with the tattoos snorted, looking Julia up and down. "Not bad lookin' for a cancer chick," he muttered under his breath to his partner. The taller one ignored the comment, his eyes still locked on Julia's face, searching for any sign of a lie.

Julia's skin crawled, but she kept her cool. The empty bag that Cain had left was just a few feet away, hidden by the door, and she had to keep them from finding it. She crossed her arms over her chest, trying to look more annoyed than scared. "Are we done here? I've got my own shit to deal with."

The taller one tilted his head, as if considering her words. He lingered just a moment too long, his gaze drifting past her, toward the room behind her. She could feel the tension building, a dangerous game of cat and mouse playing out in silence. One wrong move, one wrong word, and they'd be inside her room, searching for the one thing that could get her killed.

Finally, the taller man nodded. "Yeah, we're done."

Julia let out a breath she hadn't realized she was holding, watching as the two men walked away. They didn't look back.

The two Artemis operatives made their way down the hallway, their steps almost silent on the cheap carpet. Once they were out of earshot, the shorter one spoke up again, his voice low. "She's hidin' something."

"No shit," the taller one replied, his tone sharp. "But we'll deal with her later. Let's check the other room first."

They approached Lee Cain's room, the door still locked from when he'd last left it. But locks didn't mean much to these men. The taller one pulled out a sleek device from his pocket, something that looked like a cross between a smartphone and a scanner. He placed it against the lock, and within seconds, there was a soft click. The door swung open.

Inside, the room was empty, but not untouched. They knew how to spot the signs—subtle disturbances, things that normal people wouldn't notice.

"Let's do this." The shorter man pulled out a small ultraviolet flashlight, shining it across the room. The blue light revealed traces of footprints, fingerprints, smudges on the walls that weren't visible to the naked eye.

They moved methodically, sweeping the room like the professionals they were. The closet, the bathroom, the bed—it all told a story. A story that confirmed their worst fears.

"Diablo was here," the shorter one muttered, crouching down and running his gloved fingers over a faint stain on the carpet. He touched the tip of his finger to his tongue, tasting the faint trace of chemicals.

"Yeah, but he's gone now. Something bad happened here," the taller one replied, his eyes scanning the room with a practiced intensity. "You think he went rogue?"

The shorter man shook his head. "No, not on timeline. This doesn't feel like that."

The taller man stood up, cracking his knuckles. "No, this was someone else. Cain. It has to be. He's the only one who makes sense."

The two of them exchanged a glance, unspoken understanding passing between them. They'd seen enough. They knew enough.

The taller one turned toward the door, his voice cold and deadly. "Tell Razor to get everything he can on this motherfucker. He's gonna want to know who he is, where he's been, and why the hell he's trying to fuck with our operation."

As they walked out of the room, the hunt for Lee Cain had officially begun.

Down the hallway, Julia sat on the edge of her bed, her hands trembling as she tried to steady her breathing. She had done it. She had managed to keep them out of her room, to keep them from finding the bag. But the relief was short-lived.

She glanced over at the empty bag hanging in the closet. Whatever Cain had left behind, it was already working. She could feel it. The pain, the sickness that had been gnawing at her for months—it was fading. She felt stronger, healthier.

But that only made things more dangerous. If Artemis found out what she had, if they realized what was happening to her, they would kill her. No hesitation.

She needed to move. She needed to get out of there before they came back.

Because now, more than ever, she knew one thing for sure: no one was safe.

CHAPTER 41

Thursday, January 25, 2023. 3:15 p.m.

Artemis Headquarters, Geneva, Switzerland

The conference room at Artemis Headquarters was a fortress of cold steel and glass. Its walls were lined with monitors displaying shifting data streams, each charting the pulse of a world oblivious to the predators circling in the shadows. At the head of the sleek obsidian table sat Olivier, his posture as rigid as the chair beneath him. Across from him was Razor, Artemis's head of security, the man who handled the dirty work when whispers turned to roars.

Razor always had an edge of unpredictability about him—a glint in his eyes that made even Olivier take note. He leaned back in his chair, fingers drumming lightly on the armrest, his sharp features etched with mild amusement.

"What's on your mind, sir?" Razor began, his voice gravelly and casual.

Olivier's fingers tapped a rhythmic beat on the table, the only sound in the cold, sterile room. His pale, almost skeletal face betrayed no emotion. When he finally spoke, his voice was smooth and deliberate.

"Lee Cain," Olivier said. "I want an update on your investigation. Particularly regarding the Silverman incident."

Razor's smirk faded, replaced by a grim seriousness. "Cain . . ." He exhaled sharply, leaning forward. "He's a ghost wrapped in muscle and bad decisions. Tough as they come. Stupidly resilient. His connection to Silverman—I'm finding it hard to believe it's just a coincidence."

Olivier's gaze sharpened. "Cain survived this long and we can't find him yet? That's no small feat. Tell me, Razor, why does he persist?"

"Luck," Razor replied flatly. "And a hell of a lot of anger. But luck runs out, and anger only gets you so far. The question is why he's burrowing into Artemis like a tick."

Olivier's lips curled into a faint, calculated smile. "He's a survivor. And survivors interest me. They defy odds, Razor. And we . . ." Olivier gestured to the room around them, "are in the business of defeating odds."

Razor tilted his head, his tone laced with skepticism. "Business is one thing. Obsession is another. And let's be honest, Olivier, you've been obsessed with this idea of immortality since the beginning. But what does that have to do with Cain?"

Olivier's voice dropped to a near whisper. "Everything. Cain represents a raw, unrefined version of what Artemis strives for. Survival at all costs. He is nature's answer to our question of endurance. But he is flawed. He's human. And that makes him expendable."

Razor chuckled darkly. "So what's the plan? Study him? Use him? Kill him?"

Olivier's faint smile didn't waver. "All three, perhaps. Tell me, Razor, do you ever question what we're doing here?"

Razor's demeanor shifted. His smirk returned, but it was bitter this time. "Oh, I question it all the time. I question why we're playing God, why we're pulling strings that aren't ours to pull. But then I remember: I'm good at what I do. And what I do keeps me alive."

Olivier leaned back, his expression unreadable. "Do you think the world deserves to survive, Razor? Truly?"

Razor's eyes narrowed. "Deserve? No. Deserve has nothing to do with it. The world's a mess. Weak people living off the scraps of the strong. That's nature. That's balance. But what you're doing . . ." He shook his head. "You're not just pruning the garden. You're trying to scorch the earth."

Olivier's voice turned icy. "The Earth is dying, Razor. The weak are killing it. We're not scorched-earth tacticians; we're preservationists. The Great Reset is necessary. A controlled burn to save the forest."

"And the viruses?" Razor asked pointedly. "The designer plagues? The engineered diseases? What's that about—saving the forest? Or wiping out the ants?"

"Both," Olivier admitted without hesitation. "The weak drain resources, Razor. Resources the planet doesn't have. Artemis is ensuring a future where humanity's best can thrive. The rest . . . they are collateral."

Razor's laugh was hollow. "And Cain? Where does he fit into your utopia?"

"He doesn't," Olivier said simply. "He's a threat. But he's also a tool. Every action he takes, every move he makes, it teaches us something about our future enemies. About survival. About resilience. When he's no longer useful, he'll be dealt with."

Razor's jaw tightened. "And what about the rest of us? What happens when we're no longer useful to you?"

Olivier's smile was chilling. "That depends, Razor. Are you strong enough to survive?"

The room fell into a heavy silence, broken only by the faint hum of the monitors. Razor's eyes lingered on Olivier, his mind turning over the weight of the conversation.

Finally, Razor stood, adjusting his jacket. "I'll keep looking into Cain," he said.

Razor left the room, his footsteps echoing down the empty corridor. Olivier remained seated, his gaze fixed on the monitors. The world outside moved obliviously, a garden of ants waiting to be pruned. To Olivier, it wasn't a question of if Artemis would succeed. It was a question of when.

And when that time came, he would stand among the gods, untouchable, eternal.

CHAPTER 42

Wednesday, January 25, 2023. 4:05 p.m.

US-Mexico Border

The Land Cruiser's tires hummed on the hot asphalt as Jimmy gripped the steering wheel, a half-chewed toothpick sticking out of his mouth. The guy had a way of making everything seem calm, even when the situation was stressful as hell. Lee sat in the passenger seat, legs stretched out, trying to ignore the knot tightening in his stomach. He had been in some real shit over the years, but this? This felt different. This was bigger.

"Nice ride," Lee muttered, glancing around the plush leather interior. Jimmy's Land Cruiser was decked out—chrome finishes, high-end sound system, even the damn seats felt like they were made for royalty. It sure as hell wasn't what a broke guy should be driving.

Jimmy grinned, his Texas drawl smooth as ever. "Yeah, well, Hoss, it ain't exactly a car you buy with a nine-to-five, if you catch my drift."

"I catch it," Lee replied, a smirk creeping onto his face. His mind wandered back to his old 1975 Imperial LeBaron. "Hell, remember that time I had that boat of a car? Thing was practically indestructible."

Jimmy let out a chuckle. "Oh, I remember. You could've driven through a damn brick wall, come out the other side just fine. We made some *real* memories in that beast."

"Before we see if we make it across or not, I wanted to thank you, brother," Lee said as he scanned the line of cars in front of them.

"*De nada*, Hoss," Jimmy said through closed lips holding his toothpick. "Always glad to help. And don't worry none, we will get across."

"I don't mean thank you for pickin' me up now," Lee answered. "It's for when you picked me up and didn't even know it."

"Fuck you talking about, Hoss?"

"When I was at the worst of it with the cancer, there were moments when I was fighting to stay alive. During those moments I was terrified to go to sleep . . . worried that I was gonna die. There were nights I'd be willin' myself not to give up. I would get pissed at myself and smack myself in the arms and chest just to make sure that my body remembered what it was like to stay alive. I said to myself, don't you die on me yet, you son of a bitch."

Jimmy sat straight-faced and nodded.

"One of the worst fucking moments, I was so weak I couldn't get out of my damn bed. Then I had to piss so bad, I got on the floor and crawled on my elbows to the toilet. But when I got there, I was so goddam weak from the chemotherapy, pullin' up on that bowl was harder than any chin up I ever tried. It broke my ass. At that moment, I was finally ready to die. I rolled on my back, and gave up."

Jimmy had never imagined Lee like this.

"But in that moment," Lee continued, "My phone buzzed on the floor next to me. Out of habit, I checked it and saw a text from you. It said, 'I don't know where you are Hoss, but I hope yer ok. Never forget yer the toughest sum bitch I ever met.' After that text, my spirit came back to me. And I got on that fucking bowl."

Lee paused and said, "You really saved my life that day, Slick."

Jimmy, understanding the power of that simple text, had a lump in his throat.

"I never knew, Hoss." He choked.

"Well, now you do," said Lee as he slapped Jimmy on the shoulder with a smile.

As they inched closer to the border, the gravity of what they were about to do started to creep in. Halfway across the bridge, the distinct smell of Acuña hit Lee's nose. It was a scent that instantly reminded him of dusty streets, cheap tequila, and lawlessness. Here, they were leaving behind the safety net of American soil and entering a different world—a world where the rules shifted depending on who was holding the gun.

Lee leaned back, staring out the window as the familiar landscape of Mexico came into view. There was a line you crossed when you came down here, not just the physical border, but a line in your mind where you knew that safety was now a memory. Once you crossed it, you were on your own. No backup. No second chances.

"Just a fuckin' dollar," Lee muttered, tossing the coins into the basket at the toll booth to cross into Mexico.

"Always worth it for the thrill," Jimmy said, his grin never fading, but even he felt the shift in the air.

They cruised into the Mexican side of customs, and Lee's pulse quickened. He'd done this trip plenty of times before, but never like this. The difference was the cargo. Before, it was always just little shit—maybe some brass knuckles or a slapjack stuffed in his bag, nothing that would get him more than a fine and a slap on the wrist.

This time? This time, they had a gold bar and a folder of files containing some earth-shattering shit stashed in the back. Shit that could put them away for a long time—well, as long as it took for his hunters to have him killed in the clink.

Lee's eyes flicked to the random checkpoint ahead. It was a crapshoot. Sometimes you'd breeze right through, no hassle. But other times, that damn red light would flash, and you'd get waved into the search lanes. And once they had you in there? Well, things could get real dicey, real quick.

"Y'know, Jimmy," Lee said, trying to keep his voice steady, "I never got too worked up about these stops before. But this time, I'm sweatin' bullets. You ever feel like this?"

Jimmy glanced over, his grin still intact but his eyes serious. "Buddy, don't let anyone fool you. Even the best of us get the jitters. Hell, I'm a pro at this, but it only takes one slipup. Don't matter how badass you are. Sometimes, that fear's what keeps you alive."

The tension was palpable. The line of cars slowly inched forward, and Lee could feel his heart pounding in his chest. Sweat beaded on his forehead. The closer they got to the checkpoint, the more he could feel his nerves taking over. He never got caught doing shit like this. But today? Today could be the day everything went south.

The border guard waved them through.

No red light. No bell. No alarm. Just a casual wave that signaled they were free to go.

Lee let out a long breath, his grip relaxing slightly on the armrest. Jimmy grinned again, the toothpick rolling to the other side of his mouth. "See? Told ya. Just a little luck, and we're home free."

Jimmy always was a good-luck charm. They crossed into Mexico, the landscape turning even more foreign with every passing mile. As they drove, Jimmy started explaining the state of things on La Sombra's side of the border, his tone becoming more serious.

"Shit's wild down here now," Jimmy said. "Cartels are getting smarter, nastier. Used to be they just dealt in drugs. Now? They're moving people, too. Human trafficking, illegal border crossings. They're making more money off selling people than they are off coke or heroin."

"Human trafficking," Lee repeated, the word hanging heavy in the air. It wasn't new to him, but hearing it laid out so bluntly still turned his stomach.

Jimmy nodded. "Yeah. It's big business. You've got the drugs, the guns, and now people. They run it all, and it's a tight operation. I mean, fuck, man, they've even got the politicians down here and in the United States in their pocket. Ain't nobody safe from the cartels."

Lee leaned back, letting it sink in. Jimmy was a bad guy. He had always known that, but somehow, it didn't matter. He was Lee's best shot at getting through this alive. Maybe Jimmy was in deep with the cartels, but in a world where the enemy of your enemy is your friend, sometimes you had to play the game.

"You're a real piece of work, Jimmy," Lee said with a smirk, shaking his head. "You're in deep with these fuckers, aren't you?"

Jimmy's grin returned, and he let out a low chuckle. "Oh, I'm neck-deep, brother. But let me tell you something: sometimes, being in with the bad guys is the only way to survive. You play the game right, and you might just come out on top."

Lee knew it was true. They weren't going to make it through this unless they played their cards right. Artemis was after him, and the only way to survive was to team up with the very people he hated. The Scar was their ticket to survival, but getting in front of him would be the hardest part.

Thirty minutes later, they reached the meet-up location—an isolated stretch of road outside the city where two blacked-out SUVs waited for them. Armed men leaned against the cars, guns hanging loosely from their shoulders.

Jimmy pulled up next to them, his face suddenly serious. "All right, here we go. Showtime."

Lee's stomach tightened again as the men approached. One of them, a massive guy with a scar running down his cheek, motioned for them to step out of the car. The tension in the air was suffocating.

They were ushered out of the Land Cruiser, and before Lee could even get a good look at the situation, a black bag was yanked over his head.

"Fuck," Lee muttered under his breath as rough hands pushed him forward.

The world around him went dark, but the real darkness, the real danger, wasn't with these men. It was with the Scar.

CHAPTER 43

Wednesday, February 7, 2018. 7:00 p.m.

Saint Moritz, Switzerland

The man stood at the edge of the bobsled track, his sharp, tailored coat hugging his athletic frame against the alpine chill. Monaco had always been lavish, but this was something else entirely. The snow-covered mountains of Saint Moritz glittered in the moonlight, and the crowd of ultra-elite socialites gathered around him were all buzzing about one thing: the Legends Party—an invitation-only event that could turn the lucky few who attended into legends themselves.

He was not like the others. He had worked for this moment. His success wasn't inherited. It was earned, clawed from the jaws of obscurity. Every decision, every maneuver had led him to this night. His black hair was slicked back, his thick eyebrows giving his face an intensity that matched his ambition. He had movie-star looks, and they didn't hurt in a world where appearances meant everything, but his edge was something deeper—something forged in fire.

He watched the bobsleds cut through the ice like knives, but his mind was elsewhere, thinking of what lay ahead. His heart raced. Then, a man in ski gear approached from the shadows, his goggles still on, obscuring his face. Without preamble, the man spoke in a clipped tone.

"You've been invited to a party."

The well-dressed gentleman felt a jolt of excitement race down his spine. *This was it.*

"Albert has invited you personally," the skier added, nodding once.

Before he could walk away, the dark-haired man stepped forward, his voice calm but pressing. "Where is it?"

The skier gave a faint smile. "Be at the alpine gondola at seven p.m. sharp."

He hesitated. "And?"

The skier turned, walking away into the night, but left behind one last cryptic instruction. "It's an invitation for one."

The well-dressed man stood there, breathing in the frosty air, watching as the skier vanished into the crowd. His heart hammered in his chest. *He had made it. Finally.*

The penthouse of the chic hotel gleamed with opulence. He had already received congratulations from an acquaintance named Norman LeGrande in the lobby bar who was also attending the party—one of those "first-timers" who had connections, not grit. Another guy born on third base and thought he hit a triple. Already overweight and getting soft. It didn't matter. Tonight, they were equals.

Back in his suite, he opened his closet, smoothing his fingers over the finely tailored suits. Tonight, he'd wear the one that had been custom-made for him by a designer in Milan. The fabric was smooth as silk, dark as midnight. He dressed with care, adjusting his cufflinks and tie, glancing at his reflection. This wasn't just a party; it was a coronation. The man who stood before the mirror wasn't just another rich guest. He was someone who had cracked the code, who had earned his place among the elite through sheer willpower.

He had been punctual all his life, and this night was no exception. At precisely 7:00 p.m., he arrived at the gondola station, the lights of Saint

Moritz twinkling below him like a galaxy of stars. Two beautiful women, both models, stood near the entrance in skintight dresses with short skirts and fur-lined parkas. The cold air didn't seem to faze them. It was like they were impervious to discomfort—just like the world they inhabited.

One of the women, her red lips parting in a professional smile, handed him a glass of glühwein. The spiced wine warmed his body as he took a sip.

"Your name?" she asked.

After he gave it, the woman checked her list and nodded, her perfectly manicured hand motioning him to step inside the gondola.

The gondola was lavishly draped with exotic fur and animal skins. He settled into the plush seat, his back to the mountain, staring out at the town below as the gondola began its ascent. Saint Moritz was shrinking beneath him, but his world was expanding. The sun had already dipped below the horizon, leaving behind a sea of glittering lights and the quiet hum of the gondola cables. He still didn't know exactly where he was going, but it didn't matter. He was going up, rising into a world he had fought his entire life to enter.

When the gondola reached the top, the doors slid open with a soft mechanical hiss. A second woman, just as beautiful as the first, took his empty cup and replaced it with a glass of champagne. "Right this way, sir," she said, pointing toward a red carpet that stretched across the snow. "Knock when you get to the door."

The man stepped onto the carpet, the soft crunch of snow under his polished shoes barely audible against the howling wind. Tiki torches lined the path, flickering wildly in the cold night air, casting eerie shadows over the snow. Ahead, the grand silhouette of a European chalet came into view—an enormous structure, ancient and regal, perched at the top of the mountain like a king overseeing his kingdom.

This was old money, the kind that had passed down through generations, untouchable and unreachable by ordinary men. But tonight, he would walk through those doors and join them. *He had earned this.*

When he reached the heavy wooden door of the chalet, he knocked twice. A moment later, the door creaked open, revealing another beautiful woman, this one even more striking than the last.

"Your name?" she asked, checking a list as if the gates of heaven themselves could only be opened to those with the proper credentials.

He gave it without hesitation, his voice steady, "Keith Larsen."

"Do you have your cell phone, Mr. Larsen?" she asked, extending a hand.

The man handed it over without question. In this world, privacy was everything.

"Thank you," she said, ushering him inside.

The party was already in full swing when he stepped into the grand hall. Music pulsed through the air, a heavy, intoxicating beat that seemed to match the rhythm of his own excitement. Beautiful people, dressed to the nines, moved across the floor in a dance of excess—draped in designer clothes, sipping champagne that cost more than most people's cars. This was Prince Albert's world, where the absurd met the exclusive.

Tables were lined with silver platters of hors d'oeuvres, caviar, and truffles. The waitstaff moved seamlessly through the crowd, offering everything from exotic cocktails to delicacies flown in from the farthest corners of the globe. But even among the glamour and decadence, there was an undercurrent of something more. This wasn't just a party. This was *a test*.

Larsen knew that much. He wasn't just here to celebrate. He was here to prove himself.

Prince Albert stood off to one side, laughing with a group of men. Even in a crowd of billionaires, Albert's presence commanded attention. His bobsled obsession was well-known, as were his tastes for fast women and faster cars. But tonight, he was hosting more than just a social gathering. He was scouting. *Recruiting.*

The well-dressed Larsen weaved his way through the crowd, shaking hands, sharing drinks, doing what he had always done best: blending in.

But as he sipped champagne, keeping his cool, he noticed something else. Several men—serious, well-dressed—were talking in hushed voices near the far end of the room. These weren't ordinary guests. These were men with power. Real power.

By the time midnight approached, the atmosphere had changed. What had started as a party now felt like a secret society meeting. Larsen felt it, too—the shift, the gravity of what was really happening. He had heard rumors about the party being a recruiting ground for something bigger than just business. A club. *A society*.

After the party, Larsen was guided to another location—a private celebration at the Dracula Club. As he stepped inside the exclusive members-only club, he was greeted by the smell of woodsmoke and expensive cigars. The walls were dark, adorned with crimson velvet and dim chandeliers that cast flickering shadows. It was like stepping into another world, one where rules didn't apply.

The waitstaff were all little people, dressed in matching tuxedos, carrying trays of drinks and exotic foods. But what really caught his attention were the guests. The true power players. Men and women whose names were whispered in boardrooms and political circles. And there he was, among them.

At the height of the party, one of the club's members—a man whose face was barely visible in the dim light—opened a large door and released a flood of chickens and goats into the room. The crowd erupted in laughter and chaos as the animals scattered.

People swung from chandeliers, dancing wildly. It was the kind of spectacle that only the absurdly wealthy could create, and for the first time in his life, Larsen felt like he truly belonged.

He had earned his place.

But it wasn't the party that mattered. It was the man sitting at the head of the table. Olivier. The mastermind behind Artemis.

As the night drew on, Olivier, with his dark hair slicked back and his eyes gleaming with intelligence and something darker, gathered a select few into a private room. Larsen was one of them.

"You've all proven yourselves," Olivier said, his voice smooth, almost hypnotic. "But there is more. Artemis is not about wealth. It is about power. Control. The world is on the cusp of something extraordinary. And we, gentlemen, will be the ones to control it."

The man listened, enraptured, as Olivier detailed the goals of Artemis—the pursuit of immortality, the control of the world's resources, the manipulation of society from the shadows. It wasn't just about money. It was about *transcendence*.

Olivier lifted his glass, the dark liquid inside shimmering like blood in the low light. "We are not bound by the rules of ordinary men," he said. "We will shape the future. We will become gods."

Keith Larsen raised his glass, joining the others. He was no longer an outsider. He was part of Artemis now.

And there was no turning back.

CHAPTER 44

February 27, 2023. 3:45 p.m.

New York Athletic Club, Manhattan

Keith Larsen sipped his espresso, savoring the sharp bitterness as he gazed out over the Manhattan skyline from the rooftop terrace of the New York Athletic Club. The cold winter breeze cut through the air, but Keith stood tall, unfazed, his coat hanging open to reveal a crisp dress shirt beneath. The towering glass windows of the club reflected the city back at him—a panoramic reminder of everything he'd conquered. The view wasn't just a spectacle; it was a scoreboard, with each shimmering high-rise representing a level he'd cracked and every floor climbed an affirmation that he was exactly where he belonged.

But it had all started somewhere much smaller.

Keith grew up in New Jersey, in a neighborhood where the middle-class dream meant a steady nine-to-five, a modest home, and the hope that your savings would last you through a retirement that you might not even live to enjoy. His parents were no different. They slogged through life with a kind of quiet resignation, chasing a future that never quite seemed worth the struggle. His mother's words echoed through his memory: "There will always be someone better than you." Her voice carried a tone of acceptance that made Keith's blood boil even now, years later. What if that didn't have to be true?

Keith had known early on that he didn't want the life his parents had. He watched as his father came home each night, defeated after hours at a job he despised, stopping at the bar more often than not before collapsing in front of the TV with a bourbon in his hand. The monotony was suffocating, and Keith vowed he would never settle for less just because it was "good enough."

His neighbors lived the same script—carpenters, plumbers, and small business owners, each one scraping by, complaining about taxes, and discussing meager retirement plans that offered no true escape from the grind. To Keith, they were all trapped, stuck in a system rigged to keep them satisfied with mediocrity. They were consumers. Keith wanted to be a producer.

Keith refused to accept that he had to play by the same rules. He had drive, ambition, and a simmering anger that pushed him to question the boundaries everyone else seemed so willing to accept. It was Mr. Tomlinson next door who first made him see that there were other paths. A former wrestler who had never married, Tomlinson didn't have kids of his own, but he took a special interest in Keith. Maybe he saw a kindred spirit—someone who wasn't satisfied with a life lived small.

Tomlinson was the one who lit the fire in Keith, teaching him to see beyond the American Dream's lie. "You don't have to settle, kid. You just need better strategies," he would say. He explained that the people who lived large lives didn't do so because they were better—they did so because they had better ideas, better connections, and better mindsets. They played a different game entirely. And Keith believed him.

Together, they crafted a plan. Keith needed a Trojan horse, something to get him into the world of the elite, and they both knew sports were a golden ticket. Wrestling was Tomlinson's passion, and it became Keith's, too. He wasn't particularly tall or heavy, which made him a perfect fit for the sport. Every day, they trained, pushing Keith beyond his limits, breaking him down and building him back up, stronger each time.

Wrestling wasn't just about grappling with opponents; it was about learning to dominate, to bend others to his will. On the mats, he found that he could control more than just his opponent—he could control his own destiny. Tomlinson made sure Keith's focus didn't end at the gym. "Your brain's a muscle, too," he would say. "You need to train it the same way." Keith devoured books on strategy, psychology, and success, and his grades soared as a result.

The plan worked. His achievements in wrestling earned him invitations to train at the New York Athletic Club, a prestigious institution that attracted the elite of both the sports world and society. It was a world far removed from New Jersey, where even the air seemed infused with power and privilege. The club exposed Keith to another level of life—one that included sailing, equestrian events, polo, and squash. But it was fencing that caught his attention.

Fencing was elegant yet violent, a sport that demanded both physical agility and mental acuity. It felt like a refined form of combat, and with his wrestling background, Keith adapted quickly. The club's elite members saw his potential, and within a year, he was ranked and had caught the attention of several Ivy League scouts. With his grades, SAT scores, and athletic achievements, Yale was no longer a dream; it was a stepping stone.

Step 1 complete.

2003

Yale University, New Haven, Connecticut

When Keith arrived at Yale, he didn't just see it as an escape from his New Jersey town; it was his entrance into a new world of wealth and status. The campus was filled with students who came from old money, their names associated with legacies of power. Keith had spent his entire life preparing for this, but the reality was even more intoxicating than he had imagined.

He quickly found his place on the fencing team, earning the respect of his teammates through sheer skill and determination. His popularity grew, and with it, his network expanded. He wasn't just learning from textbooks; he was learning from the people around him—sons and daughters of billionaires, political dynasties, and CEOs. Keith studied them as if they were part of his curriculum, picking up the way they spoke, the way they thought, the way they carried themselves.

He took the classes they took—finance, economics, international relations—building not just his academic résumé, but also his social capital. He learned to navigate conversations about yachts and foreign investments, about art collections and ski vacations in Aspen. The more he acted like them, the more they accepted him. And the more they accepted him, the closer he got to the circles of real power.

Keith's relentless drive made him insatiable. He developed expensive tastes—luxury cars, high-end suits, and women who had never known a day of struggle. The finer things weren't just rewards; they were validations of his success.

When he was invited into the Skull and Bones society, he felt like he had reached a new pinnacle. The ritualistic nature of it, the secrecy, the exclusivity—it all reinforced the belief that he was destined for more. Being part of Skull and Bones wasn't just about membership; it was about understanding the allure of secret societies. It taught him that power wasn't just about what you did, but also about what you knew and whom you kept in the dark.

2010

New York City

Graduating with honors in finance, Keith had little difficulty landing a prestigious internship at one of New York's most respected firms. His network from Yale paid off in spades, and within a few years, he was earning more than his parents had saved in a lifetime. It wasn't just about the money; it was about status, influence, and—most importantly—access.

His roommate at Yale had once told him, "More levels, more devils." It was true. Each new level in his career brought a different set of challenges, more cunning opponents, and more ruthless rivals. But Keith had learned to thrive on competition. For every devil he faced, he found a way to slay it. He moved through the finance industry with the precision of a fencer, slicing through obstacles and acquiring assets, companies, and secrets.

As his career soared, so did the exclusivity of his circles. The clubs and societies became smaller and more elite. And each one unlocked new opportunities that those outside the circle could only dream of. He wasn't just part of these circles—he was shaping them, using his connections to build a reputation that went far beyond the office or the boardroom.

Keith had lived what Mr. Tomlinson taught him: "Act the thing you want to become, and you will become what you act." Now, he wasn't just playing the role—he was the role. He was the elite. And when an invitation from Artemis arrived, it didn't feel like a surprise; it felt like the next logical step.

The Artemis meeting atop Saint Moritz was the culmination of Keith's life's work. The setting was exquisite—models draped in fur, champagne in crystal flutes, and a backdrop of the Swiss Alps. It felt like he had finally reached the summit, but the ceremony's end brought a sobering realization: There was no final summit. The journey was endless. The men and women around him weren't content with what they had achieved; they were obsessed with what they hadn't.

And so was Keith.

The higher he climbed, the fewer people he could trust, and the more he had to fight to stay on top. But he was prepared for it. Every step of his life, every mentor, every secret society had led him to this point. He was not about to falter now.

His phone buzzed, snapping him out of his thoughts. An encrypted message from Artemis: "Annual meeting in Zurich. Details to follow." Keith's heart quickened. This was the kind of challenge he lived for. He was ready to face whatever new devil awaited him.

As he tightened his grip on the fencing bag slung over his shoulder, he saw his reflection again. The ambition burning in his eyes hadn't dimmed. If anything, it had grown fiercer. Keith Larsen wasn't just escaping his past anymore; he was determined to rule the future.

CHAPTER 45

Wednesday, January 25, 2023. 8:45 p.m.

Jiménez, Mexico

The world came back to Lee Cain in fragments—bright lights, a thick haze of cigar smoke, and the uncomfortable pull of ropes binding his wrists to the arms of the chair. He blinked hard, trying to orient himself as his vision sharpened. The room came into focus—a lavish office, far too opulent for the violent underworld he had just crossed into. Ornate gold fixtures lined the walls, leather-bound books filled shelves, and a deep red Persian rug covered the floor beneath his feet. This wasn't just an office. It was a throne room, fit for a king. Or a man who thought he was one.

Across an oversized, elaborately carved wooden desk, a figure sat in a leather chair, shadowed by the dim light of the room. The smell of cigar smoke hung thick in the air, curling around the man's figure like a serpent. Cain knew him immediately. The Mexicans called him *Cicatrix*. To Lee, he was Scar.

The man before him was massive. Dark, hairy, and radiating menace, he looked like a beast barely contained by the fine, tailored suit he wore. His face, scarred and pitted, was unmistakable. It was the kind of face that could scare children and silence a room with a glance. But it wasn't the scar that caught Lee's attention—it was his eyes. Cold, calculating, and dangerous.

"Wake up, gringo," Scar's deep voice broke the silence, a twisted smile playing on his lips. His thick accent carried a mix of Spanish and English, the words tumbling together in a harsh cadence that only added to the tension.

Cain blinked again, fully conscious now. His gaze fell to the desk in front of Scar—a bottle of expensive tequila, a gold bar, and a stack of manila folders filled with documents. The contents of Silverman's house. *His leverage.*

Scar picked up the bottle, studying it for a moment before pouring a glass for himself. He lifted it to his lips, savoring the taste like it was a fine wine, his eyes never leaving Cain.

"The only reason you're not dead," Scar began, placing the glass down, "is because I can't believe anyone could be this fucking stupid. I have to hear this story, gringo."

Lee shifted in his chair, feeling the ropes cut into his skin, but his voice stayed steady. "It's not stupidity, Scar. I brought you something valuable. Very valuable. Something I know you'll want to hear."

Scar grunted, unimpressed. He leaned forward, picking up the gold bar from the desk with his massive hand. He turned it over slowly, feeling its weight, letting the cold metal rest against his palm. Then, with a soft chuckle, he dropped it back onto the desk with a heavy thud.

"You have five minutes to explain what the fuck this is and why I shouldn't put a bullet in your head," Scar said, flipping through the hundreds of pages in the manila folder. "And let me tell you something, *cabrón*. If you waste my time, you're going to regret it. I'll hurt you in ways that'll make you wish you were dead."

Lee met his gaze without flinching, his voice even. "That bar is for the past. What's in those files—that's your future."

Scar's eyes narrowed, but he leaned back in his chair, giving Lee a slight nod. "Okay, *pendejo*. Speak. But do it fast before I change my mind."

Lee took a deep breath. This was it. He had to convince Scar, or he was a dead man. "I'm not asking for much. Just listen. Artemis isn't what you think it is. They're bigger. More dangerous than any enemy you've ever crossed paths with. And they've been pulling strings in the shadows for decades—controlling governments, economies, and lives. They control the cure for cancer. *They decide who lives and who dies.*"

Scar raised an eyebrow, still unimpressed. "Artemis, huh? Yeah, I've heard the name. Rich pricks think they can play God. So what, gringo? Why the fuck does that matter to me? Why should I care about some rich *blancos* with too much time and money on their hands?"

"Because it's not just about them," Lee said, his voice lowering. "It's about control. They want to live forever, and they'll burn everything else to the ground to make sure it happens. What they've started can't be undone. They'll kill anyone who gets in their way, including you."

This is when Cain pulled the only card he had to stay alive.

"Look at the files. You are on their list. You and your entire organization. In their master plan, you are going to be eliminated. And if you dig into the shit in there, you will see they have already killed some of your people."

Scar's face darkened. He took another drag from his cigar and exhaled a plume of smoke that clouded the space between them. His fingers drummed on the desk as he thought about what Lee was saying. He remembered certain unexplained incidents where people he had cared about had inexplicably disappeared. Incidents where no one was ever found to blame. And one incident in particular in which he lost someone he loved.

"You know what I think, gringo?" Scar said, leaning forward with his massive arms resting on the desk. "I think these rich fucks have no idea what real power is. They've lived their whole lives behind walls, protected by their money. They think they can just buy immortality? No, *pendejo*. Life doesn't work like that. Not in my world."

Scar's eyes glinted with a dangerous light. "I grew up in the dirt, eating scraps while these *cabrones* dined on gold plates. But I'm still here.

I built this empire with my bare hands. And now, these rich fucks think they can come into my world and take what's mine? No. I don't think so."

He paused, taking a slow sip of the tequila, savoring it before continuing. "You see, gringo, they may have their money, their science, their fancy ideas about living forever, but they underestimate people like me. They think they're better because they were born rich, because they have their little clubs. But my people, *mi gente*, we've fought for everything we have. We've bled for it. And I'll be damned if I let them take it from us."

Lee could feel the shift in Scar's tone, the anger simmering beneath the surface. This was his opening.

"I know you're a man who doesn't take shit from anyone, Scar. And I'm not asking you to. I'm telling you that Artemis is coming, and if we don't stop them, they'll take everything from you. They don't care about La Sombra, about borders, about *su gente*. They want to control everything. And they have the means to do it."

Scar stood up slowly, towering over Lee. His massive frame cast a long shadow across the room. "You think I'm afraid of these rich boys? I've been fighting since I could walk. They don't know what real power looks like. They think they can buy the world, but I'll show them what it means to bleed."

Scar was silent for a moment, his dark eyes locked on to Lee's. Then, a slow grin spread across his scarred face. He walked around the desk and stood in front of Lee, leaning down until their faces were inches apart.

"You know something, gringo? I should thank you."

Lee frowned, unsure where this was going.

Scar's smile widened. "Do you remember the first time we met? In Acuña?"

Lee had been unsure if Scar knew it was him on that New Year's Eve. The bar. The fight. The guy who almost stomped him to death.

Scar laughed, a deep, rumbling sound. "You gave me this," he said, dragging his finger along the jagged scar that ran across his face. "But you also gave me something else. You gave me something to recover from that made me stronger. You taught me that pain is a gift, that weakness is temporary."

Lee stared at him in defiance and said, "I was young. And you punched out my brother."

"Don't worry," Scar cut him off, his voice low and dangerous. "You gave me the best gift I've ever received. And now that you've brought me this tequila and information . . . you can call me Salvador."

"Don't forget the gold . . . Salvador," Lee said, looking over to the valuable bar.

He straightened up, the smile never leaving his face. "I'm going to look deeper into these files. If they have done what I think they have done, I'm going to make Artemis bleed. By eight a.m. tomorrow you need to make a decision about what side you are on."

CHAPTER 46

March 1993

Lubbock, Texas

Lee Cain sat in the jail cell near the campus of Texas Tech. His bruised knuckles and throbbing temples served as a brutal reminder of last night's chaos—a house party that spiraled out of control. His life had been a relentless collision of rage and raw talent, and last night he'd damn near destroyed both.

Lee wasn't the fastest linebacker on the field, but he seemed to always be in the right place at the right time on the gridiron. After topping out at six foot, four inches, and 240 pounds, with shoulder pads that made him look like a human freight train, Lee had instincts that turned him into a predator. He was mean, relentless, and feared. Football had pulled him out of Del Rio, Texas, where his future could have meant prison or a shallow grave. Now it was threatening to drag him back.

Lee's arrival at Texas Tech was not major news. He was a good player—raw, untamed, and ready to hit anything that moved—but not on the national radar. High school football had been a breeze; Lee was a quarterback and a defensive end, smashing through smaller players with reckless abandon. But college was different. Coaches don't tolerate freelancing, and players twice as fast with NFL dreams were waiting to humble freshmen like him.

The Tech coaches moved him to middle linebacker. The first few months were a struggle. Defensive schemes were a foreign language, and Lee didn't have time for translators. But once he figured it out, it clicked. By the end of his freshman year, he wasn't just playing—he was starting. His ferocity on the field had earned him a spot, but his demeanor off it had earned him something else: fear.

Lee wasn't interested in being anyone's friend. He didn't care about team bonding or other player's accomplishments. He cared about making tackles, cracking helmets, and reminding everyone who the toughest bastard on the field was. If that meant popping a teammate in the mouth during practice for running his mouth, so be it. The message was simple, and the Texas Tech team learned it pretty quickly: don't fucking mess with Lee Cain.

By junior year, Lee was leading the team in tackles, but he wasn't leading the team. He was a lone wolf, a predator who stalked alone. His teammates respected his ability but kept their distance. Lee didn't care. Football wasn't about friendship. It was about survival.

Off the field, survival meant drinking. It meant rage. It meant lifting motorcycles at parties and throwing them into swimming pools just to prove he could. It meant bar fights and blackouts, and, last night, after a wild game of "Kill the Keg," it meant a broken nose, three unconscious bodies, and cops dragging him away in cuffs.

The headline in the *Lubbock Avalanche-Journal* the next morning read: "Texas Tech Linebacker Arrested After Party Melee." The president of the university was livid. The athletic director had called it "an embarrassment to the program." And now, Lee was sitting across from Head Coach Hugh "Rocky" Lehman, waiting to hear his fate.

"Cain," Coach Lehman growled, his voice heavy with disappointment. "This ain't fucking Del Rio. This is Texas Tech. We're not here to babysit thugs."

Lee sat silently, his hands clasped tightly in front of him. His face was a mess of bruises and cuts. Two black eyes glared back at the coach, unyielding.

"You're one hell of a player," Lehman continued, his tone softening slightly, "but you're a damn liability. The university's got rules. And those rules say I gotta cut you."

The words hit Lee like a freight train. For the first time in years, he felt something he didn't recognize: panic. Football wasn't just a game to him. It was his ticket out, his shield against a world that had tried to chew him up and spit him out.

"Coach," Lee said, his voice gravelly and low. "This can't be it. You can't do this."

Lehman shook his head. "You think I want to? You think I like this?" He leaned forward, lowering his voice. "You did this to yourself. You've got talent, kid. But talent doesn't mean shit if you can't keep your head straight. You're a walking PR nightmare."

"I'll fix it," Lee said, desperation creeping into his tone. "Whatever it takes. I'll do it."

"It's too late for that," Lehman said, though his voice wavered. The man's stern facade cracked for just a moment, enough for Lee to see a sliver of hesitation. "The university wants you gone. My hands are tied."

Lee clenched his fists, his knuckles white. For a split second, Lehman tensed, as if preparing for the younger man to lash out. But Lee didn't. Instead, he stood, his towering frame casting a long shadow over the desk.

"This is horseshit, Coach," Lee said, his voice quiet but seething with anger. "Fucking horseshit." And to Lehman's relief, Lee stormed out of his office and hopefully his life forever.

Lee left in shock. Maybe that was the only reason he stumbled out of the meeting instead of doing something drastic like tearing the coach's office or the coach himself apart. This shock luckily gave Lee time to think. Actually, it gave him all night since he couldn't sleep. He was terrified to let his family and hometown know he had let them all down.

Lee decided that night he wasn't going to give up that easy. By dawn, something had shifted. Maybe it was desperation. Maybe it was resolve. Either way, Lee found himself standing outside Coach Lehman's office at 6:00 a.m., waiting. Lehman arrived, his briefcase in hand and coffee steaming in a to-go cup. He froze when he saw Lee. For a moment, the coach looked almost frightened. But then he noticed the tears in Lee's eyes.

"Coach," Lee said, his voice cracking. "I can't leave. This is all I got. Gimme a chance. I'll do whatever it takes."

Lehman sighed heavily, running a hand through his thinning hair. "It's not up to me anymore, Cain. The program's embarrassed. The team's embarrassed. Hell, I'm embarrassed."

"Please," Lee said, his voice barely a whisper. "Don't do this to me."

Lehman studied him for a long moment, then nodded slowly. "All right, Cain. You want back on this team? It's up to your teammates. You plead your case, and they'll vote. Majority rules."

The locker room was silent as Lee stood before the team, his hulking frame somehow smaller than usual. For the first time, the indomitable Lee Cain looked vulnerable.

"I messed up," he began, his voice steady but low. "I've been a selfish asshole, and I've let all of you down. I'm asking for another chance. I'll do better. I'll be better."

He paused, scanning the room. Some faces were blank, others skeptical. A few teammates wouldn't even meet his gaze. He took a deep breath.

"This team means everything to me. Football means everything to me. I know I've been a fucking pain in the ass, but I'm done with that.

I want to be part of this team. I want to fight for you guys, not just for myself."

A long silence followed. Then a voice from the back—one of the senior captains, a wide receiver named Jackson.

"Why should we believe you, Cain? You've been a selfish prick since the day you got here. What makes this any different?"

Lee didn't flinch. "Because I've got nowhere else to go. This team is all I have. And I'll prove it to you every damn day if you let me."

The room dissolved into whispers, players muttering among themselves. Finally, Jackson stood.

"All right," he said. "Let's vote."

Hands went up, one by one. Lee watched, his heart pounding. When the votes were counted, it was close. Too close. But he'd made it. By one vote, he was back on the team.

From that day forward, Lee Cain began to change. It wasn't easy. Years of anger and selfishness don't dissolve overnight. But he worked at it. He started showing up to practice early, staying late to help younger players. He stopped picking fights in the locker room. He even started going to team dinners, forcing himself to be part of something bigger than just Lee Cain.

By the end of his senior season, he wasn't just leading the team in tackles—he was leading the team. The lone wolf had found his pack. And for the first time, Lee understood what it meant to fight for something other than himself.

Football had taught him to hit, to hurt, to survive. But almost losing it had taught him something far more valuable: how to be a teammate, a leader, a man.

CHAPTER 47

Thursday, January 26. 8:15 a.m.

Jiménez, Mexico

The bar was tucked into a crumbling side street. Inside, the air still stunk of cigarette smoke from the night before. It was the perfect place for a conversation no one was supposed to hear.

Lee walked through the door and the bartender glanced up, his face a road map of hard years and bad decisions. Recognition flickered in his eyes, but he said nothing, just poured a glass of something dark and strong.

Lee didn't sit. He stayed standing, his jacket stretched tight across his broad shoulders. His strength was coming back every day since leaving New York. Maybe it was the old chemo exiting his system. Maybe it was his new purpose coursing in his veins.

His eyes scanned the room, taking in every face, every exit, every potential threat. Old habits didn't die—they just sharpened. And in Mexico, caution was more than survival for Lee. It was his religion.

At the far corner of the bar, Salvador Salazar waited. Dressed in a crisp white shirt with the top two buttons undone, Salvador looked more like a wealthy businessman than the leader of La Sombra. But the way his dark eyes locked on to Lee told a different story. This was a man who had carved his name into the underworld with blood and fire. He was about to address the old enemy who he had kicked the signature scar into his face.

"You're fucking late," Salvador said as Lee approached.

Lee pulled out the chair across from him and sat, the scrape of wood against wood loud in the quiet bar. "You're lucky I came at all."

Salvador's lips twitched into something that could have been a smile, but it didn't reach his eyes. "If I were lucky, we wouldn't be having this conversation."

Lee leaned back in his chair, letting the silence hang for a moment before he spoke. "Did you go through the files?"

Salvador reached into his pocket and pulled out a folded piece of paper. He slid it across the table without a word. Lee picked it up, unfolded it, and felt his stomach twist. It was a list. Names. Locations. Dates.

"What am I looking at?" Lee asked, his voice flat.

"That doctor must have been keeping his own records of Artemis as his own insurance policy. All the shit he knew. He had lists of the members and lists of people Artemis killed," Salvador said. "People who got too close to their secrets or pissed off the wrong person. Journalists. Whistleblowers. Scientists. All dead now."

Lee stared at the list. "And?"

Salvador leaned forward, his voice dropping to a dangerous whisper. "There is some horrible shit he suspected these bastards are doing. Scary things. They don't just kill people, hombre. They erase them. Whole lives, gone. And they'll do the same to you if you don't stop playing lone wolf."

Lee set the paper down and met Salvador's gaze. "You think I don't know what they're capable of? I've seen their work up close. But this . . ." He gestured to the list. "This doesn't prove anything. You want me to join your war?"

Salvador's jaw tightened. He took a slow sip of his drink, then placed the glass carefully on the table. "I read the files you gave me, Cain. The ones you bled for. You don't know half of what Artemis is doing."

Lee's eyes narrowed as he took a sip of whiskey. "Then tell me."

Salvador hesitated, his fingers drumming against the table. "I can't yet. Not everything. Not until I have confirmed something."

"Convenient."

"Fucking necessary," Salvador shot back, his voice sharp. "This isn't about trust. It's about survival. Yours. Mine. Theirs." He nodded toward the bar, where a couple of his henchmen sat hunched, oblivious to the storm brewing just feet away. "Artemis doesn't leave loose ends, Cain. And you? Your end is looser than the whores upstairs."

Lee's hand clenched into a fist on the table. He hated how right Salvador was. Hated that the scars on his body and the nightmares in his head were proof. He didn't want to fight for La Sombra. Hell, he didn't want to fight for anyone. But the alternative wasn't peace. It was annihilation.

"So what's the play?" Lee asked finally.

Salvador leaned back, the tension in his shoulders easing slightly. "What would you do, Lee Cain?"

Lee thought during an inhalation and breathed out the words, "We hit them where it hurts. Hard. Fast. We still have an advantage because they don't even know we're coming. But their guard will be up after that."

Salvador just nodded.

Lee arched an eyebrow. "And you think I'm just going to dive into this with you?"

"No," Salvador said. "I think you already have. Otherwise, you wouldn't be sitting here."

Lee realized he had no choice. "When it's you versus me," Lee said, his voice low, "I'm for me. But when it's you versus them . . ."

Salvador waited, his dark eyes boring into Lee's.

"I'm for us," Lee finished spitting out the words in almost painful disgust.

Salvador smiled then, his scar twisting like a snake from the facial muscles grinding underneath. It was sharp and dangerous, but there was something else in it, too. Relief. Maybe even respect. "Then let's get to work."

Lee looked again at the paper and said, "Okay, if we are going to really fuck with these bastards, here's what I would do."

He didn't trust Salvador. Not yet. Maybe not ever. But trust didn't matter right now. The only thing that mattered was the fight for his own preservation.

And Lee Cain never backed down from a fight.

CHAPTER 48

Thursday, January 26, 2023. 1:00 p.m.

Jiménez, Mexico

La Sombra's world was one that Lee had always feared but never fully understood—until now. The moment the bag had come off his head, Lee knew he was in a different kind of world. Not the sleek, cold elegance of Artemis, but the raw, bloody underbelly of Mexico's La Sombra-controlled territories. This was a world where rules didn't apply, and morals were a distant echo. Where life was fleeting, and survival was a game with ever-changing rules. Here, the strong didn't wait generations to grow like trees—they killed today to survive tomorrow.

Salvador, the man sitting across from him, had the presence of a bullfighter—a *matador*—but with the cunning and ruthlessness of a predator who had learned to live with the horns of the beast. He was the king of the arena, but unlike the matador, he did not seek to kill the bull quickly. Salvador preferred to drag out the fight, to savor the fear in his enemies before delivering the final blow.

As they sipped Silverman's expensive tequila, Lee explained how he had taken the doctor's life to get the information he needed. Salvador's eyes gleamed with interest as he listened, but he was also sizing up Cain. There was something about Lee, a wildness that Salvador could relate to—a survival instinct that came from years of fighting in the trenches. But he also sensed that Cain felt he had the moral high ground—that Cain looked down on him as a villain because of La Sombra's reputation.

Salvador took a long sip of his drink, then placed the glass down softly, his eyes narrowing as he leaned forward. "Lee, you think I give a fuck about some homeless vagrants in Portland? Or LA? Or New York? I don't. You know why? Because I'm not taking care of *their* people. I'm taking care of mine. My people are starving."

His voice was calm but lethal, each word like a blade slicing through the air. "You want to talk about morals? You wanna tell me that feeding your family with money from rich white kids snorting coke is wrong? Supply and demand, man. They want the drugs, we sell it to them. *Que se mueran*. Let them die. You think I care if some rich white kid in Beverly Hills overdoses? Nah. That's not my problem."

Lee leaned back in his chair, taking in Salvador's words. The more he listened, the more he began to understand the brutal simplicity of it all. Salvador wasn't just a criminal. He was a *provider*, a Robin Hood for the forgotten. He fed his people with the same blood money that poisoned others. It was twisted, but it made sense.

"Look around here, Cain," Salvador continued, gesturing to the world beyond the luxurious walls. "You've lived here before. You know what it's like. We have *nothing*. My people are barely surviving, and you think I'm gonna turn down money from gringos who are desperate to escape their lives for a night? *Chinga su madre*—fuck that."

Salvador's hands tightened on the arms of his chair. "I have kids to feed. Families depending on me. And you want me to care about *climate change*? Don't drive my car? Fuck you. That's a luxury I don't have. Outside of your American walls, it's a jungle, Lee. *Un verdadero infierno*. And I am the lion here."

His words hung in the air, heavy and undeniable. Lee could feel the weight of Salvador's conviction, the desperation in every decision he made. This wasn't about right or wrong. It was about survival.

"These Artemis scumbags," Salvador said, "they think they're saving the world? Science is a lie. All they care about is preserving *their* world. The rich white man's world. But what about us? *Mi gente*. The Mexican people. The ones starving to death while they build their fucking rockets to Mars. You think they give a shit about what happens down here?"

Salvador's voice had risen, his anger palpable. But then, just as quickly as it had come, he calmed. A smile tugged at the corner of his lips. "But we're not weak. We fight back. The world's a jungle, and in the jungle, only the strong survive. And I . . . I represent the jungle."

For La Sombra, life was like a *corrida de toros*, a bullfight. There was no elegance in what they did, no carefully orchestrated plan stretching over decades like Artemis. Their fight was bloody, brutal, and immediate. Like the bull charging into the arena, knowing its chances were slim but fighting anyway with all its might. Sometimes the matador won, sometimes the bull did.

And Salvador, despite his matador-like cunning, knew La Sombra was more like the bull—powerful, less sophisticated, but deadly when it counted. La Sombra's moves weren't subtle; they were bold, direct, and violent. They didn't hide in shadows like Artemis. They charged headfirst into battle, horns out, ready to gore anything that stood in their way.

Salvador smiled, thinking of the bullfights he loved so much. "You know what they say about the bull, *hijo*? They say even if the odds are against him, sometimes, if he fights hard enough, if he fights with enough *coraje*, he can take down the matador. It's rare, but it happens."

He paused, swirling the tequila in his glass. "Artemis might be the matador in this fight, but we're the bull. And we fight like hell, because sometimes, just sometimes, the bull wins."

Salvador may have been a killer, a drug lord, and a criminal, but he was also a protector of his people. In the squalor of Mexico, where the government failed and the people were left to fend for themselves, men like Salvador stepped in. He gave food to the poor, built schools, and ensured that the people in his territory were taken care of. It wasn't out of kindness—it was out of necessity. If he didn't take care of them, no one would.

"You think I do this just for me?" Salvador asked, his voice softer now. "I've fed more people here than your American government ever has. I've built homes where there were none. I take care of *mi gente* because no one else will. I'm their Robin Hood, Cain. I steal from the rich, and I give to the poor. That's how it works down here."

Lee couldn't help but admire the twisted morality of it all. Salvador wasn't a good man, but he wasn't a bad man, either. He was a product of his environment, a man doing what he had to do to survive and protect his people.

As they sat in that smoke-filled room, going over the final points of their attack on Artemis, Lee realized something. He and Salvador were two sides of the same coin. Artemis and La Sombra were both monsters, but they were different kinds of monsters. Artemis was cold, calculating, and patient, working behind the scenes to slowly shape the world to their vision. La Sombra was brutal, aggressive, and immediate, fighting for survival in a world that had forgotten them.

Both were funded by vast amounts of money. Both had soldiers ready to die for their cause. And both, in their own twisted way, were right.

The Earth was a sinking ship, and while Artemis was trying to save the world by killing the weak, La Sombra was helping the ship sink while scrambling to survive in the chaos.

"Who decides who's weak, Salvador?" Lee asked, breaking the silence. "You both got money. You both got power. But what happens when you two butt heads?"

Salvador smiled darkly. "That's when the real fight begins, *cabrón*. It's a jungle out there, and in the jungle, only one thing matters—who's willing to do whatever it takes to survive. This is just the beginning, gringo. You know what they call the first stage of a bullfight? *Levantado.*

It's when the bull still has its full strength, before it learns the real danger. That's where we are right now. With the files you gave me, I finally know who they are and where they are. Artemis doesn't even know the bull is charging yet. But they will."

CHAPTER 49

Friday, January 27, 2023. 5:15 a.m.

Various locations across the United States

It was a perfect morning in the wealthiest neighborhoods across America. Expansive green lawns stretched like mini estates, dotted with manicured hedges, gazebos, and sparkling pools—quiet, pristine sanctuaries hiding in plain sight. Inside these homes, the occupants slept soundly, wrapped in luxury and unaware that anything could disrupt their morning rituals.

And then, the silent shadows began to move.

In affluent neighborhoods, the dawn was marked by the soft hum of lawnmowers, leaf blowers, and hedge trimmers. These sounds, unnoticed and routine, signaled the arrival of lawn service workers—people rarely seen as individuals, more like passing blurs wearing sun-bleached shirts, dust-streaked pants, and tired caps. These workers had become as much a part of these neighborhoods as the grass they cut and the weeds they pulled, blending seamlessly into the background of elite American life.

But that morning, the faces behind the lawn mowers were different. They weren't the usual crews. They were Los Demonios, a fearsome La Sombra arm trained not in tending to lawns but in taking lives. And today, under Salvador's orders, they were there not as workers but as silent assassins. Using information from Silverman's files, they had their targets—Artemis members living in sprawling mansions with more square footage than entire neighborhoods in Mexico.

La Sombra's plan was simple and brutal: strike where the elite felt safest, where their money and security systems offered them the illusion of invulnerability. They were to deliver a bloody message—that no matter how well-hidden Artemis thought they were, La Sombra knew exactly where to find them. And so, La Sombra's foot soldiers, skilled in stealth, drifted silently across green lawns and through open gates that recognized familiar access codes.

The strategy was cunning. La Sombra knew that in these gated communities, no one would look twice at the lawn service guy slipping through a side gate or punching in a garage code. They had these codes memorized from years of working for these people, cultivating trust, becoming invisible. For years, La Sombra had been preparing for a scenario like this. They'd positioned men under the guise of hired help, watched and learned the rhythms of these wealthy homes, and knew exactly where to strike.

One Los Demonios operative, a muscular man with heavily tattooed arms bearing dark inked skulls, death motifs, and faint reminders of his past hits, quietly entered the gate code of a high-profile fund manager's mansion in Scottsdale, Arizona. He'd worked in the area enough to know the neighborhood's rhythms. His faded work shirt hung loosely over a body hardened by violence, the only hint of his real purpose hidden beneath the loose folds of his clothing—a long blade, gleaming and ready.

The gate swung open with a soft buzz, and he slipped inside. His steps were light, soundless on the cobblestone driveway. He approached the front door, punched in the house alarm code he'd memorized, and stepped inside, leaving the rich man's fortress vulnerable from the inside out. He closed the door with a quiet click, silencing any intrusion alarm.

The house was a testament to wealth. He stalked through an entryway larger than most homes he knew, passing designer furniture arranged like museum pieces. Mahogany bookshelves lined with antique volumes, oil paintings, and marble busts glared down at him as he passed. A massive chandelier cast a ghostly glow over the entrance as he moved farther in, unfazed. He turned left down a corridor lined with framed family portraits and equestrian trophies gleaming from their glass cases, displayed as if they were meant to be admired by anyone passing by.

He could feel the quiet confidence of wealth in each room—the meticulously cleaned Persian carpets, the enormous flat-screen TVs, the fresh white orchids in ornate vases. Every item in this house screamed abundance, complacency, a life of safety that could never imagine a threat would come so close.

But La Sombra knew, and they were here to shatter that illusion.

He moved deeper into the mansion, where the hum of a shower could be heard in a master bathroom. It was his target, the fund manager who had no idea he'd made enemies far beyond the boardroom. He was a man who saw himself as invincible, surrounded by layers of security and money.

The Los Demonios operative leaned against the wall, calm, breathing slow, waiting for the right moment.

When the shower turned off, he knew it was time. His hand tightened on the grip of his knife. The bathroom door swung open, and the fund manager, wrapped in a plush white towel, stepped out, looking as satisfied as if he owned the world.

In the fraction of a second it took for Norman LeGrande to register that someone was standing there, the assassin moved forward. The target's eyes widened, a strangled scream caught in his throat as he took in the sight of the muscular, tattooed stranger in his hallway, his dark eyes gleaming with a promise of violence.

The blade plunged forward before the fund manager could react, piercing through layers of soft flesh and into his belly. Blood blossomed instantly, a rich, red stain spreading across the towel. The man's body buckled, and he crumpled to the floor, clutching his stomach as he looked up in horror.

"*¿Que pasó, cabrón?*" the assassin sneered, voice low and taunting as he pulled the blade free and watched blood spatter across the white tile, painting it in dark crimson. Norman struggled, blood seeping through his fingers, eyes glazing over as the realization of his fate sank in. His fortress of wealth had failed him; he had been breached, not by hackers or rivals, but by the very people his wealth exploited, by a man who knew that in the jungle, weakness is a death sentence.

The assassin looked down at him, relishing the power he held over a man who had looked down on people like him his entire life. There was no fear in the assassin's eyes, only a dark satisfaction as he watched the life drain from the man's face, the last spark of defiance flickering out as he slumped back against the cold, blood-splattered tile.

When the man was finally still, the Los Demonios operative went to work for the real prize he was there for. Then he wiped his blade on the man's towel, sheathed it, and walked calmly out of the house. He moved through the same rooms, leaving a trail of bloody footprints on the carpet and out the front door. His mission complete, he slipped back out through the gate, vanishing as silently as he had arrived.

Across the country, similar scenes unfolded—La Sombra operatives moving through mansions in silence, stepping over priceless artifacts, untouched food, luxury, opulence, all of it meaning nothing to men who had come for blood. They moved with precision, striking quickly, leaving trails of red on marble floors, drowning out the screams of their wealthy victims with the sharp echo of silence once they left.

The wealthy in America, those who had once trusted their lawn workers, cleaners, and household staff, had been lulled into complacency. They never thought to suspect the men and women working in their homes, let alone consider the hidden threat lurking behind a familiar face. La Sombra, with its network of seemingly invisible soldiers, had used this arrogance, this blindness, to make its first move against Artemis.

As the sun rose over wealthy neighborhoods, the screams of the housekeepers who discovered the bodies pierced the morning calm. Police and ambulances flooded into neighborhoods that had never known such violence, confusion and horror evident on the faces of residents who had always believed their wealth protected them.

This was just the beginning.

In a single morning, La Sombra had done what few could imagine—they had infiltrated the homes of the world's wealthiest, men and women who were used to controlling the world. La Sombra had shown Artemis that they weren't safe, not even behind high walls and armed guards. And they had done it with the silent efficiency of an ancient predator, reminding Artemis that their power wasn't absolute, that there were still people they couldn't control.

It was a declaration of war, the first of many strikes to come. La Sombra was the bull charging into the ring, raw and unrestrained, ready to gore its opponent or die trying. Artemis, the matador, had no idea yet that the bull was in the ring. They thought themselves untouchable, surrounded by their wealth, their science, their carefully constructed walls. But now, blood was in the sand.

Salvador's message had been clear: Artemis might be willing to sacrifice the world to achieve their version of perfection, but La Sombra was ready to tear down that world to protect their people, their families, their own kind. Artemis sought control; La Sombra sought vengeance. And for the first time in history, two titanic forces were on a collision course, a war that would decide the fate of both the oppressors and the oppressed.

There was no going back.

CHAPTER 50

Friday, January 27, 2023. 6:45 a.m.

Greenwich, Connecticut

The morning sun filtered through the windows of his expansive home, casting sharp lines of light across the pristine hardwood floors. It was a mansion built to the exact specifications of a man who demanded perfection in every aspect of his life. Everything from the stainless steel kitchen counters to the library of first-edition books screamed of success earned through relentless ambition and a refusal to settle for anything less.

He was Keith Larsen, the same dark-haired Ivy Leaguer who had once stood on the side of a bobsled track and cracked the code to the elite inner circle. But now, standing shirtless in his workout room, sweat still glistening on his chiseled frame from his morning routine, this man was no longer thinking about power or wealth. He was thinking about survival. Keith had always been driven to be the best, the smartest, the strongest—and today, that drive would be tested in a very different way.

Keith had spent his entire life cracking codes. It wasn't enough to be smart. He had to be *the smartest*. It wasn't enough to be strong. He had to be *the strongest*. Now, as a man of extraordinary wealth and influence, he was ready to conquer the world. But today, the world was coming for him.

His security system had been tripped just moments earlier. The cameras had shown a figure moving through his front yard, a shadow passing through his perfectly manicured rosebushes. Another one of those garden workers? No, this one didn't look right. His instincts, honed from years of calculated preparation, kicked in immediately. He finished his protein shake, set the glass down on the marble countertop, and turned up the volume on his house-wide speaker system.

Vivaldi's *Summer* from *The Four Seasons* blasted through the house, the fierce, rapid tempo mimicking the violent storm he was about to unleash.

The Los Demonios assassin, a muscular man covered in tattoos from his neck to his wrists, had entered the residence just like the other operatives around the country had done that day. He moved swiftly, machete in hand, his eyes scanning for the prize he had come to claim—the head of an Artemis member. But this time, it wasn't a surprise. This time, he had walked into a prepared battlefield.

As the operatic strings thundered around him, the killer caught sight of his target. Standing in the center of the room, bathed in the sunlight streaming through the floor-to-ceiling windows, was the homeowner, shirtless, in Yale shorts, and holding a gleaming saber in his hand.

A smile spread across the Artemis man's face, cold and calculated. He had been training for moments like this his entire life. He didn't know what form his next challenge would take, but he always knew one was coming. His body was a weapon, honed through countless hours of martial arts, fencing, and strength conditioning. He wasn't just an elite scholar or businessman; he was a man forged in fire, someone who had destroyed every obstacle in his path—and now he had the chance to destroy a living, breathing threat.

The assassin, still brandishing his machete, hesitated for a moment. The pounding strains of Vivaldi's *Summer* were disorienting, the violin's sharp notes reflecting the violence in the air. His dark eyes scanned the room, landing on the man before him—shirtless, composed, and looking more like a predator than prey. The operative tried to steel himself, taking a step forward and raising his machete.

"I'm going to kill you," the Los Demonios man growled, his voice laced with venom, trying to assert dominance over this wealthy gringo.

The Ivy League fencer didn't flinch. He stood there, the saber in his hand catching the light, a smirk curling on his lips. Keith had heard those words before, in a thousand different ways, from a thousand different opponents, whether in the boardroom, on the fencing strip, or in his own mind. And every time, he had come out on top.

"Kill me?" Keith laughed, low and dark, as he took a step forward, the saber poised expertly in his grip. His voice was icy calm, full of arrogance and cold confidence. "You can't kill me. I killed myself a long time ago, you fucking piece of dog shit."

With that, the gap between them closed.

The assassin rushed forward, swinging the machete in a wide, brutal arc. It was an attack meant to overpower, to crush an opponent in one devastating blow. But the Artemis man had seen this before. He could read the muscles in the Los Demonios operative's arm, the angle of his approach, the amateur way he gripped the machete like a crude butcher's tool rather than a weapon.

Keith moved with precision. As the machete cut through the air, he ducked beneath it, the sharp edge of the blade whistling just inches above his head. He spun quickly, bringing his saber up in a quick, controlled arc, slicing across the would-be killer's forearm. The blade cut deep, and blood spurted from the wound as the man let out a pained roar.

But the operative wasn't done. He lunged again, this time with more fury, more desperation. The machete came down in a vicious, overhead swing, aiming to split the man in two. But the Ivy Leaguer sidestepped it effortlessly, moving like water, fluid and unstoppable. His saber flashed again, this time slicing across the man's chest.

Blood poured down the Los Demonios man's body, staining the floor beneath him. He staggered back, breathing hard, his eyes wild with rage and pain. The music swelled around them, the strings of Vivaldi reaching a fever pitch as the two men circled each other.

The Artemis man was breathing heavily now, but it wasn't from fear. It was from the thrill. The adrenaline coursed through his veins like fire, every fiber of his being alive with the raw, primal energy of combat. This was what he had trained for—what he had *always* trained for.

"You really thought you could walk into my house," Keith said, his voice dripping with contempt, "and kill me? You've got no idea who you're fucking with."

The assassin, gasping for breath, raised the machete for one last desperate attack. He swung with everything he had left, a wide, reckless strike aimed at Keith's throat.

But the Artemis man was faster. He moved in a blur, dodging the swing and stepping inside the Los Demonios man's reach. With a swift, precise motion, he drove the point of his saber deep into the man's gut, twisting the blade as it slid through muscle and bone.

The operative let out a strangled gasp, his body convulsing as the blade pierced his flesh. His eyes bulged, his hands clutched at the saber still buried in his abdomen. Keith stepped back, ripping the blade free in one fluid motion, sending a spray of blood across the floor.

The Los Demonios man collapsed to his knees, blood pooling around him. His vision blurred, the strength draining from his body as he stared up at the man who had bested him.

The Artemis man stood over him, his chest heaving, the saber dripping with blood in his hand. He looked down at the dying man, his expression cold and unfeeling.

"This is your world, right?" Keith said, his voice low and mocking. "Welcome to *my* world."

With one final, swift motion, he raised the saber and brought it down, severing the man's throat in a clean, brutal cut. The man's body slumped forward, lifeless, as blood continued to pool beneath him.

The Artemis man stood there for a moment, breathing heavily, the adrenaline still coursing through his veins. He looked down at the dead man at his feet, the operatic strains of Vivaldi still echoing through the house. And then, with a calm, practiced motion, he wiped the blood from his saber and walked out of the room.

The swordsman had to make a call.

CHAPTER 51

Friday, January 27, 2023. 4:00 p.m.

Artemis Headquarters, Geneva, Switzerland

Fridays were supposed to be quiet.

Olivier was sitting in his office, watching the last rays of sunlight break over the rolling hills outside the large glass windows. His office was immaculate, as orderly as his mind, the walls lined with art from ancient cultures and artifacts gathered from around the world. It was his sanctum, a place where he could focus on his mission: orchestrating the plan to unlock immortality, to save the most deserving while leaving humanity's weak behind.

The vibration of his phone ended his calm. Razor's name appeared on the screen, the message marked urgent. Olivier's brow furrowed, irritation flickering across his face. Razor never disturbed him like this unless something was drastically wrong. He swiped to open the message, a photo popping onto his screen. His grip tightened as he stared.

Seven bloody bags, lined up on a rough concrete floor.

Seconds later, his phone buzzed again, and this time it was a message from Razor himself: "Sir, we need to meet immediately."

Olivier stormed down the hall, his thoughts racing, each step more purposeful than the last. He had heard whispers of resistance, the occasional rumor of some fool daring to interfere with Artemis's plans, but this—this was something different. Something targeted, orchestrated. Razor was waiting for him in the security suite, his expression grim.

"Someone has declared war on us," Razor said, his voice heavy. He handed Olivier another phone and pointed to the screen. The next image appeared. Seven severed heads, lined up on the floor, their lifeless eyes staring out into the void. Blood pooled around them, smears trailing across the floor as if the heads had been dragged.

"Impossible..." Olivier muttered. His hands clenched as he studied each face. They were all familiar, each one a loyal Artemis member. These were not just random victims; they were his people.

"Not only do they know who our members are," Razor said, the tension etched deep into his face, "but whoever they are, they're coordinated. These people weren't even in the same state. This... this took planning, manpower, advanced transport—possibly aircraft or helicopters to get those heads to one location within hours of the hits."

Olivier paced, his thoughts a twisted labyrinth of fury and dread. He stared at Razor, his eyes narrowing. "How many were hit?"

"Nine houses were targeted across the United States. Seven heads were found—two members are still unaccounted for, and their fates are... uncertain." Razor glanced down, and then his phone buzzed again, his face paling as he read. He turned the screen to Olivier.

Another photo. Another message.

Mr. Keith Larsen of Connecticut. The man had been prepared, sending an image of a bloodied, dead intruder sprawled across his marble-tiled floor.

"Had this visitor at my house today. Please advise."

The message was curt, detached, as if Larsen were reporting a pest problem rather than an assassin in his home.

Olivier couldn't help but let a cold smile creep across his lips. "At least someone followed protocol. Send a security team to Larsen's estate.

Congratulate him for his skill, and ensure every camera and piece of evidence is erased."

Razor nodded. "Understood."

Olivier and returned to his office with Razor, his mind a storm of chaos. He closed the door, shutting out the world for a moment. His gaze drifted to a framed photo on his desk—a black-and-white image of him as a child with his father, walking through a vast, ancient forest. The trees had towered over them, silent witnesses to their secrets and ambitions. His father had taught him about strength, about survival, about growing in the shadows. Those memories had been his bedrock, guiding him, pushing him to bring Artemis's vision into reality.

Now, it was all under threat. Someone dared to interfere with his mission. Olivier clenched his fists, his knuckles white, a single word pulsing through his mind.

War.

He turned back to Razor, a steely resolve in his eyes. "We need to strike back. Whoever did this, whoever orchestrated this—"

"They know more than they should," Razor finished. "Could Silverman have been working with another group? And I have a strong suspicion it's connected to Lee Cain. He's been in the wind since the Silverman incident."

Olivier's jaw clenched. "We have to believe now that this breach of information may have blown open every safeguard we've spent decades putting in place. This isn't random; this is this man Cain. He must be connected to someone powerful enough to move an entire organization against us."

Razor smirked, a dark glint in his eye. "You realize what this means, don't you?"

Olivier looked him in the eye, his expression cold as ice. "Yes. We will discover who they are and we will respond. Ruthlessly."

A slow, calculated smile spread across Razor's face. "I already have teams preparing. I will put together a report and have it for you in the morning."

Olivier straightened, his gaze as hard as stone. "Go. I want every single person connected to this—anyone with a history, any contact, every backchannel burned to the ground. Bring the weight of Artemis down on them, and make them regret ever crossing our path."

Razor's voice was low, lethal. "Consider it done."

CHAPTER 52

Saturday, January 28, 2023. 8:00 a.m.

Artemis Headquarters, Geneva, Switzerland

"The left ears are gone. They know intricacies of Artemis right down to small details," Razor said as he threw his report onto Olivier's desk in frustration.

The photograph landed on Olivier's desk with a muted slap, its weight amplified by the dozen papers within Razor's report. The faces stared back at him—eight severed heads, mouths agape, eyes lifeless. Their expressions varied, some frozen in fear, others in defiance, but all were marked by one glaring mutilation. The left ears were gone.

Olivier leaned back in his chair, the leather creaking softly beneath him. A polished glass desk stretched before him, empty except for the report and a sleek computer. He studied the image, his sharp features unmoving. Olivier had the kind of face that seemed carved from stone—high cheekbones, a sharp jawline, and deep-set eyes that betrayed neither fear nor warmth. His black hair, perfectly combed, caught the faint light filtering through the overcast sky outside. To the world, he was the epitome of control and refinement. To those who truly knew him, he was a predator, and he was close to his ultimate prize.

Razor stood in front of the desk, his frame a contrast to everything around him. The man looked as if he'd been assembled from raw violence—thick shoulders, a chest that strained against the tactical jacket he always wore, and arms like wire cables covered in naturally tan skin. His weathered face gave him the appearance of a soldier permanently stuck between wars.

"They could potentially know everything," Razor said, his voice low and gravelly. He didn't sit. Razor never sat during briefings. He stood like a coiled spring, radiating energy that could erupt at any moment. "Whoever did this knew the message they were sending."

Olivier's hand hovered over the photograph, his long fingers brushing the edge of the glossy paper. "Our men," he murmured, his voice soft but lethal. "Tracked, monitored, equipped, and still . . . gone. Their deaths are one thing. The message is another."

He gestured to the missing ears, his expression darkening. "This wasn't just murder. This was precision. They cut the ears off to remove the microchips. Do you understand what that means?"

Razor nodded, his jaw tightening. "They know our protocols . . . and probably much more."

"Exactly," Olivier said, standing abruptly. He paced to the window, the soft soles of his designer loafers muffled against the marble floor. His tailored suit—a deep gray that matched the storm clouds outside—hung perfectly on his tall, lean frame. He stared out at Geneva, his reflection a ghostly outline in the glass. "Someone out there knows our secrets. Someone out there wants me to know what it feels like to bleed."

"Lee Cain," Razor said bluntly.

Olivier turned, his eyes narrowing. "Of course Cain has something to do with this." His voice sharpened, cutting through the air like a whip. "That man had cancer, but to our organization he is a cancer. But this . . ." He gestured to the photograph. "This is more than him."

Razor shifted his weight, his boots clicking softly against the floor. "You think he's working with the Israelis? The Albanians?"

Olivier didn't answer immediately. He walked back to his desk, the cold light from the windows catching the silver in his hair. He picked up the photograph again, staring at the faces. "Cain's involvement is certain. But this... this requires coordination, resources. Cain's smart—a survivor, but he's not a strategist. Someone else is pulling strings."

"Who?" Razor asked.

"That's what you're going to find out," Olivier said, setting the photograph down. He tapped a button on the tablet, bringing up a series of satellite images. "Isn't this what I pay you for? Find the fucking trail."

Razor, who was unused to seeing Olivier distressed, stepped forward, studying the photo.

"This wasn't random," Razor said, his voice colder now. "They had intel. They knew our members. Depending on what else was in Silverman's safe, they may know a lot more. Virtually everything."

"And they had the nerve to act on it," Olivier added, his tone filled with venom. He looked back to the final image—close-up at Edward Thurston, one of the dead Artemis members. His neck was slashed, his face battered, and the left ear crudely hacked off. "He was a good man. Joined Artemis in order to save his sister. MS, I believe." Oliver dropped the photo back on the desk in disgust. "They're taunting us."

Razor's eyes narrowed. "Do you think they're stupid enough to believe we won't respond?"

Olivier smiled faintly, but there was no humor in it. "They don't believe. They *hope*. They want to test how far they can push us." He paused, his fingers resting on the edge of the desk. "They'll regret it."

Razor straightened. "I'll take a team. Track them down."

Olivier's smile disappeared. "Yes," he said sharply. "But this is personal." Olivier opened a drawer and pulled out a special satellite phone.

Razor recognized the phone and his brow furrowed slightly. "The Russian?"

"Exactly," Olivier said. "If Cain is involved, Gromov will sniff him out. And if he's not..." Olivier let the sentence hang in the air, the implication clear. "We eliminate everyone who is."

Razor hesitated for a moment—he hated not being the first choice for a job. There was a flicker of doubt that Olivier noticed immediately. But the hesitation vanished just as quickly. Razor nodded. "Understood."

"And Razor," Olivier said, his voice dropping to a deadly whisper. "This isn't just an operation. This is a hunt. I want Lee Cain's head on my desk. No delays. No excuses."

Razor smirked, his lips curling into a wolfish grin. "Consider it done."

When the door closed, Olivier sat down again, his hands steepled in front of him. He stared at the photograph for a long moment, then reached for his phone. He dialed a number, his fingers moving with practiced precision. When the line connected, he spoke in Russian.

"Privet Grisha," he said. "I want you in the field. Tracking just one man. This should be easy for you and you will make more money than any job you have ever done for me. I will see you here first in Geneva to explain. The plane is already on the way. *Spacebo.*"

The voice on the other end mumbled an acknowledgment before the line went dead.

Olivier leaned back in his chair, his gaze drifting to the photograph once more. He picked it up, his fingers tracing the edge of the glossy paper. Eight heads. Eight failures. When they found out the truth, the other members of Artemis would be in a panic. One of those people could expose everything. Just when Olivier was so close to the objective, it was time to move fast.

No, this was Lee Cain's fault. And Cain would pay for it.

Olivier placed the photograph down carefully, like a chess piece being moved into position. He glanced out the window again, the storm clouds outside darkening.

This wasn't just about revenge. This was about survival.

And Olivier planned to survive forever.

CHAPTER 53

Saturday, January 28, 2023. Dawn.

Hope Lodge

Julia took a slow, steady breath, letting the morning's crisp, cool air fill her lungs. Each inhale was a promise, each exhale a quiet thrill, a reminder of the strength coursing back into her body. She hadn't felt like this in years—not since the illness had taken root, defining her world with sterile walls and whispered conversations about life expectancy. Now, as she stepped out through the lodge's double doors and into the warmth of the sun, she felt alive. Not merely surviving but fully, thrillingly alive.

Julia paused on the steps, savoring the sensation of her heartbeat, steady and confident. She reached up, touching the soft stubble growing over her scalp, a surprising rush of pride spreading through her. Each small patch of hair represented something she never thought she'd feel again—hope, recovery, strength. For years, her life had felt like a series of limitations, defined by what she couldn't do, where she couldn't go, and the shadow of a future she hadn't dared to plan for. But that Julia, the one weighed down by fear and rules, was gone. What had risen from the ashes of illness was something fiercer and unafraid.

Her gaze drifted toward the world outside the Lodge. The bustle of New York City seemed almost to pulse in time with her new heartbeat.

She was no longer the girl trapped in the background, watching life pass by through hospital windows; she was ready to be part of it. *It's my turn now,* she thought, her hands curling into fists. All her life, Julia had played it safe, or rather, safe had been imposed upon her. But now she was ready to take risks—to chase the highs, face the dangers, and savor every unpredictable thrill. She had survived death more times than most people ever would. Now, finally, she was going to learn how to face life.

As she looked out at the city, Julia's mind lingered on Lee Cain. The man who had saved her life in ways she still couldn't quite fathom. Whatever he had done, whatever that mysterious gift he had given her was, it had given her a second chance—a chance she would not waste. It was time to repay the debt. She knew he was out there, and if the men who'd been snooping around were any indication, he was in danger. Whether he knew it or not, she was coming for him.

Julia felt a flicker of suspicion stir in her. The Lodge staff had started watching her differently, as if they, too, saw something impossible in her sudden recovery. She'd heard their whispers—"miracle," "anomaly." Rosa, one of the attending nurses had even dared to call it divine intervention. But Julia knew better. Miracles didn't just happen; they were usually followed by questions, sometimes tests, and always cages. She knew if she stayed, she'd end up a specimen under someone's microscope. She had spent enough of her life as someone's patient. She wouldn't allow them to make her a prisoner.

"Are you sure you're ready for this?" Rosa had asked that morning, her face a mix of admiration and worry as Julia packed her bag with the confident hands of someone finally in control.

Julia had smiled, her tone resolute. "I've been ready my whole life. I just didn't know it until now."

Julia took her first few steps away from the Lodge, feeling her pulse quicken, her muscles responding with a strength she didn't think she'd ever possess. The lightness in her step felt like freedom itself, an open invitation from the world to step out and claim her place in it. She had no home, no family waiting, nowhere she was expected to go. But she had a direction—Lee. The only man who had given her hope, even if he hadn't meant to. Wherever he was, he was the only compass she needed. She'd find him, even if it took her across every city in the country.

"Where will you go?" Rosa had pressed, her voice tight with concern.

Julia had shrugged, a small smile playing at her lips. She didn't have the answer; she didn't need one. The Julia who had longed for certainty, who had waited for others to save her, was gone. This Julia was willing to face the unknown, willing to fight for the life she had been given. Somewhere out there was Lee, the man who had rewritten her fate. And now, she'd take on the world if it meant she could repay him in kind.

With each step, her confidence swelled, her mind echoing with a single truth: *I am alive.* It was time to catch up on all she'd missed, to live the life she'd been denied. And now, with her lungs full and her heart daring her forward, she was ready to chase every moment.

For the first time, she'd be taking on the world not as a victim, but as a survivor. And in the back of her mind, she knew that wherever he was, Lee Cain was waiting. This time, she'd be the one to save him.

CHAPTER 54

Saturday, January 28, 2023. 2:00 p.m.

Artemis Headquarters, Geneva, Switzerland

Olivier Malraux reclined in the hyperbaric chamber, its airtight seals hissing softly as it began the prescribed cycle. The chamber was sleek and custom-built, its titanium interior gleaming under the low lights of the room. The faint hum of pressurized oxygen filled the silence as Olivier closed his eyes, his mind churning even as his body rested.

A timer on the wall counted down in soft blue digits. Thirty minutes—time carved out of his meticulously scheduled day to rejuvenate his cells and stave off the inevitable march of age. For Olivier, this chamber wasn't luxury. It was necessity.

He opened his eyes, staring at the inside of the glass dome above him. His reflection stared back—dark hair immaculately combed, sharp cheekbones unmarred by time, and the faintest shadows under his eyes that no serum could erase. At almost sixty, Olivier looked like a man in his late thirties, but he knew the truth. He felt the truth in every joint, every bone.

Mortality was a curse, and he was too close to escaping it to allow distractions.

"Mr. Malraux," came the soft voice of his assistant through the intercom. It was Marie, always precise, always unobtrusive. "Razor said his report is ready, and the members are ready for you."

Olivier pressed a button inside the chamber, lowering the oxygen flow to respond. "Five minutes."

"Yes, sir."

The chamber hissed again, releasing him from its embrace. He stepped out, his bare feet brushing the cool marble floor as he reached for the robe draped nearby. Every movement was measured, deliberate. Control extended even to the smallest gestures.

The office was a testament to Olivier's philosophy: minimalism and efficiency. No personal photos adorned the walls. No unnecessary clutter marred the clean lines of the furniture. The only decorations were objects of subtle power—a rare sculpture from ancient Mesopotamia, a single bonsai tree that stood as a metaphor for his vision: growth shaped by discipline.

Olivier sat at his desk, opened his computer, and started the virtual meeting.

Dozens of other Artemis members—politicians, CEOs, heirs to empires—watched him in silence. He was their leader, the man behind the curtain who had crafted the illusion that held them all together.

"Ladies and gentlemen," Olivier began, his voice smooth but commanding, "our progress is remarkable, but our timeline is shortening. The world will occasionally try to impede us from completing our mission."

Although the members were muted on the call, Olivier could see some shifted uncomfortably in their seats, others nodded in silent agreement.

"I have received intelligence indicating that our secrecy is at risk," he continued. "Some members have been noticed by others who wish to exploit or disrupt what we are building. The greatest danger to our immortality is not time itself—it is interference."

He let the words hang in the air, their weight settling on each member like a shroud. "If anyone interferes with our mission," Olivier said, his voice dropping to a near whisper, "we will remind them that while death is an enemy we are working to conquer, it is still a weapon we know how to wield. You have my promise I will resolve this situation with the utmost prejudice."

Olivier ended the call and closed his computer, his mind already moving to the next step. He walked to the bonsai tree on the low wooden table near the window, picking up a pair of pruning shears. The tree was small, carefully cultivated, each branch a testament to precision and patience.

He clipped a single branch, the sound sharp in the stillness of the room.

As he returned to his desk, Marie entered, carrying a tray with a small vial and a syringe. "Your treatment, sir," she said softly, placing it on the desk.

Olivier nodded, rolling up his sleeve as she prepared the injection. The serum was the culmination of years of research, a prototype from the Lazarus Protocol. It wasn't perfect—yet—but it was progress.

"Do it," he said.

Marie pressed the needle into his vein, injecting the luminous liquid. Olivier felt the familiar burn as it spread through his bloodstream, a mix of pain and vitality. He clenched his fist, letting the sensation wash over him.

"How close are we?" he asked, his voice low.

"The final trials are ongoing," Marie replied. "Dr. Bader has requested additional subjects."

Olivier's gaze flicked to her, sharp and unyielding. "He'll have them. No delays."

"Yes, sir."

Marie bowed slightly and left the room, leaving Olivier alone with his thoughts.

"We are so close," Olivier murmured, his lips curling into a cold smile.

He set the tablet down and turned back to the bonsai tree, picking up the shears once more. One by one, he clipped the branches, shaping the tree into his vision of perfection.

ACKNOWLEDGMENTS

I've heard it said there's always room for another story—so here's one more about this book.

Lee Cain has been fighting to get out of my mind and onto the page for over 30 years.

It's bittersweet that it took one of my best friends getting cancer to finally set him free.

This book began as an attempt to help my U.S. bobsled teammate, Todd Hays. We've raced at 90 mph, flipped upside down, and burned across the ice on our shoulders—but his second bout with cancer was far scarier than anything we ever faced in a sled.

At first, this book was just a distraction. While Todd starved himself and endured chemo, I developed the idea as a way to help pass the time, to take his mind off the pain.

This book was almost derailed by my own procrastination. But once I ran out of every excuse not to write, I finally put down the first words. And then the real pain began.

I worked hard.

I pushed myself.

I took chances.

I wrote dangerously.

I wrote about the antihero I wanted to read. I wrote about what I knew and the places I'd been.

I rewrote.

I suffered.

I edited.

I doubted.

And only after I typed the final period and submitted my manuscript was I reminded that no book is written alone. There are people without whom this story would never have become a reality.

And so, to the characters of my life who helped shape this book—thank you.

To my teachers:

Thank you to my high school English teachers—Mr. Malara, Mrs. Pellechia, and Ms. Carltock—who dared me to believe I could be a writer (and gave me the ability to hold a conversation about Beckett, Brontë, and Dickens). A nod as well to my Furman University professor who declared no freshman should ever earn an A in English. That B+ I received is still a trophy I carry with pride.

To the fighters who shaped me and this book's action:

When you get comfortable with being punched in the face and choked unconscious, writing a book starts to seem easy. My thanks to the warriors who gladly put their fists in my face to further my education: Maestro Renzo Gracie, Dr. Tony Caterisano, Ricardo Almeida, Rolles Gracie, Igor Gracie, Roger Gracie, Alan Teo, Joe Sampieri, John Derent, Gene Dunn, Jamal Patterson, Gianni Grippo, Frankie Edgar, and the UFC's all-time winningest fighter, Jim Miller.

To the NYAC Judo Club:

In the dojo, I learned the pain of being a student and the mantra: *you ain't shit if you don't walk with a limp.* Special thanks to Dr. Arthur Canario, Shintaro Higashi, Jimmy Vennitti, Barry Friedberg, and my Olympian sensei, Teimoc Johnston-Ono, who put it best: *Martin, you have two speeds—asleep and ferocious.* Deep bow.

To the U.S. military:

I was honored to contribute what knowledge I could to those who stand for something greater than themselves. My time spent with the U.S. Army Rangers, Army Airborne, and Navy SEALs was not only a career highlight, but also a lesson in integrity. Salute to Dr. Nick Barringer, CSM Chad Acton, and frogman Ajay James.

To Bill Parisi:

The wizard of all things speed. I can't imagine where I'd be if I hadn't taken that flight to Tyler, Texas.

To Lucas Noonan:

Photographer superstar. Without you, I'd have no proof of all the insane adventures I tell stories about—the ones that always make people ask, *Is that really true?*

To Luca Atalla:

Obrigado for letting me sharpen my writing skills on the editorial council of *Gracie Magazine* for over a decade.

To Dr. Rob Gilbert:

Although this book isn't about motivation, your lessons always kept me going.

To my Training For Warriors familia:

You have all pushed me to be ready on this battlefield called life. *Kiitos, tak, gracias, danke schön, takk fyrir, merci, shukran*, cheers, and good on ya, mate.

To the athletes I've coached and the coaches I've worked alongside:

I know I've learned more from you than you learned from me. You're not used to seeing this side of me, so please don't hold the cursing in the book against me.

To Jeffrey Gitomer:

Thanks for being a mensch and introducing me to editor extraordinaire Zach Schisgal. And a huge thanks to Zach for connecting me with my editor for this book, Michael Campbell. Mike, thanks to you and Skyhorse Publishing for handling me in the perfect way (which my wife will attest is not easy).

To my dad, Martin Rooney:

My lifelong editor and biggest fan. He's the most well-read guy I know, and the fact that he said this book stands up among the others he's read was all the feedback I needed.

To my mom, Jeanne Rooney:

She always said she wasn't surprised I was writing this book. I just wish she could have held it in her hands and given me a simple, *Not bad, Mart.*

To my wife, Amanda, and our daughters—Sofia, Kristina, Keira, and Sasha:

You are my balance. Since I spend so much time around alpha males, I believe the universe put you five in my life to keep me grounded. I want this book to be a reason to be proud of your dad.

And finally, to you—the reader:

I've always wanted to play in the action-thriller genre, and I hope I did right by you. Now that Lee has bled through these pages, I hope you've enjoyed meeting him—and that he's challenged you, too.

And for the best part of this story?

By the time this book was finished, my buddy Todd beat cancer, too.

ABOUT THE AUTHOR

Martin Rooney is no stranger to the fight. An internationally renowned fitness expert and combat sports specialist, he has spent over three decades in the trenches of physical and mental warfare. With a Master of Health Science and a Bachelor of Physical Therapy from the Medical University of South Carolina, as well as a BA in Exercise Science from Furman University, Martin's journey has been anything but ordinary.

A former Division I javelin thrower, U.S. bobsledder, and two-time Guinness World Record holder, Martin is also the founder of the Training for Warriors system, which has transformed over a million lives across the globe. A Kodokan Judo black belt and Brazilian Jiu-Jitsu brown belt, he has trained UFC champions, Olympic medalists, and world-class athletes in multiple disciplines. His expertise extends beyond the cage and the mat—he has designed hand-fighting programs for the New York Giants, New York Jets, and University of Notre Dame football teams.

As a sought-after speaker, Martin has delivered keynote presentations for Fortune 500 giants like Nike and Prudential and visited with elite military units, including the Navy SEALs and Army Rangers. Now serving as Chancellor of Lionel University, he has authored 12 books, but *BloodFeud: Raising Cain* marks his explosive debut into thriller fiction.

Martin lives in North Carolina with his wife and four daughters—who, as you might imagine, keep him on his toes every day.